# BEER MONEY

## A TALE OF THE IOWA CITY BEER MAFIA

# S.C. SHERMAN

**Post Hill**
PRESS

A POST HILL PRESS BOOK
ISBN: 978-1-64293-394-9
ISBN (eBook): 978-1-64293-395-6

Beer Money:
A Tale of the Iowa City Beer Mafia
© 2020 by S.C. Sherman
All Rights Reserved

Cover art by Cody Corcoran
Cover photo courtesy of the Johnson County Historical Society

Post Hill Press
New York • Nashville
posthillpress.com

Published in the United States of America

**Also by S.C. Sherman**

*Leaving Southfields*
*Hell and Back: The First Death*
*Moxie*
*Mercy Shot*
*Lone Wolf Canyon*

# FOREWORD

THE "Northside" neighborhood of Iowa City, Iowa has a long history and a checkered past. The following is a tale of Iowa's heritage, but it is also a much larger story, an American story, that illustrates our passionate individuality and the struggles that go with it.

This story is wrought with entrepreneurialism, connected neighborhoods, sharp divisions along the lines of politics, country of origin, customs, language, and religion. It is a story of just how difficult the details of our beautiful melting pot were in the past and still are today.

The tale found in this book is classified as "historical fiction," which can mean many things. What it means to me and this book is that the vast majority of major events found on these pages really happened. The overwhelming majority of characters actually lived in Iowa City and were a part of the happenings you will soon discover.

Historical fictions are full of educated guesses and this one is no different. I endeavored to portray the story dramatically as well as factually. Thanks to many wonderful historians who've gone before and archived so much detailed information that made my goal achievable.

Enjoy a tale of blood and beer in America's Heartland.

# AUTHOR'S NOTE

MY romance with the "Northside" of Iowa City, Iowa started in the fall of 1988. I was an eighteen-year-old freshman at the University of Iowa. I spent orientation with a couple of other Iowa boys in Burge Hall located on North Clinton Street.

My first act as a resident of Iowa City would forever tie me to the story I now share with you all these years later. I committed a crime. The very same crime committed by the characters in my book. I broke the state laws of Iowa and illegally purchased and consumed beer.

My new friends and I walked, since we had no vehicle, to a Quik Trip gas station formerly located at the corner of Market and Linn Street. I had no idea it was sitting right between what had been Englert's City Brewery and Graf's Union Brewery.

We simply wanted some beer like thousands of young lads who had gone before us. We were undeterred that the state of Iowa had declared that at age eighteen, we were not allowed to buy or drink beer. We had no idea people had broken the law and fought for their right to drink beer more than a hundred years before us at that very same location.

Open a bottle of your favorite beer and enjoy the story of the northside that is a fascinating part of Iowa City history and learn of the deeply rich heritage that is literally under the streets!

FYI: I've discovered many people do not know the term *Teetotaler*. This term is frequently used in the story. It stood for people who were completely abstinent and drank zero alcohol. They became known as teetotalers which derived from "Tee" for Total and "totaler" for total abstinence.

Also, you will find the word Bohemian used a few times, which is a more period accurate term for people who would commonly be called "Czech" today.

1 - Church Park
2 - St. James Hotel
3 - St. Mary's Catholic Church
4 - First United Methodist Church
5 - Union Brewery -  Graf
6 - Union Public House and Bakery
7 - Great Western Brewery - Dostal
8 - City Brewery  - Englert
9 - Baker Property
10 - Old Capitol and State University

**1**

## November 5th, 1881. Iowa City, Iowa

ANTON Stein applied more grease to his unruly shock of dark hair in an attempt to tame it. He crooked his neck and hunched his shoulders to better see himself in the mirror that was obviously hung too low for his height. He wet his fingertips with his tongue and straightened his mustache.

With a final glance he adjusted his suit coat and re-checked each pocket to be sure of their contents. Inhaling deeply, he exited the small room containing only a single bed, a small three-drawer dresser, and the mirror. The single window was trimmed with white lace and birds were announcing a glorious day just outside.

Mrs. Spryng ran a respectable boarding house on Dubuque Street, which was the heart of Iowa City. She worked hard and kept a clean establishment that regular travelers returned to again and again. Spryng Boarding House was known for an affordable room with a hot breakfast in the morning and a pleasant landlady.

No one asked what happened to Mrs. Spryng's husband. The story was he died back east before she made her way to the frontier. She was no longer thin of body and her hair was always pulled back, which showed much more gray than it used to.

She heard the heavy footsteps of a man coming down the stairs. She knew who it was. He was the last one to rise. All her other boarders had already gone at a respectable hour. It was eight o'clock and a man coming down at this hour was peculiar, as if he was sick or a man of leisure. She took him for neither, which made her wonder.

At the sight of him dressed elaborately in a full dress suit she gasped. "Oh my, Mister Stein, don't you look dapper today."

"Thank you, ma'am. I'll take breakfast."

"I'm sorry, but breakfast has already been served. All I have for you is coffee. Would you like a cup?"

His stare hardened at the landlady and his steely eyes caused a chill to run up the matron's spine.

"Uh, I have hot coffee. M-Maybe a biscuit?" she stuttered.

His cold stare gradually turned to a strained smile. "Thank you, mum, I'll be on my way."

"Yes, Mister Stein. Please come again," she said, though it was obvious she didn't mean it.

Mr. Stein placed a stylish round hat upon his head and carefully tipped the bill to Mrs. Spryng as he promptly strode out the front door.

"Whew." Mrs. Spryng exhaled loudly, glad he was gone. Not many people made her nervous, but that man did. She went to the window and watched him making his way south toward Market Street. Her gaze lingered until he disappeared from her view.

Something about him just felt off. It wasn't because of the divorce business either. If truth would ever be told, Mrs. Spryng's husband hadn't died back east, she'd left him and all the beatings that went with being his wife. She'd made her way out west and started a new life in Iowa. It was simply easier to tell people he had died. There was no judgment in that.

ANTON Stein walked straight and tall like a man who knew what he was about. Something about wearing a fine suit just made you stand taller. He ducked down an alley and came back out on the street front right where he meant to. He paused for a moment and peered through the front glass of Luse's Shoe Shop.

Several men inside were hard at their craft. He was looking for one man in particular. It didn't take long, and he spotted his father-in-law. Peter Hess was a well-liked man with a careful way about him. His gray hair and sweet disposition meant almost everyone instantly enjoyed his company. He was meticulously working at his bench with a hammer, gently tapping the sole of a leather shoe held in a bracket before him. He did not notice his son-in-law across the street.

Mr. Stein stared with contempt for a moment, wishing he could see the look on his self-righteous face when he found out. His vision was interrupted when his stomach growled loudly. He unconsciously put his hand to it. "Dang Mrs. Spryng and her breakfast!" he muttered.

He was hungry and the smell of bread baking down the street made it worse. He turned to go as he'd seen all he was hoping for anyway. Mr. Stein made his way directly toward the smell. He didn't glance up at the simple sign overhead stating Union Bakery.

He let the door shut behind him. No one else was in the bakery save the man behind the counter. He was a stout man in his fifties and had the round look of a healthy baker.

The baker raised his gaze at the sound of the door and with a glance realized he did not know his patron. A grand smile came across his face and he waved his flour covered hands. "Welcome to the Union Bakery, my friend. I am Alexis Bushnagle and everything we bake is delicious. What would you like?"

Mr. Stein approached the counter and carefully admired the selections like a man picking his last meal. After some time, Mr. Bushnagle pointed to a few items, "This is sourdough, that one is cinnamon, and that is French pastry. I've been working on it with my good friend, Mister Bloom. He was born in France. He says we are very nearly perfect!"

Mr. Stein nodded at the pastry with a smile. "I've never had a French pastry, perfect or not. Today's the day to try it."

"Fantastic!" The baker carefully slid the large pastry onto a paper. "Ten cents."

Mr. Stein took a coin from his vest pocket and paid the baker. He promptly took his pastry and turned to leave without a word.

As the door was closing behind him, the baker hollered, "Come back and let me know what you think of my pastry!"

Mr. Stein gave a sideways glance at the single-story house next to the bakery and turned his back, making his way to the Union Public House only a few steps away.

Once inside, he spotted a man behind the bar in a white apron. He appeared to be counting beer casks that lined the back wall. The room was empty, as it should be at this time of the day. Most men were working.

The man behind the bar noticed his presence. "Good day to you, sir," he said with a fine baritone.

Mr. Stein stepped up to the bar and set his pastry out before him. The bartender approached.

"That's a fine pastry. Al's very nearly got it perfected, or so he says. What can I get you to wash it down? I'm boiling some sausage if you want some meat to go with it? But that won't be ready for a bit. I have a pot of hot coffee, and of course, we have the best beer in town."

"I'll take a beer, thank you," Mr. Stein said.

"Never too early for a glorious Graf Golden Brew, I always say." The bartender laughed and went about his business of pouring the suds.

He returned and placed the beer before Mr. Stein. It was a beautiful golden color with bubbles rising to the top, just a slight foam on the surface. "There you go, sir."

"Thank you," Mr. Stein said.

"I don't know you. From out of town?"

"Yes, I'm from Cedar Rapids. My wife's family lives here and we are in town on some legal matters."

"Well my name is Max Geiger. My great-uncle Anton founded this brewery with his friend Simeon Hotz and let me tell you, it's the best one in town." He stuck out his hand.

Mr. Stein shook the bartender's hand firmly without a word.

"I know most everyone on the northside. Who is your wife's family?"

Mr. Stein glanced out the window, suddenly uncomfortable with all the conversation. "The Hess family is my wife's family."

"Yes, I know them. Fine people. And you are?"

"I am Anton Stein. I married their daughter Lizzie. Do you have a paper I could read while I eat my pastry and enjoy my beer?"

"Why yes, sir." Max reached behind the bar and handed the paper to Mr. Stein. "Here you go, sir." He laid the day's copy of The Iowa Post on the bar. "It's half in German, half in English. Enjoy."

Max had bartended long enough he knew when to walk away, but there was something about this man. All dressed up like he was going to a wedding or a funeral and Max had heard of neither on that day. His attire was definitely something strange for so early in the morning on a weekday, but to each his own.

Mr. Stein carefully ate his pastry and enjoyed his beer, while Max kept on with his inventory. He knew he had to have the sausage ready by noon and prepare for a steady crowd of hungry workers the rest of the day. Mr. Stein and his pastry didn't matter in the slightest.

Mr. Stein was savoring his last bite of pastry when the front door burst open. A serious-looking man in a white shirt and a dark vest closed the door behind him.

His sleeves were rolled up, his open collar showing the dark curly hair of his chest. He strode through the public space and went straight behind the counter to speak with Max.

"Are we ready? Sausage smells good. Ida is bringing a huge pot of kraut and Alexis is bringing over bread as usual." The man had a strong voice. He was obviously all business and he scanned the room with his penetrating eyes, suddenly noticing the man at the bar decked out in a full suit.

"Hello, sir, I don't know you. May I introduce myself? I am Conrad Graf. This is my place. May I ask you a question?"

"Yes, sir, of course," Mr. Stein said, clearly nervous.

"What is a man dressed as fine as you are doing in here at this time of day?"

"I am in town with my wife for a brief time," Mr. Stein said, glancing at the door.

"May I be of service? I know everyone in town and am well connected. Are you in town on business?" Conrad asked with a quizzical look on his face.

"No, sir," Mr. Stein answered and offered nothing more.

Conrad's curiosity was obviously piqued. "What do you do, sir?"

Mr. Stein again looked out the window. After a long pause he said, "I used to work for Magnus Brewers in Cedar Rapids." The corner of his left eye twitched a bit.

"Yes, I know Magnus. What did you do for them?"

"I was in the caves."

"Oh, good work in the summertime! Cool down there!"

"Yes, it is cool." Mr. Stein turned his back to Conrad and shuffled slowly out the front door.

Conrad and Max watched until he was gone, then Conrad asked Max, "What's the deal with that guy?"

"I don't know. Kind of strange. Are you bringing up a few more casks?"

"How many?"

"Maybe ten. We are fine for mid-day, but later we will need some more. Later on, they'll be thirsty."

"I will send them over," Conrad said, marching off to his next task.

Max threw away the pastry paper and wiped down the bar where the odd fellow had stood. He discovered a penny left as a tip. With a smile Max tucked it into his pocket.

Mr. Stein left The Public House and turned a hard right, making his way past the bakery to the simple house next door. He stepped behind the bushes near the back entrance, leaned up against the clapboards, and exhaled slowly, looking back toward the alley.

Two boys walked down the alley. They each carried a school pail and Mr. Stein could see their breath in the cold November air. The temperature was hovering around freezing, but the bright sun and absolute stillness made it quite pleasant outside to those accustomed to the midwestern climate. Stein could hear the soft sounds of a woman singing inside the house.

He swore under his breath and muttered, "What the hell does she have to sing about?"

At twenty-five years old, Lizzie was stunning in her beauty. She had blonde hair, a shapely figure, and a sweet countenance that endeared people to her instantly.

She hugged her daughter tight to her chest. Lizzie knew that at five years old she'd already seen too much. Her blonde locks fell around her shoulders and her little blue eyes shone like a lake bathed in sunlight. Her son brooded. His eyes were always dark and downcast. Ever since their father had died, things had not gone well. She feared he would never recover and be the giggling boy he once was.

She'd been known as "The Widow Goering" since her childhood sweetheart had died suddenly from an accident with a horse. She was too young to be thought of that way. When a new suitor had shown up so willing to accept her children and love her she quickly remarried.

Lizzie discovered her mistake on her wedding night as her new husband apparently enjoyed inflicting pain upon her more than wedding night intimacy. She had her first black eye the next morning.

Lizzie learned a few months later that his name wasn't even Stein. It was Skierecki. Everything he'd promised her had been a lie. He had no money and seemed to only find enjoyment in punching and kicking her. She had hoped and prayed it would get better, but it did not. When he began beating her children as well, she knew she had to do something.

Her friends and even her parents told her to endure it, but she knew she could not. Divorce was the only answer...or run away, but the thought of leaving and losing her family was too much. She decided to try divorce, despite the shame it would bring. There was no other option and now it was done.

Only two days earlier she'd stood in the Johnson County Court before Judge Hedges and told her tale as best she could.

The scar on her lip and the yellowing bruise on her cheek helped illustrate the dire situation. Lizzie couldn't help but smile as her divorce request was granted. Her smile disappeared when she looked across the courtroom and locked eyes with Anton. They were cold, dead eyes. She was afraid.

Judge Hedges saw Anton's eyes as well. He slammed his gavel. "I also do hereby grant an injunction that Anton Stein not be allowed near the home listed or any future homes in which Lizzie Stein may be living."

The Judge pointed right at Anton. "You stay away from her! Do you understand?"

"Yes, Your Honor. I'll stay away," Anton said as he exited the courtroom. And with that, he was gone. A weight lifted from Lizzie's chest, with a requisite amount of fear lingering in the back of her mind from his haunting stare.

She took her children and moved back into her parent's house right next to the Union Bakery. The divine aroma was enough to stay forever. It was time to make a fresh start even if it meant she never married again. She'd decided to live an old maid for her children and nothing else.

Her mother joined them in the front room and sat down near her grandchildren with a book in her hand. "I have a story to read you," she said.

Lizzie smiled. "Thanks, Mother. I'll be in the kitchen."

She picked up her water can and began watering the flowering plants that sat on the window ledge. Lizzie didn't even notice that she was humming a tune. Did she dare entertain happiness?

She heard the back door open and assuming it was her father she turned. "Hi, Papa..."

She screamed a bloodcurdling scream at the sight of Anton Stein. He stood completely still with his finger up to his mouth to force her silence.

"What do you want? You aren't supposed to be here!" she cried. "Mother, he's here!" The house was small enough anyone talking loudly could be heard in the other rooms.

"I want my journal and the picture of my mother. Nothing more," he said with the icy cold look that was his way.

"It's in the other room. I'll get it, you stay right here, but then you must go." She went to the front room and grabbed the journal and the picture from the shelf. She motioned to her mother to stay where she was with the children. Both of them looked terrified in her arms. They'd seen Anton's outbursts before.

Lizzie gave them a forced smile and re-entered the kitchen. She handed Anton the journal and the photograph. He accepted them and tucked them into the inside pocket of his suit jacket.

In one motion he withdrew a long knife he'd concealed under his coat. With no more words and in a movement as swift as a cat he was on Lizzie. She screamed a terrible sound as his right hand raised high and slammed down hard. The blade entered the left side of her chest just above her breast, crushing through her ribcage and piercing her lung. She continued to scream as the knife was withdrawn and stabbed into her body a dozen more times.

Her life's blood flowed like a torrent down her body, spraying the floor. Lizzie pushed away with all her remaining strength and lost her footing in the slippery mess covering the wood floor. She landed on her back. Anton was instantly on her with his knee pressing hard against her chest. She blinked and faded to darkness as a chortle emanated from her throat.

With a handful of Lizzie's golden hair in his left hand, Anton kept sawing with the knife in his right until his mother-in-law screamed and hit him with full force.

He fell from Lizzie's body and focused on Mrs. Hess, who stood before him. He regained his footing and slashed her way with his bloody reaper.

"No! No!" She put up her arms to protect herself. Anton felt the meat on her forearm cut like a beef steak with each swipe. She cried out and dropped her arms. With a slashing motion from left to right he clipped her throat.

Blood sprayed forth between her fingers as she clutched her wound.

He heard a strange whimpering sound and turned to see Lizzie's children staring at the scene. Mrs. Hess took her opportunity and bolted out the front door. Mr. Stein could hear her screaming for all the world to take notice.

"Murder! My daughter's been murdered! Help! Help!"

Mr. Stein glanced down at himself and could see his fine suit was covered in bright red blood. He turned his attention to the two children who stood motionless, staring at the remains of their mother.

He laid them side-by-side in the front room after slitting their throats. Peering down at them, he was surprised that he felt nothing at all.

The noise was growing out front. Mr. Stein stepped out the front door and stood for a moment staring at the gathering crowd. Mrs. Hess lay on the ground, blood all around her. Several men were attending to her wounds.

He was a picture of terror, dripping in the blood of his slain victims, carrying a large knife in his hand.

The bulk of the crowd stared at him in horror. An image they'd not soon forget. He realized the knife was still in his hand. He raised it and waved it at the crowd menacing their advance.

Several women screamed and covered the eyes of their children from the carnage. Several adult men had arrived, and they froze at the sight of Mr. Stein covered in blood, brandishing a large knife.

Mr. Stein could see they didn't know what to do. Should they charge him? Go get a gun? Wait for the sheriff?

He knew his time was short, but he smiled at his success. All who saw it were forever haunted by that demonic smile. Mr. Stein stepped back into the home as Dr. Lytle arrived. Anton reached into his pants pocket and removed a small glass vial with a cork top. He pulled the cork and tossed it aside. He put the vial to his lips and threw his head back as if it was a shot of whiskey. With not a drop remaining Mr. Stein dropped the small bottle as the acid found its way home.

He stood in the doorway to the kitchen for a moment. Dr. Lytle pushed by him and went to Lizzie. The doctor glanced up in time to see Mr. Stein cough hard and blood dripped from his mouth. Without warning, his eyes rolled back in his head, leaving only the whites showing, and he fell flat on his back, convulsing like a man with seizures.

After a few moments his body relaxed, and Mr. Stein never moved again. His eyes glossed over in death, frothy blood dripping from his mouth and nose.

Dr. Lytle glanced sideways when a man in a uniform stepped up next to him. He was a young man new to town but eager to do well and make a name for himself in law enforcement.

"Who might you be?" asked Dr. Lytle with a sideways glance. "We've not met."

"Deputy Parrot. Samuel Parrot. I just moved here from Pennsylvania."

"Well, welcome to town, son." Dr. Lytle chuckled a little with a wicked wry sense of humor he'd picked up during the war. "Have you ever seen a dead body?"

"Uh, yes, one time," Deputy Parrot said. "My grandpa in a coffin."

"Get ready, this ain't nothing like that!" Dr. Lytle said, leading the young officer into the kitchen.

Young Deputy Parrot's face blanched whiter than white and his jaw hung slack for a few moments. He'd obviously never seen anything as horrific as the scene before them.

"Doc, he cut her head clean off!"

"Not all the way. There is a slight bit of tissue on the right side there," Dr. Lytle said matter-of-factly, like the seasoned doctor that he was.

"Holy Mary, Mother of God..."

"Yeah, Jesus and Joseph too. Did you see the two kids in the other room?"

The young constable looked into the other room and abruptly ran to the back door. He slipped in the blood but caught himself on the table and made it out the back door just in time to vomit in the bushes.

He wiped his mouth and shut the door behind him. Dr. Lytle gripped Lizzie's head with both hands and placed it more where it should be on her neck. Parrot heaved again but kept it down.

Dr. Lytle glanced up at him. "I think you need a task. You better get the sheriff and send for Doctor Clapp. I'll need his help. Also, get Father Edmonds, and somebody better go find Peter Hess. His family's been destroyed. He should know straightaway. News like this will spread like wildfire."

# 2

DEPUTY Parrot stepped out of the little house into the cold, clear day. He stood motionless for a moment on the top step of the porch. A large crowd had formed, and he could see Mrs. Hess was already in a wagon and heading toward the hospital. He noticed Deputy Sheriff Tom Fairall pushing his way through the crowd and he was glad for it.

He was at a loss for words and he knew Fairall would know what to do. He was as tough as they came. He'd served at Gettysburg, and after that nothing shook him. He stopped at the bottom step and sized up the look of the young constable.

"How bad is it? You look like you've seen a ghost," Fairall said.

"It's bad. Worst I've ever seen. They're all dead. The young mother and her two children. They just took the old mother to the hospital all cut up."

"Who did it?"

"He's dead too. Doctor Lytle is inside. He says it was the husband. He killed himself with a poison. He's in the front room."

Fairall nodded. "Alright. We need to take care of these bodies. Alright?"

"Yes, sir." Parrot looked like he wanted to say more.

"Spit it out, man, what is it?"

Parrot took a step closer and whispered, "He cut her head off. I saw her spine sticking out of her neck."

Fairall exhaled and shook his head. "I'm sorry, young man. The first time is the worst. I hate to say it, but you'll get used to it."

"I won't ever get used to that. She looked kinda like my sister." He dry-heaved again.

"Get a hold of yourself, man. We've got a job to do and it's you and me. You see this crowd over my shoulder?"

Parrot nodded.

"We have to get them to disperse. We can't haul out bodies in front of the friends and family who love these people. Have you notified next of kin yet?"

"No," Parrot said. "I just walked out here to get some air. Doctor Lytle wants Doctor Clapp and Father Edmonds right away."

"Definitely. Both those men will help." Fairall scanned the crowd and pointed. He saw two boys pushing their way through the crowd to see what they could.

Fairall pointed at them, waving for them to come near. They complied immediately. "I want you two boys to help with what's happened here today. It's an important job and I'm trusting it to you. Can I count on you?"

They both nodded with wide eyes.

"I want one of you to run and fetch Father Edmonds and the other to go find Doctor Clapp at his office in the Sisters of Mercy Hospital. Can you do it?"

They both agreed and were off running. After they had disappeared from sight Fairall patted Parrot on the shoulder. "Let's go inside."

"I'll stay out here and control the crowd if you don't mind," Parrot said.

Deputy Fairall nodded and went in to have a look at the scene. Deputy Parrot stood like a sentry as the crowd continued to grow. A man with graying hair and a leather apron over his shoulders pushed through the crowd and burst toward the door.

Deputy Parrot stopped him as his hand grabbed the knob. "Sir, please get back out with the crowd. This is a crime scene."

He looked incredulous. "A crime scene? This is my home. What's happened?"

It was like a kick in the gut. Deputy Parrot strengthened his resolve. "I'm sorry, sir, what is your name? I'm new to town."

"I'm Peter Hess. I'm going inside."

"Mister Hess, I hate to tell you this but...your daughter, she's gone."

"What do you mean gone? I had breakfast with her just a bit ago."

"I mean she's dead, sir. Killed by her husband we believe."

"What? No! My wife, the children?"

"I believe your wife has been taken to the hospital. I do not know the extent of her wounds, but she was hurt. And, sir, the children are both dead as well." Deputy Parrot did his level best to remain steadfast. He could see the turmoil in Peter Hess' eyes as he tried to comprehend what he was hearing. The loss was more than a soul could bear.

He lunged toward the door. Deputy Parrot stopped him. "I implore you, sir. Do not enter. Remember your breakfast with your sweet daughter. You don't want to see her now."

Hess' face twisted in pain like the young deputy had never seen before. Tears streamed down the older man's cheeks. "I must see," he insisted.

Deputy Parrot shook his head and a tear slipped from his eye. "If you must, I will not stop you, but—"

Just then Dr. Clapp pushed his way through the crowd with Father Edmonds right behind him. They gathered on the porch in an awkward silence.

Dr. Clapp was a fine-looking middle-aged man. His appearance commanded authority and the unique trimming of his beard marked him in an instant. Each corner of his chin had its own magnificent growth of whiskers separated in the middle. His medical brilliance was known far and wide.

Father Edmonds was a legend. The "Prairie Priest," Mazzuchelli, had been the first priest in the territory and founder of St. Mary's, but Edmonds had done more to spread the Catholic faith than any before him west of the Mississippi.

Both men sensed the situation they'd walked into and they all knew each other well from life lived in a common neighborhood. Father Edmonds had eaten in this very home with the Hess family. Dr. Clapp had examined the children when they were sick.

"Deputy? How can we help?" Father Edmonds asked.

"Mister Hess would like to go into his home and see what has happened. I've cautioned him that might not be a good choice given the nature of the...murders."

"Murders?" Dr. Clapp echoed.

"Yes, sir. Doctor Lytle is inside and told me to send for you. The Hess daughter and her two children are both dead. Mrs. Hess has been taken to the hospital and is severely wounded."

"A loved one has the right see their dead," Father Edmonds said.

"I agree, Father, but it's not a vision you will forget," Parrot said. "At least I never will."

Father Edmonds turned to Peter Hess. "Do you want me to go in first and look? Let me see if I think it's a good idea or not?"

Peter Hess was getting angry and visibly shaking from the grief already taking hold. "No, Father! I'm going in. None of you can stop me. I *will* see my daughter!"

Father Edmonds nodded and looked at Parrot. "Right or wrong, we're going in." He glanced at Peter. "I'm right here with you, Peter, and may God be with us at this desperate hour of need."

Deputy Parrot opened the door and stepped out of the way, allowing them to enter. He closed the door after they'd gone in. He could hear Peter Hess wailing though the glass and thin plank walls. A somber mood fell over the crowd as they all heard the sounds of a man who had lost control of his emotions. Some left about their business while others patiently waited for a word or statement.

After a time, Father Edmonds came out of the house, his hands stained with blood. He nodded at Deputy Parrot and walked to the crowd. "Dear friends and neighbors, a great tragedy has taken place. Three souls snuffed out by the evil one and a fourth taken to damnation. Lizzie Hess and her two children are dead, murdered at the hand of her own husband, Anton Stein. We will have a candlelight mass tonight at the church to pray for the dead and our community. Now pray with me." He raised his right arm high. Everyone, Catholic or not, removed their hats, bowed their heads, and prayed aloud.

*"Hail Mary, full of grace, The Lord is with thee. Blessed art thou amongst women, and blessed is the fruit of thy womb, Jesus. Holy Mary, Mother of God, pray for us sinners now, and at the hour of our death. Amen."*

Father Edmonds pushed through the crowd, struggling to conceal how rattled he was to his very core. Most of the crowd turned and found somewhere else to be.

News of the murders spread exactly like Fairall had predicted. Within an hour every person in Iowa City knew of the slayings and news of the grisly murders was on its way to Des Moines for the next day's statewide papers.

CONRAD Graf was standing at the bar talking to Max when fellows started coming in from the house just a block down. The somber mood was hard to miss.

"What's happened, lads?" Conrad asked.

"The family Hess has been killed," a solid looking man with a mustache answered, placing his arms on the bar.

Max set beer in front of the men and began to place sausage, kraut, and bread on a plate for each. At the Union Public House if you were buying beer, you got a nice meal compliments of the house.

"Peter Hess? The shoemaker? What do you mean killed?"

"No, Peter is alive, but his daughter Lizzie and her two little ones are dead. The old mum, she's been injured, and they have taken her to the hospital. Don't know how bad, but it didn't look good for her either."

"Who did this?" Conrad asked, incredulous.

"The young woman's husband they say," the man continued. "Stein."

Conrad and Max locked eyes.

"That was the guy from this morning!" Conrad exclaimed. Max nodded. Conrad slipped on his coat. "I'm going to go see if I can help." More men were coming into the pub as he made his way out the door.

It was only a moment before Conrad stood in front of the Hess house. Dr. Clapp was standing on the porch talking to Deputy Fairall and noticed Conrad.

With a somber countenance Dr. Clapp immediately walked toward his friend. "Sad day on the northside."

"What the hell happened?" Graf asked. "They're dead?"

"Yes sir. Three murdered and one suicide. The young gal and her two children were killed by her husband, then he killed himself rather than face the hangman."

"He had a beer in the pub just before he walked down there and killed them. I talked to him. Doc, this is bad."

"Sure is. I guess the husband didn't take kindly to his wife divorcing him. Judge Hedges just passed judgment a day ago, along with an injunction for Stein to stay away from her."

"Oh my." Conrad shook his head. "Anything I can do?"

"I'm not sure. Peter is in shock. I'm going to go see to his wife. We've called for the undertaker. I'm taking the murderer to see if I can determine the poison that killed him."

"You send the bills for anything you do to me, do you understand? No bills to Hess," Conrad said. "My father-in-law worked in the shoe shop with Peter years ago when they were young men."

"I'll be sure to send you any bills. That's real nice of you to do that, Conrad."

"Only the right thing to do."

"Father Edmonds is having a special prayer mass tonight for the neighborhood. Spread the word."

"Will do. See you there, Doc."

Golden light bathed the Old Capitol dome as the sun dropped low, bringing a day chilled by cool breezes and death to a close. The hollow gong of the bell at St. Mary's rang out across the town calling all who would come to mourn together and try to understand the senseless.

Father Edmonds stood at the front of the sanctuary watching the pews fill with his friends and neighbors. He noticed all three of the neighborhood kings had entered together as if royalty. The three successful breweries and the men who owned them were titans of industry and celebrities within Iowa City and Johnson County. Conrad Graf owned The Union Brewery, John P. Dostal owned the Great Western Brewery, and John J. Englert the City Brewery. They were widely known as the "German Beer Mafia" and they controlled all things on the northside whether they meant to or not.

First came Conrad Graf and his wife Anna with their children, followed by John Dostal, his wife and children, and finally J.J. Englert and his children. They knelt and made the sign of the cross before sliding into a pew.

The ushers closed the back doors and Father Edmonds raised both arms, beginning the meeting in Latin prayer. Of course, none present spoke Latin other than the priests, but the repetitiveness of the prayers provided comfort to the saints in the seats no matter the language.

After Father Edmonds finished his prayers, he continued in English. "My friends, we are gathering tonight to pray for our neighborhood, as mere steps from this very altar, the evil one has stretched out his wicked hand and slain our brothers and sisters in the faith.

"We are all shocked by the viciousness of this attack. It's hard for a civilized mind to understand such horror inflicted so viciously upon the innocent. We must pass our petitions on to God and pray for the Hess family in this time of unspeakable loss. Peter Hess, our friend, has lost much. His wife may survive, but his daughter and grandchildren are gone. We will have a wake and burial services for them in the coming days, but for now cry out as one voice for mercy upon our community in the coming days as we try to make sense of this senseless act and go on about our business. Do all you can for our brother Peter in this time of unspeakable trials.

"Remember to love your family and protect them from all evils. Love your neighbor as yourself and look to help one another in the name of the Father, the Son, and Holy Spirit, Amen.

"The common room is open to any who wish to stay and talk or if anyone has a special request you can find me there."

Father Edmonds switched back to Latin and closed the abbreviated session with a conclusory song and prayer then made his way down the center aisle.

No one went to the common room. Parishioners filed by Father Edmonds on their way home either by foot or carriage. Darkness had fallen, and the air had a bite to it as bitter as the death on everyone's mind.

The three brewers stood before Father Edmonds.

"Father, we'd like to sponsor all costs associated with the funeral mass and we will each be donating to the benevolence fund in the name of Hess," J.J. Englert said with a clear and melancholy tone. "Anything we can do, don't hesitate to ask, Father. I know Peter would never ask us directly for help, but maybe through you and the church we could do some good."

"Thank you, sirs, and may God bless you and yours tonight. It's times like these we all fill our roles and we must stick together like the family we are," Father Edmonds said.

"Goodnight, Father," Conrad said, shook his hand, and turned to go.

"Bless you, Conrad," said Father Edmonds.

"Bless you, Father." J.J. Englert clasped the priest's massive warm hand.

"And you, J.J."

John Dostal looked a bit uncomfortable and turned to go. "Goodnight, Father."

"Bless you too, John," Father Edmonds said. He turned to the next of his flock to bless them all one at a time.


The three brewers paused in front of the church while their families waited in their carriages. Conrad noticed his wife Anna nod to him as if to say, *please hurry*. It was cold, and the children needed to be fed and bathed.

He nodded back to her and turned to his compatriots. "Sad times, gents."

"Indeed. Never heard of man killing children like this," Dostal said.

"Well he didn't father them...horrible, nonetheless. Too bad the coward killed himself," J.J. added.

Conrad glanced down the block. He could see lights and people coming and going from Methodist Church that dominated the opposing corner of Dubuque and Jefferson Streets. The entire block was divided up between St. Mary's on the Southeast corner, First United Methodist on the Southwest corner, and the entire Northern half of the block consumed by The Union Brewery and its various buildings.

"Looks like the Methodists are having a meeting," Conrad said.

J.J. glanced down the block. "I must be going."

"Yes, we all do," Dostal agreed. They shook hands and went their separate ways.

27

JOE Lund shuddered in his coat. The wind was colder than he'd expected. The stone church stood before him with a light emanating from the arch topped windows. He glanced down the street toward St. Mary's. He stretched out his hand and grabbed his friend by the shoulder, "Hey, Richard, look at that."

Three men were standing together, obviously talking.

"The Catholics probably had a mass or something," Richard Jones said. "Let's go in, its cold."

"Look closer, it's the mafia," Joe said.

Richard squinted in the poor light. "It is indeed. All standing together."

Joe sneered. "Yes, probably plotting ways to destroy God's light."

"They just came out of church, Joe. Leave them be."

"For now." He gave his friend a shove and trotted up the steps into church.

# 3

JOE was surprised to see such a large group in the sanctuary. He'd only just heard there was going to be a meeting an hour before. There were only five other men in the room and at least twenty women.

The men congregated together toward the back pews. Joe nodded to the fellows, as he knew them all well. Mrs. Vernice Armstrong stood at the helm. She was a strong looking woman, but not attractive, and always dressed modestly. She commanded attention if nothing else.

"Thank you all for coming on such short notice. Thank you, ladies of the Christian Temperance Union, for venturing out on this cold night. Also welcome, Sons of Temperance." She waved her hand toward the men. "I'm sure you've all heard of the horror inflicted on our community today. A man slaughtered a mother and her children and killed himself. This is yet another blot on Iowa City's history. A stain on the Christian presence in Johnson County. It is now a mark in time that things are about to change.

"How does this happen in our town? A town so educated and enlightened that our state university is known as the Athens of Iowa? A town where God's word and our Methodist church has been established since 1839. I'll tell you how this happens here in a place where God's light is predestined to shine. Beer. That's how. Beer and strong liquor are the wide path to destruction. These brewers and their *mafia* are a den of wickedness and must be stopped.

"Did you know that this murderer stopped in the Union Public House and imbibed a beer right before he committed his heinous crimes? Did you know that none other than the owner of the Union Brewery himself, Conrad Graf, drank with this murderer and did nothing but entwine himself with the devil and drink down his wicked ways?"

A young woman in the front raised her arm. "Yes, Matilda?" Vernice said.

"What can we do, but pray?" Matilda asked. "They run the city."

"Pray yes, but we must take action. Bold action like Jesus when He cast out the demons and turned the tables on the money changers. We must cast these beer men out and shut down their vile breweries. Only then can the light of God return to our city. They don't run this city anymore. God is in control and will deliver us our desires."

"How? What can we do?" Matilda continued.

"We will agitate them. We will give them no peace. We will rally more to our righteous cause. We will march in the street. We will distribute pamphlets all over the county. My husband will print them in our shop. We will get the politicians to change the laws. Every God-fearing Christian will know we are not going to sit idly by and let our neighborhoods and our children be corrupted by this foreign way, this ungodly way of living! These Germans, and these Bohemians, they even let their children drink!"

"You are talking prohibition," Joe said from the back.

"Yes. We have friends in Des Moines. Some of our senators and representatives and the local constabulary are sympathetic to our cause. Schrader, and the new Governor Sherman too. The time is now to stretch out the hand of God and strike off the head of these serpents and beer peddlers. We must agitate them right here in our own streets. We can't wait for the legislature to do God's work. *We* must do it. Are you with me?" Vernice escalated the intensity of her voice while her passion spread to everyone present.

"We are with you!" cried an older woman with tears streaming down her cheeks.

"What should we do?" Matilda asked.

"By noon we will have pamphlets printed and ready for distribution. They will say in big letters on top, 'MURDER ON THE NORTHSIDE.' Under that it will say 'INTEMPERANCE is the root of all evil. Breweries Must Go! Johnson County Needs Prohibition!' Then it will say in small print our name. Women's Christian Temperance Union."

"Simple and to the point. Place blame where it's due and let the people know what we want."

"We should march around the Northside neighborhood singing songs to the Lord and passing out the pamphlets," another woman suggested.

"I couldn't agree more. Let's meet here at two. I'll bring the pamphlets. Invite all who are united in our glorious cause," Vernice said.

Joe raised his hand. "Mrs. Armstrong, I think we will not be joining you for the march. The existence of the Sons of Temperance is only rumor at this point. I'd like to keep it that way for now if you'd agree. I don't want the brewers to know who we are exactly, not quite yet. My brother Eli works for Great Western Brewery. He hauls ice and supplies. He has won their trust. I'm afraid if they see me marching with you, it could jeopardize him."

"Your brother is with us?"

"Oh yes," Joe said.

"He is not a drunkard?"

"No, ma'am. He got work as a driver and has been employed by the brew men ever since. They don't know he is on our side. He lets me know anything he hears."

"God bless your brother's work. You will be called to service when you are needed most. God will use your resolute will and temperant heart to smite our enemies. It is the mothers and daughters of the light who will begin this fight against the abomination that has been flourishing in our midst for far too long."

The crowd erupted in enthusiastic clapping.

VERNICE left the meeting and walked alone toward her husband's print shop. The night was cold and she was anxious to be inside. Warm light poured from the window of their establishment. The sound of the door opening could not be heard over the machines printing out pamphlets. The aroma of ink and paper filled the air.

Vernice stepped behind the counter and into the back room. Robert Armstrong stood with his back to her, watching the machine printing out papers as he slowly cranked the mechanism. His longtime business partner, Randall Martin, stood next to him with his hand upon his shoulder.

"Robert," she said loudly. The two men jumped apart when they heard her voice.

"Vernice, I've told you not to sneak up on me when the machines are running," he said after a brief glance at his partner.

"How do they look?" she asked.

He handed her one with "MURDER" in big, bold letters across the top.

"Vernice, are you sure you want to go through with this? I don't want the attention brought on us," Robert said nervously.

"The attention will be on me," Vernice said.

"I prefer we just do our job and people leave us alone," Robert said. "We created an advert for Conrad last year."

"The devil's money," Vernice spat.

Robert rolled his eyes and shook his head. "Vernice, we need all the jobs we can get. The money all spends the same."

Vernice scowled at the two men. "I'm going home."

"I will obviously be late finishing your pamphlets for tomorrow," Robert said.

"Stay as late as necessary. I won't wait up. You have Randall for company." She leveled her gaze at Robert's business partner. "Goodnight, sirs." Without another word she marched out the front door.

Once the door was closed behind her, the two men looked at each other.

"I don't know how you do it," Randall said.

"We have no choice. People would talk if I wasn't married to her. She lives her life, and we live ours."

"I know, I know, you're right."

Robert turned back to the machine. "Let's get this done."

CONRAD Graf was in his office before the sun came up as usual. The brewery was a busy place in the morning. He entered notes in the ledger as quickly as possible. He hated the paperwork, though he loved working with the men. The brewing process from start to finish was exhilarating. He'd learned his craft as a boy in Bavaria and knew nothing else.

When he left Germany, he never could have dreamed the success waiting for him in America simply doing what he loved.

He left the office and found his Master Brewer on the top floor.

"Good morning, Hans. How are we looking?" Conrad clasped his man firmly on the shoulder. Conrad was famous for his intense grip and large hands from years of hard work.

"Right on schedule, Mister G. We will need the hops shipment by the end of the week, but I expect it tomorrow." Hans Albrecht spoke in English with a thick

German accent. Both men spoke fluent German, and sometimes they slipped into it, but they both liked using their English. Hans was a man of medium build and slight of shoulder. He had sandy hair and kind eyes. He dressed as a working man should and his hands were tough as leather. His mustache entirely covered his top lip from sight and he walked with a slight limp. A barrel had rolled onto his ankle in his youth and he never walked the same again.

"Be sure to let me know if the shipment doesn't show up on time."

"Yes, Mister G."

"Can you believe the murder?"

"No sir, terrible news. Peter is a good friend. I've shared many a beer with him. I don't know how a soul recovers from such a terrible thing," Hans said with a sour look to his face.

"I don't know either. We'll have to do all we can for Peter. I heard that his wife might survive, but she'll bear some nasty scars on her arms and throat."

"I'm sure she'll wish she had perished, with all her family killed like that," Hans said.

"Perhaps so," Conrad conceded. He patted Hans on the shoulder. "I've got to go check the caves. Have a good day."

"Every day is a good day making beer!" Hans smiled with a grand smile, minus an incisor on his left side.

With a smile and a nod, Conrad made his way down several flights of stairs. Every man he encountered had a task and was busy about it. Conrad climbed into the elevator and slammed the iron gate shut for the descent. He lit the whale oil lantern that was right where he'd left it the day before. He was a creature of habit.

The creaking and grinding sounds of the elevator descending would have terrified most anyone who didn't know the sounds were normal. The elevator dropped thirty-five feet into darkness. A faint light could be seen at the bottom and the temperature grew warmer the farther down Conrad went. At the bottom it was as a constant fifty-five degrees.

Fifty-five degrees felt like cool heaven on an August day and toasty compared to a frosty November morn. The caves were one of Conrad's favorite places in the world. He slammed open the gate and exited the elevator. Several lateral openings big enough for man and cart disappeared into darkness both to the east and north toward the other breweries.

Conrad could hear the cave hands just up ahead. He entered the main finishing cave to find his two men arguing about something. He paid them no mind and began counting barrels.

All three lamp niches were lit with lamps at the end of the cave and several others burning on the side walls. The dome shaped roof and the dancing firelight caused it to be an eerie room to many, but somehow it felt like home to Conrad. When the beer left the caves, it went straight to the people who loved to drink it.

Not all caves were the same. The one along Market Street directly under the Union was more than one hundred feet long, twenty-five feet wide, and fifteen feet high, lined with bricks in an arch overhead. The ceiling had been built using an ancient Roman technique employed by German masons for centuries.

Venting and piping brought in fresh air and allowed the beer to flow down with gravity from the upper "hot" floors. The wooden vats were between six and eight feet in diameter and allowed the sweet aroma of fermentation to spill out into the atmosphere.

Maybe that was what Conrad liked so much about the caves...the aroma. It reminded him of his father. His father had first taught him the art of brewing and he knew he'd never see him again. Somehow the aroma of the brew brought his presence close.

The two men arguing suddenly noticed they were not alone. "Mister G, how are you today, sir?" the taller man asked.

"Very well, and you?"

"Can't complain. Beer is looking good. We'll be barreling on schedule today."

"Good. I'll check with Max and see how many we need at the pub. I'll let you know myself or I'll send Hans to tell you how many."

"Yes, Mister G."

Conrad turned his back and made his way into another cave south of the elevator. He passed a small workshop area and then walked down a center aisle containing shelves stacked high with wooden keg barrels on either side.

He couldn't help but count them as he walked. Old habits died hard. The lantern lit only a certain area around the man carrying it and then darkness reigned. Conrad didn't mind the darkness as he knew every inch of this cave.

He couldn't stop thinking about the tragedy.

What would he do if everyone he loved was suddenly gone? Murdered. What if everything he loved was taken from him and there was nothing he could do about it?

The thought brought a shiver up his back. He even raised his lantern to peer further back into the cave, pushing a slight twinge of fear back down where it belonged. He turned to go, and glanced over his shoulder, spinning around holding the light high over his head as if something was coming for him. Nothing.

He chuckled at himself, shaking his head as he climbed into the elevator.

*Jumpy as a child.*

He raised it to mid-level and slammed open the gate once more. He exited the contraption and turned north, crossing under Market Street to come up in the back room of the Public House.

He found Max wiping down the bar and preparing for the day. "Good morning, Mister G."

With a nod for a good morning greeting, Conrad started right in. "Can you believe that guy came in here and then killed those people?"

"No, it's been bothering me all night. Should I have noticed something?" Max asked.

"My conversation with him was unimportant, but his clothing should have been a clue. He was dressed up. That should have stood out. It didn't fit." Conrad shook his head. "I should have stopped him or something."

"How the hell could we have known?"

"I know. But I wish we could have known. We'd have beat that son-of-a-bitch and saved those folks."

"Mister G, you know we would have, but how were we to know he was crazy?"

With a shake of his head Conrad agreed. "We couldn't have known. Just so sad. I feel for Peter."

Max nodded. "Me too."

"Did you know that Anna's dad used to make shoes with him years ago before he worked with Louis Englert and got into the beer business?"

"No, Mister G. I didn't know that."

"It was before he partnered up with your grandpa and started the Union."

"Does Simeon know about what happened?"

"I don't know. I guess I should go ask Anna if she's told him. He doesn't get out of the house much. I'm sure he's heard, but I could go see him anyway. It's been too long since I've seen him."

"We're all family around here!"

Conrad grinned and clamped his hand on Max's shoulder. "Do you have the food figured for today?"

"Yes, sir, I got it handled."

"What would I do without you, Max?"

"Find someone else, of course," Max said with a laugh.

"Impossible. Thanks for all you do." Conrad headed out the door.

CONRAD pulled the collar of his coat up against the wind. His father-in-law's house wasn't far and he decided to walk to it. It had been too long since he simply stopped in to talk and he was going to do it now. He made it three blocks when he noticed a carriage make a wild turn around the corner a block away.

Then he realized it was his carriage and his wife was driving.

She pulled back hard on the reins and the chestnut horse skidded to a stop. He could see she'd been crying. Her bright blue eyes always appeared even more blue than normal through her tears.

"Get in!" she yelled. "It's Father!"

"I was just walking to go see him."

"Doc Clapp sent for us. He's had an episode!"

"That's all they said?"

"They said to come quick. He might not make it this time!" As soon as he was halfway in the carriage, she snapped the reins and the gelding was off in a flash, his hooves clacking on the brick road.

In a few moments the carriage came to a sliding halt in front of a stately Victorian style home that was stunning in its detail. Her father had grown up poor in Germany and often wondered if the house was simply "too much."

The horse had barely come to a stop and Anna was on the ground running toward the door. A neighbor boy was standing nearby. While she ran to the house, Conrad handed him the reins.

"Can you take this horse around back and stable him?"

"Yes, sir," the boy said with a nod.

"Thank you, son." Conrad handed him a penny.

Conrad hurried himself along to the house. He didn't knock and made his way inside to find his mother-in-law and his sister-in-law holding hands and crying in the front room. He went to them and offered his hand without a word.

They each offered a strained smile and nodded uncomfortably. "What's happened?" Conrad asked.

"Conrad, come on up," Dr. Clapp said from the top of the stairs. "I'll tell you."

Conrad hurried up the stairs. He stood close to Dr. Clapp since the hall was narrow. The door was open to the master bedroom and his father in law was in bed, lying on his back. Anna was sitting in a chair holding her father's hand.

"Is he...?" Conrad asked.

"No, but soon. He had an episode while getting dressed. They'd told him what happened to the Hess girl and he said he had to go see Peter. While he was trying to get himself ready, he clutched at his heart and fell to the floor," Dr. Clapp explained.

"Like last time?" Conrad asked hopefully.

"No. This one is much worse. Conrad, you should go make your peace with him. He'll not survive this. It could be any time now. I've already sent for Father Edmonds."

"Thank you, Doc. You're a good friend."

Conrad's steps caused the wood floors to creak as he ambled toward the heartbreaking scene. He put his hand on his wife's shoulder. Without looking she put her hand on top of his. Her shoulders were shaking as she wept.

After a moment, she stood and hugged her husband, burying her face into his chest.

"I'm going to talk to Mama for a minute. You can have a moment with him if you like," she said and left the room.

Conrad stared down at the body of Simeon Hotz, the man who had taken him in when his daughter fell in love. They shared the love of beer, politics, Anna, and arguing. Conrad sat down in the chair. He reached for Simeon's hand. It was all he could do not to pull away. It felt cold and bony, nothing like it once was.

Conrad strengthened himself. He didn't know if Simeon could hear him or not, but he decided to try speaking to him anyway. He gently squeezed his hand.

"Simeon, it's Conrad. I just want you to know the brewery will be just fine. Anna will be just fine. I'll take care of everybody. You have my word. Thank you for taking me into your family. I'm glad my children have your blood. May God bless your soul."

Anna and her sister entered the room. Conrad immediately stood and wiped a tear from his eye. The sisters stood at the foot of their father's bed staring at him for a time. Conrad reached for his wife's hand. After a light squeeze, he smiled and walked out, descending the stairs to the front room.

Dr. Clapp was there talking to Conrad's mother-in-law, Barbara. She had never been a strong woman, but now she looked as frail as only an aged woman could. Conrad sat next to her. She'd always been fond of him and his presence was a comfort.

"Barbara, if you feel you need to see him alive again, we should get you upstairs. What do you think?" Dr. Clapp asked.

She wiped her eyes with a napkin and shook her head. "No. I have said my goodbyes. I'll see Simeon in the great by and by soon enough."

Dr. Clapp patted her shoulder comfortingly.

"He just wanted to go be with Peter," she added.

"Yes, he would want that. He was a good man and Peter was his friend," Conrad said.

Barbara wiped her eyes. "What's happening in the world if a husband butchers his wife and children?"

"I guess he was a bad man all along and she tried to divorce him," Conrad answered.

The sounds of a big man coming up the steps on the porch foretold the rap on the door. Conrad stood and opened it to find Father Edmonds. He entered like he was about his business. With a curt greeting to Conrad he went straight to Barbara.

"My dear Barbara, is it his time?"

She wept and leaned into Father Edmonds.

Dr. Clapp nodded to the priest.

"He lived a full life and will pass with those who love him all around him. That is a blessing without measure," Father Edmonds said. "He will soon be with the Father in heaven and more who love him."

Barbara pushed back from him. "Thank you, Father. Please go see him while he still lives and pray for him."

"Yes, ma'am. I will." He stood and made his way upstairs.

Conrad watched his priest with love and admiration. Father Edmonds was not a young man anymore, but he was always about the work of the church and it never ended. He obviously loved it as much as Conrad loved making beer.

An hour later, Simeon Hotz took his last Earthly breath.

Anna found Conrad in the kitchen. "I think we should go and get the children. They should see him before they take him away."

"Do you want me to go get them?"

"I'll come along. I need some air." They embraced again.

"I should stop at the brewery and let them know. Many of them loved your father," Conrad said.

"Yes, that's fine."

Conrad prepared the carriage and they were off. The day was clear and cold like the day before and the one before that.

"I can't believe it," Anna said.

"What?" Conrad asked.

"I can't believe he's gone. I thought he was going to die four years ago after the train accident at Little Four Mile, but he pulled through. I know I shouldn't be surprised, but I can't believe he's gone." She leaned into Conrad and wept.

"He was a good one," Conrad said. "He loved me. I loved him too. He was good man. I can't believe it either." Conrad wiped his own tears away.

They pulled up in front of the brewery and left the carriage on Linn Street. They were heading to the main entrance when a commotion began a block down at the Hess House.

"What's that?" Anna asked.

It was the sound of women singing. "I don't know," Conrad said. They were carrying signs. As soon as he read one of them his heart sank.

In big block letters it read, TEMPERANCE NOW!

Another one said, NO BEER! And another said, DRINKING LEADS TO DEATH!

A group of women was marching straight toward him. Conrad recognized the woman in front. Vernice Armstrong. She'd been trouble before, but nothing like this.

They were singing a hymn and marching east down Market Street. The streets were filling with his friends. Most people simply gawked at the spectacle.

"What are they doing?" Anna asked.

"I guess they think this will get us to stop drinking beer," Conrad said.

"Why?"

"I don't know. They think it's going to ruin us all."

"Don't they know it's beer that keeps this town alive?" Anna scoffed.

"I guess they don't care about that. Let's go inside. I don't want to be out here when they go by."

It was too late; Vernice had spotted him.

"Conrad Graf, you have blood on your hands!" she shouted.

He stopped cold in his tracks and walked down the steps. She stepped up in his face completely unafraid. "You have blood on your hands! The Hess blood is on you and your brewery!"

"What are you talking about? I had nothing to do with that!" he yelled right back at her.

"Beer is sin. The wages of sin is death! This is on you! Turn from your wicked ways and tear down this brewery of death!" Vernice screamed.

Conrad's anger boiled. He'd never wanted to hit a woman until that moment. How could she say that? He had done nothing wrong!

Suddenly Max was by his side and grabbed his arm. "Mister G, let's go inside."

He let Max lead him inside as the Women's Christian Temperance Union marched on without incident.

They continued past the other breweries and turned right in front of Baker's store on Gilbert Street, disappearing around the corner. Conrad heard later they kept marching around town until they were sure everyone had seen them. They ended up in front of the Old Capitol where they took to the steps and gave a good oration decrying the evils of alcohol to a crowd of interested townspeople.

Once they had gone, Max let go of him. Conrad found himself shaking with anger. He'd had an emotional couple of days and he'd never been so mad.

Max handed him a flyer. They had littered the streets with them. The top read, "MURDER ON THE NORTHSIDE!"

"Have some boys follow around town and pick every one of these up," Conrad said to Max.

"Every one? There's a lot of them just here," Max argued.

"I said pick them up!" Conrad snapped. "All of them! Every damn one!"

He'd never yelled at Max before and it showed on his face. "I'm sorry, Max. Just pick them up. Any man who helps gets a free beer."

"Yes sir," Max said. "No need to apologize."

"Simeon just passed on."

"Oh, I am sorry," Max said with a glance at Anna. "Very sorry, ma'am, he was a good man."

Anna nodded. "He was. Thank you, Max."

After Max left, Anna grabbed Conrad's hand. "Let's go get the children. Nothing else will happen here today."

**4**

THE funeral of Simeon Hotz was as if a founding member of the town had died, and in many ways that was true. Virtually anyone who had been in Iowa City for more than a year knew Simeon.

He used to spend hours in the Public House telling stories about Brentano's Army. The story got a little larger every time he regaled the crowd with the fact that Duke Leopold had abandoned his post and ran like a coward, leaving his duchy to Brentano. Then Leopold returned with the Prussian Army to regain his former status, and everyone associated with Brentano was exiled.

He fled the Baden lands for the liberty-loving republic of America! It was a winding tale that led him to be a co-founder of the Union Brewery. From shoemaker to a minor partner with the legend, Louis Englert. He'd learned enough of the beer business to know he wanted to be his own boss. Why else come to America? With his knowledge and Anton Geiger's hard work, the Union Brewery was born.

Simeon was a happy man who loved to drink beer as much as profit from making it. Everyone loved him. He was a willing supporter of anything people asked of him and the first to give at any offering. After the train wreck at Little Four Mile he wasn't ever quite the same. The injuries had aged him more than physically.

He died a beloved man and the overflowing crowd at a church the size of St. Mary's was a testament to his life well lived. Conrad would later say he was glad Simeon hadn't lived past 1881. Everything was changing.

The first week of November 1881 was nothing like Father Edmonds had ever seen. He'd been priest at St. Mary's since 1858 and thought he'd seen everything. He'd overseen a prairie town growing into a modern city. He'd delivered mass in the woods, in cabins, and in a storeroom. Father Edmonds helped establish as many as forty-four new parishes and watched many of them build grand churches.

And still, November of 1881 stood out among it all. The horrible Stein Murders on the 5th followed up by the death of a beloved town patriarch on the 6th, left everything that was certain...uncertain. The only thing that felt true was that times were changing, and unseen forces were squaring off against one another. Father Edmonds did what he always did. He kept the faith and did all he could to guide those around him back to it.

## November 15th, 1881

CONRAD Graf sat in his office as the sun came up, like he had a thousand times before, to the sounds of the brewery coming to life all around him. He was reading the *Iowa City Post,* a copy of the *Iowa Methodist* at his side. He shook his head in disgust. Both papers had front page articles about a Prohibitory Amendment to the Iowa Constitution. The two papers wrote from opposite perspectives, but both were written as if the idea of an amendment coming to the Iowa Congress in the spring 1882 for an actual vote was a foregone conclusion.

The idea of prohibition actually passing the legislature was like a kick in the stomach. It would kill their entire business overnight. The entire empire would be illegal. Generations of labor and love gone with the stroke of a pen. It was not the America he'd dreamt of.

Max walked in without knocking. He had a paper in his hand which he promptly slammed onto Conrad's desk.

"Not another pamphlet!" Conrad said.

"Oh yes, take a look," Max said.

It read:

**Temperance and Prohibition Lecture**
**Tonight at the Methodist Church**
**By Professor Moffat.**
**Everybody Come Out!**

Conrad exhaled loudly and ran his hands through his hair. "What am I gonna do with these people?" He was incredulous. "I'm going to the meeting."

"No, you are not!" Max said. "It'll turn into a shouting match and they'll be shouting at you!"

"I need to know what they are saying at that meeting."

"I agree with that, but you can't go," Max said. "You know you can't."

"Yes, I know, and I also want to know who is there."

"Who can we send?" Max asked.

"I don't know, I have to talk to the others."

Max walked out the front door of the Union with Conrad. They paused for a moment. "Do you ever feel like everything is going out of control?" Conrad asked.

"Ever since that guy butchered his wife and kids, I've been a little out of sorts," Max answered.

"Out of sorts," Conrad said with wry glance at Max. "I'll stop in and see you after I talk to the others."

"Sounds good," Max said. He crossed the street on his way back to the Public House while Conrad headed east down Market to the other breweries.

J.J. Englert was standing on the front boardwalk to his brewery as Conrad approached.

"What the hell took you so long? I've been standing here waiting for you for an hour!" J.J. shouted.

"Bah...you have not."

"So you've seen the latest pamphlet?"

"Yes, that's what I'm here about. We need to talk," Conrad said.

"We sure as hell do!" J.J. stated solidly. "Let's go over to the Great Western and drink some of Dostal's crappy Erlanger while we talk." J.J. would never admit that Erlanger was tasty.

J.J. tossed his arm around Conrad's shoulder and they made their way across Market Street.

"Don't look so glum. It's all going to work out," J.J. said.

"Maybe. It's been a rough couple weeks."

"I'm sorry about Simeon. How's Anna?"

"She's good. He'll be greatly missed."

The Great Western Brewery was the largest of the three breweries. It was half a block long and a four-story brick behemoth. It had its own blacksmith, wagons, a massive icehouse, caves, and a well-trained crew that could put out more brew than anyone else, not to mention it had three different public bars on the premises to help northsiders with their thirst.

They knew where they were going. John Dostal had an office, but he was rarely in it. He could almost always be found in his bar on the second floor with windows looking out to the west and south. This bar was the one for *"Important"* people or dear friends of John. The other two bars were open to the public, but not the Second Floor Club. You had to *be* somebody to get in there.

A tough looking fellow stood sentry at the bottom of the stairs. He smiled at the sight of Conrad and J.J. coming his way. "Hello, gents. Mister Dostal will be glad to share a pint with you."

"I'm sure he will, Frankie, but is he buying?" J.J. asked with a laugh. Conrad smiled. He was glad to spend some time with J.J. He needed a good laugh and J.J. was always good for that.

They were both second generation brewers and that somehow brought the two of them together. As much as J.J. liked to have fun, Conrad knew there would be no better friend to have in a fight.

They climbed the stairs two at a time as if in a contest. J.J. reached out his hand at the top, the victor.

"Let's have a beer!" he exclaimed.

"Let me catch my breath. I'm not twenty-four anymore!" Conrad laughed, but continued right on without pause.

They stepped into the Second Floor Club and paused a moment, shoulder-to-shoulder. With a quick scan of the room, they saw two bank presidents, one city councilman, one state congressman, one doctor, a table of professors, and half a dozen lawyers arguing in the corner.

"Too many lawyers," J.J. whispered.

John Dostal was behind the bar when he saw them. "Hello, my friends, welcome to my humble establishment."

"Humble? Something you've never been accused of!" J.J. laughed. "Well-connected by the looks of this room. That's what I'll accuse you of, but humble? No."

"You say that like it's a bad thing. People in business always need friends who are powerful. What brings my fellow mafiosos to call?"

"We just want to try your beer. Right, Conrad?" J.J. joked.

Conrad laughed. "Yeah, we're here for the beer!"

"I'm sorry about Simeon," Dostal said to Conrad. "He was loved by all."

"He sure was," Conrad said.

"Just like us," J.J. said.

"Right!" Dostal exclaimed. "Come join me over here. Let's talk about our detractors."

Dostal led them to a corner table that had views of both the City Brewery and the Union.

"Nice views," J.J. said.

"I like to keep an eye on the enemy," Dostal laughed.

"Then you should look right over there." Conrad pointed to the spire of the Methodist church a couple of blocks away that stood tall and proud.

"I'm not afraid of a few angry Methodists."

"You should be. Have you seen this?" Conrad laid the latest flyer out on the table between them.

Dostal quickly read it, pulled it from the table, and put it in his pocket with a glance around the room. "What do you propose we do?"

"We need someone at that meeting," Conrad said.

"I'd like to know who is there. What they're saying or planning," J.J. added.

"The papers are all talking like there is a constitutional amendment coming that will outlaw everything we do! Have you guys heard that?" Conrad barked.

"Yeah, I read the paper," Dostal said. "Calm down."

"Calm down? Everything I've built in America would be lost if that happens. Calm down? You calm down!" Conrad slammed his fist on the table.

The sound caused everyone in the area to look. Dostal slammed his own fist on table and laughed out loud, perhaps a little too demonstrably, but it was a good cover for the most part.

"Okay, it's agreed we need someone at that meeting. Who?" J.J. asked.

"Know any Methodists who like to drink?" Dostal asked with a preposterous look on his face as if his request was sheer fantasy.

"Holy crap!" J.J. laughed. "I do know one!"

"Who?" Conrad asked.

"He's like a brother, or at least a cousin or something."

"Who is he?" Conrad asked with a doubtful glare.

"Oh my, he's perfect. His name is Theodore Miller. Can you get any more Methodist than that?"

Dostal and Conrad shared a glance and a chuckle as another round of beers were delivered.

"He's just arrived in the last month. He's from Mankato, Minnesota. My father served with his father in the Greybeards. I'm not kidding, Teddy's dad literally died in old Louie's arms. Louis promised him on death to care for his family. If you know anything about my father, it's that he keeps his promises. He's been sending Teddy's mother money ever since."

"What's he doing here?" Dostal asked.

"He's finishing medical school that we are sponsoring. He's almost a doctor. He's interning with Doctor Clapp. He's literally a Methodist. I swear."

"Then he's a teetotaler!" Conrad shouted. "They all are."

"No, he's not. He could drink any of us under the table right now, as I live and breathe!"

"I don't believe it," Conrad said. "If that's true, then they make Methodists different in Minnesota!"

"He owes my family like no other, he drinks beer, and no one knows him. He's perfect. He's our mole!"

Dostal had to smile. "I have no better idea."

"Let's use the temperance meeting as our trial run," Conrad said. "Send him in. Get all the information he can and report back. We'll see how he does. Meet back up here at noon tomorrow. I want to see him drink a beer."

"He doesn't know anyone. How's he going to tell us who is at the meeting?" Dostal asked.

"Trust me. He's smart. He's good," J.J. said. "You'll see."

"Another round?" Dostal asked.

"Of course. This Erlanger isn't as bad as I thought it would be!" J.J. laughed.

LIGHT snow was falling straight down. Giant flakes an inch across floated to the ground, covering everything in a frosting of white brilliance. The temperature was near thirty and the complete absence of wind made it almost surreal as people made their way to the meeting at the Methodist Church.

A fine white fence surrounded the commanding stone structure that focused upon a square turret. Four imposing pillars protected the pointed spire directly in the center that was obviously added later than the original structure in a phallic attempt at supremacy.

The Methodists had been in Johnson County a long time. St. Mary's may have a loftier apex, but no one could argue the Methodists were *first* in Johnson County. From their original roots in a two-story cabin led by circuit rider Joseph

Kirkpatrick, they'd grown a strong presence that would stand the test of time. Two buildings and a spire addition later they stood ready to claim pre-eminence against the onslaught of Catholics, nearly all immigrants of a variety of heritages, mostly German, Irish, and Bohemian.

Father Edmonds oversaw church after church, literally spawning new parishes yearly. St. Wenceslaus, St. Patrick's, St. Mary's in Solon, St. Mary's in Oxford, Sts. Peter and Paul Church, and many more. The Methodists solidified their base in the heart of Iowa City intent on seeing their mission through.

The snow was weighing the limbs of the branches down so far that the lower extremities were touching the ground. It was beautiful in the lamplight that led the way for the passionate protestants on their way to a meeting that would alter the course of Johnson County.

A long line formed as the faithful Women of Christian Temperance endeavored to sign everyone in attendance in at a table near the front door. Vernice Armstrong was beside herself with worry that something would go wrong, while at the same time trusting that God would provide as needed.

Theodore Miller stepped up to the table. He spoke with his mouth pointed downward, nervous that the young woman before him would smell the beer on his breath as he signed in.

She was lovely. Her amber locks fell to her shoulders with a natural curl that bounced as she spoke. Her eyes were bright and blue as the sky on a cloudless summer day. Her modest dress did little to hide the curvaceous figure that caused Theodore to stumble over his words.

"I am Theodore...um...I mean, you can call me Teddy, but Theodore is my name."

The young lady giggled at his nervousness and that made her all the more nervous herself. She'd never seen him before and he was handsome.

"Just write your name on the paper and you can go in," she said.

When he took the pencil from her hand, he accidentally touched her finger ever so slightly, but it was like an eruption in his soul.

He spoke out loud as he wrote, "I am Theodore Miller."

"Nice to meet you Theodore. I am Matilda."

"You can call me Teddy," he looked away. "Like I already said."

"You can call me Mattie. I've not seen you around. I thought I knew everyone."

"The town is growing fast, I guess," he said. "I'm from Minnesota. I'm finishing medical school and interning with Doctor Clapp."

"Oh," she said, obviously disappointed.

"What's wrong?"

"Doctor Clapp is friends with the brewers and a German Catholic."

"Well, I am neither German nor Catholic!"

"That's good!" she said with a grand smile.

"I'm a lifelong Methodist. Does that get me anything?" he joked.

She smiled coyly at him. "Well I'm not sure, what do you want?"

He glanced around to make sure no one was listening before he spoke. "I'd love to see you again sometime after this meeting?"

"Perhaps."

"Can I call on you?"

"No, I'll find you if I want to."

He walked into the meeting, his mind spinning. Mattie was intoxicating, and he didn't need a drink. He'd never heard a woman talk quite like that and it had left him flustered. He found a seat along the outer edge and waited as the room filled in.

*What did she mean she'd find me if she wants to? Does she want to? How will she find me?*

A large man dressed in a fine suit with almost no hair upon his head waddled up to the front. He turned toward the group and scanned the room with dark eyes set close together. He saw many of his closest acquaintances.

"Welcome, friends. Most of you know me, but if not, my name is J.R. Dunleavy. I own Dunleavy Dry Goods, and you're all welcome any time. We have a full assortment of items, but that's not why I'm here.

"I'm here because an amazing thing is happening. God is changing our town, our county, and our entire state for the good. For those of us who have been praying for the temperance movement to grab hold, this is an exciting time. The time is now. Our brave ladies of temperance have thrown down the gauntlet against these evil brewers in our midst.

"Let's all give Vernice Armstrong a hand for her efforts," J.R. said, taking a moment to clap. "Thank you, Vernice. Tonight, we are lucky to have Professor Moffat with us to share what is going on around the country and our state and just how a prohibition could come about. Let's all welcome Professor Moffat."

Professor Moffat stepped to the pulpit and looked down at the papers he had laid out until the clapping began to subside. He was bald on top of his head, but the sides were a mess of wiry gray and brown hair. His chin was covered in a beard as wiry as the hair above his ears. He raised his eyes to the crowd and slowly removed his glasses, putting them in his coat pocket.

"When I was a boy, I did not know God. My mother wanted to take us to church, but my father would have none of it. Since the word of God was dear to her, she squirrelled away enough money to buy us a Bible.

"When my father found out, he beat her viciously in a drunken rage. He ripped that Bible to shreds and tossed it in the fire, forcing us all to watch it burn.

"I hated my father for the things he did to us. My mother told me not to hate him, because when he was sober, he was a good man. The problem was he was hardly ever sober. She made me promise to love God and never drink a drop.

"The last time my father was beating my mother I tried to intervene, and he beat me as well. I was just a boy and he was a strong man. After he left, my mother came to me and I told her I hated my father and prayed to God he would die.

"My mother told me to take it back and to never pray for violence or death. I did what she asked, but my father fell from his horse that night and cracked his skull. He died by the side of the road...alone. They found him the next morning."

Professor Moffat paused for dramatic effect. He had them in the palm of his hand.

"I asked my mother if God had killed him because of my prayer...if *I* had killed him. She told me to pray for his soul and she looked away, leaving me unsure. As the years went on, I was never sorry my father was gone. My mother was never beaten again. I went to school and eventually college. My brothers and sisters were safe, and why?

"Because the drinking man is an evil man. The drinking man destroys his own family. I promised my mother I would not be a drinking man, but I am here to tell you that I am taking it further than that. We can stop all men from drinking by preaching temperance and by forcing politicians to finally pass prohibitory laws that are good for all mankind."

The crowd clapped, rallied by emotion at the dream of an alcohol-free world.

"I've heard good things about what's going on here. In Kansas I heard about the Iowa City Temperance movement and the bold Methodists who are here before me. I heard you were organizing. I heard you were gathering powerful members of society to our cause—businessmen, politicians, social leaders. I heard you were marching in the streets. And all this in the shadow of the devil himself.

"Three strong kings of Satan, three breweries producing beer daily to feed the evildoers and dull the minds of the saints, but no more. I came here to encourage you in your fight. Be not afraid, be not dismayed, for many are with you. Many all across the Midwest are with you. From Kansas to Maine, Iowa will lead the fight and set an example of how men should live temperant lives.

"Remain steadfast. These titans will not fall without a fight. Stay vigilant and the Lord will strengthen you in your time of need. Fight the good fight and we shall see the floodgates of Heaven open, the brewhouses and the pubs falter and fall, but not without you.

"I thank you for your love and strength of character in a town that literally is built upon a river of beer. You will be victorious. You will take back this city and we will take back the land for our God. Amen."

The professor gathered his papers and stepped aside while the group got to their feet and enthusiastically cheered. Teddy stood, clapping as well. He noticed Matilda wipe tears from her cheeks.

Vernice stepped to the front. "Thank you for coming tonight. Thank you, Professor Moffat. You are an inspiration." The clapping continued. "Be careful on your way home, it is still snowing. Ladies, you are all invited to our regular meeting every Wednesday at six here at the church. We need all of you to accomplish our dream of prohibition. Thank you and goodnight."

Teddy glanced about the room. The crowd was easily sixty percent women. There was a man leaning against the back wall with a badge on his chest, who ducked out the door at the conclusion of the meeting.

The crowd of people milled about and socialized for a moment, basking in the glow of the professor's words. A middle-aged man with gray at the temples of his sandy hair approached Teddy.

"Hello, young man, welcome. I don't know you. I'm Stephen Dunlap. What is your name?"

"I am Theodore Miller, but people call me Teddy."

"Teddy it is then. My brother and I make furniture. What is it you do?"

"I am a doctor. Well, almost. I'm finishing my schooling and apprenticing with Doctor Clapp."

"A doctor is a useful man. Clapp is a good doctor, but he's a Catholic and a friend to the brewers."

"Yes sir, I am aware of that, but I must learn my trade and I couldn't choose only a Methodist," Teddy said with a forced smile.

"What a fine dream the professor has shared with us, don't you agree?"

"A fine dream indeed. His hopes are lofty in the face of the so-called beer mafia," Teddy said.

"Nothing so-called about it. They dominate our town, but not for long."

Matilda appeared and stood next to the man, Dunlap.

Teddy smiled and felt his cheeks flush red. "Teddy, this is my daughter Matilda."

"Yes, Daddy, we met at check in. Teddy is from Minnesota."

"Is that so?"

"Yes sir, Mankato. It's a fine place, but the state school here is the best in the Midwest for medicine."

"Well, we are lucky to have you. Maybe after you're done with your studies we could entice you to stay. Perhaps apply your trade right here?"

Teddy flashed a smile at Matilda. "I have no plans beyond completing my studies."

"Yes of course, you're young. Well, we must be going. I hope to see you again, perhaps at church?"

"Yes. Have a good night, Mister Dunlap and Miss Matilda." Teddy watched them walked away, then followed toward the door as well, keeping his eyes down and listening to all he could.

He overheard Mrs. Armstrong talking to Dunleavy and two men who looked so alike they had to be brothers. Each wore business attire and looked the part of important men. With their reddish hair and ruddy complexions, Teddy would have thought them twins, but one was obviously older than the other as his chin whiskers had almost entirely turned white, while the younger's remained rust-colored. They stood identically, with eerily similar mannerisms, each man with a thumb tucked into a waistcoat pocket, focusing their blue eyes on Vernice as she spoke, nodding in agreement. He only heard fragments, but it sounded like she said, "...with the new senate we should have the numbers to pass it..."

The older of the two brothers said, "We can't wait for that to save us. We must move at the local level. As city attorneys we are in a position to..."

The line moved on and Teddy suddenly found himself in the foyer. The door to the church was open and he could see the snow falling outside. He made his way for the door, determined to get back to his boarding house and get to his studies. He had a lot of reading to do by morning. Dr. Clapp had asked him to read up on the effects of two common poisons and he was excited to get to it.

Teddy shivered a bit and raised the back of his coat against the cold night. His breath hovered in front of him in a cloud as he rounded the corner and headed east down Jefferson street toward St. Mary's. His room at the boarding house was only another two blocks.

Suddenly two men stepped from the shadows and blocked his advance. Startled, he slipped in the snow and was in the process of falling when one of them reached out his hand and grabbed hold of his arm, preventing him from going down.

"Thanks," Teddy said. "Slippery out here."

51

"Yes, it is. Best to be careful," said the one who was obviously the leader of the two. He was not the larger of them, but he talked with a sly way about him. He was a thin man with hollow cheeks and pallid skin marked with scars from surviving the pox.

"Good night, sirs," Teddy said and went to step around them.

The leader sidestepped to remain in Teddy's path. "Who are you? We saw you at the meeting. Don't know you."

Teddy glanced at the second man. He looked much tougher than the first. Just under six feet tall and thick with muscle like a man who worked hard for a living. Snow was sticking to his thick black mustache.

Teddy looked back at the leader. "I'm Theodore Miller. Who are you?"

"Theodore Miller, what were you doing at the meeting?"

"I'm new in town. I didn't know you had a temperance group here. I saw the flyer and I wanted to check it out."

"Where are you from?"

"Minnesota. Who are you?" Teddy strengthened himself and stared right at the leader.

"I'm Joe Lund. This is my friend Richard."

"Well, nice to meet you. Have a good night." Teddy tried to push through them.

They stepped shoulder-to-shoulder blocking his advance. "So, you are a friend of temperance?"

"Of course, why else would I be here? Otherwise I'd be having a beer in the Public House right now, wouldn't I?" Inside, Teddy wished he was doing exactly that.

"Well, Theodore Miller, we are looking for strong men like yourself who are *friends* of temperance."

"What for?" Teddy asked.

Joe looked side-to-side to be sure no one was around. "Let's just say, we get things done that Mrs. Armstrong can't."

"Like what?"

"Come to one of our meetings and find out."

"Okay, when and where?"

"We meet down by the river. I got a cabin near the old Gilbert Store. Do you know where that is?"

"I can find it."

"Next Thursday at dark."

"I'll be there. What do you call yourselves?"

"The Sons of Temperance."

With a nod Teddy pushed his way through the two men and called back, "I'll see you there."

"Come alone," Joe said.

Teddy shuffled on down the walk thankful to be away from the two men. For a minute he thought it was going to come to blows, but now he found himself invited in.

He was excited for his good fortune. He knew he was supposed to get information for J.J., but all he could think of was Matilda.

# 5

VERNICE Armstrong and the two lookalike brothers marched along Clinton Street heading south, the gold dome of the former Iowa State Capitol on their right. The classic building ruled over Iowa City and promised a long and enlightened future as the heart of both the town and the state university.

Such grand and awe-inspiring architecture elevated Iowa City from all the other ramshackle Iowa towns that were scratching out an existence and bringing the civilized world to the west. Iowa City was leading the way in eastern Iowa. Civilized meant *temperant* to Vernice and her accomplices. While beer and strong drink may have been the norm in Germany or Ireland, it had no place here.

The street was full of wagons both parked and going about their business in all directions. The city was alive with activity. Vernice pushed her way through a large group of people standing outside of the St. James Hotel. She kept going without a second look. She was set about her task and nothing was going to stand in her way.

She glanced up at the shingle hanging out above a solid looking wooden door that read "City Prosecutor. A.E. Maine."

Vernice and company opened the door and immediately marched up a flight of narrow wooden stairs. By the third or fourth step the snow had fallen from their shoes and they began to feel the warmth of the building. Once they reached the top of the flight of steps, a hallway turned back directly west toward the street. Two doors presented themselves.

The first was stenciled with one word only: *Dentist.*

The second read "A.E. Maine. By Appt. Only."

The younger of the two brothers said, "Do we have an appointment?"

Vernice gave him a look that could kill as she turned the knob. "We do now."

She stepped into the front room of the office with her accomplices right behind. A young woman sitting at a desk stood and asked, "May I help you?"

"Yes, we are here to see Mister Maine. Is he in?"

"You need to make an appointment. I'm sorry, ma'am."

"He will see me." Vernice stomped toward the closed door, turned the knob, and opened it.

A man of medium build with salt and pepper hair sat at his desk shaking his head. "Vernice, we can't keep seeing each other like this."

"I need to talk to you."

"I'm sure you do, but why can't you manage to make an appointment like everyone else? I actually do have real business to attend to, you know," he said in a high-pitched voice with an angry edge to it.

"This can't wait."

"What can't wait? Be quick about it."

Vernice motioned to the men with her. "These are the Swafford brothers, John and C.G. His name is Carroll, but he goes by C.G."

Mr. Maine nodded to the men. "Yes, Vernice, I know the Swaffords. I know every lawyer in town. What can I do for you?"

Vernice sat in the chair directly across from Mr. Maine's desk while the Swaffords stood behind her like bookends.

"Our time is now," she said. "I can feel it. We are going to bring down these evil breweries and their saloons. Temperance will reign, glory be to God."

Mr. Maine shook his head. "Vernice, I am sympathetic to the cause, but bringing down the breweries in this town would take an act of God."

Vernice smiled. "Quite right. That's why it will happen and soon. The state legislature is going to pass a prohibitory amendment this next session. They have the votes, but that won't be until next year. We can't wait. We need to outlaw it now!"

Mr. Maine glanced up at the men behind Vernice. They stood motionless and appeared to believe as she did.

"We could outlaw drinking right now in Iowa City with a city ordinance," Vernice proclaimed. "We don't need the state legislature. Other towns have done it."

"Vernice..." Mr. Maine looked out the massive window framing the old capitol building, "...I admire your passion, but that is—"

"Is exactly what is going to happen."

"I was going to say that is going to be near impossible," Mr. Maine countered.

Vernice smiled. "*Near* impossible is not *impossible*."

"Impossible then."

"We need your support, Andrew. Please?"

Mr. Maine shook his head. "Let me tell you why it's imposs—"

"Nothing is impossible for God," Vernice said as a matter of fact with no regard to reality.

"Yes, I know, but for it to pass the current city council, God is going to have to kill off at least three people. Will He do that?"

"Maybe," Vernice said with a serious tone. "His will be done."

"Vernice, even if we get it presented as a city ordinance, which, of course, I can ask John Schell to do, it will go nowhere. Why do that? Why go through the fight only to be defeated? Do you remember that John Englert, owner of the City Brewery and one of the very men you are out to destroy is *on* the council? And not only Mister Englert, but also Mister Englert's confidant, lifelong friend, and First Bank President, Forrest Beck, is also on the council. He is a faithful member of St. Mary's and a financier of more than one brewery. And as if that wasn't enough, Robert Byington, who you know is a lawyer, and with his brother Otto represent the brewers in all legal matters, is on the council as well. Are you beginning to see my point? The futility? Your ordinance idea is a lost cause. Don't waste your time with it. That's my advice to you. If the state passes a prohibitory law, we will have a chance to bring down the breweries, but even then, only a chance. They're too powerful."

Vernice stood and walked to the window. Standing with her back to the men, she stared silently at the massive building across the shimmering snow-covered field. Students walked the paths between the center building and the adjacent ones that made up the main campus. It was stunning and truly majestic on the winter's day. Sunlight glinted off the gold dome, the hillside dropping away behind it culminating in the ever-flowing dark river. She shivered.

"I'm asking you to request Mister Schell to present the ordinance. Will you do it? Or will you shirk God's calling on your life?" She did not turn to face him as she spoke in a monotone voice.

Mr. Maine stared at the Swafford brothers in exasperation. "John, can you tell her it won't work?"

John glanced at Vernice and grimaced slightly, "She's right, Andrew. We can't pass it if we don't present it."

"It won't pass," Mr. Maine insisted.

"God's will be done." Vernice turned toward them. "These brewers will close, and their wicked ways will flee our city. I know this to be true. How it happens we shall see. Please tell me you will ask Mister Schell to present the ordinance? I know he is a believer."

"Yes, he is a good Methodist, but—"

"Whether it passes or not, we must let our enemies know we are not going to go quietly."

"You want a war with them?"

"No. I simply want them to tear down their breweries and stop making beer."

"You realize that means war, because they will never willingly tear down their breweries."

"God will make a way. He could tear them down in one day. So, at the next meeting Mister Schell will bring forth the ordinance outlawing the brewing and sale of all alcohol inside the city limits?"

Mr. Maine looked at the Swaffords for any last bit of help, but they stood like pillars and were both of one accord with Vernice. He shook his head in defeat. "Yes. At the next meeting. There isn't another meeting until January of the new year."

"Very good. Thank you, sir, may God bless you." Vernice turned sharply on her heel, marching back the way she'd come, the Swaffords in tow.

She paused at the door. "Mister Maine, we shall spread the word. I guarantee the January meeting will be well attended."

Vernice nodded her head in satisfaction and she was off.

"Oh, I am sure it will be," Mr. Maine whispered to himself.

THEODORE Miller entered the Second Floor Club and stood in the doorway for a moment.

A slight man with white hair and a kind face approached him. "May I take your coat, sir?"

Teddy handed the man his coat. "Yes, thank you, sir."

The man took it to a room off to the side and Teddy confidently strode to the table near the windows. All three of them waited to see what he had to say.

"What is it, man? How did it go?" J.J. prompted.

With a grand smile on his face Teddy took the seat with his back to the door. He glanced at the view out of the windows, noticing the two breweries, both spires of St. Mary's and the Methodist Church, and over it all the Gold Dome stood supreme.

Dostal waved to the bartender to bring another round. In a flash, beer for everyone and a plate of food for Teddy was placed on the table before them.

"I went to the meeting as instructed. They had no idea I was a spy." He glanced behind himself. "It was so exhilarating!"

"I'm glad you had a good time. Did you learn anything? Who did you see?" Conrad pressed.

Immediately his mind went to Matilda.

After a longer than normal pause, J.J. all but shouted, "Tell us! Come on, man!"

"Yes, I met some people. You know Vernice Armstrong. She is definitely in charge. The man who introduced the speaker was J.R. Dunleavy."

"I'm not surprised. That rotund idiot ignores me on the street. I saw him cross the street once just to avoid me," Englert griped.

"Who else?" J.J. pressed.

"Two brothers. They look like they could be twins, but one is older than the other. Reddish hair and—"

"That's the Swaffords. They are faithful Methodists and I know they're teetotalers. They've taken on some cases for the city."

"What are they planning?" Dostal asked.

"Mostly to be annoying. They are looking to be an agitation to you first. Second, they are expecting a prohibitory amendment at the state level. I heard Vernice say they had the votes."

"Good luck. That will never happen." J.J. smirked. "We even have some Republicans on our side!"

"Well, she thinks they have the votes. I'm pretty sure her plan is to wreak whatever havoc she can on you until the state finally vindicates her goals."

"What are her goals?" Conrad asked.

"She wants to see all three breweries absolutely gone."

"Gone?" Dostal was dumbfounded. "What the hell is wrong with her?"

"They feel it is their mission from God."

"From God?" Conrad said, incredulous. "Don't they know we go to church?"

"Yes, but I don't think they think much of Catholic church."

"I don't think much of Methodists! I don't appreciate that temperance hag shouting in my face ten minutes after my father-in-law dies. This isn't over by a long shot!" Conrad all but shouted.

"No, it's not." Teddy admitted. "It's just starting."

"Anything else?" J.J. asked.

"I saw a police officer in the back. He ducked out right when it ended, but he was listening more than working by how it looked," Teddy said.

"What did he look like?" J.J. asked.

"Solemn. Dark hair, a substantial mustache, and whiskers covering his chin."

Conrad frowned. "That's Coldren. That son-of-a-bitch!"

"Who's Coldren?" Teddy asked.

"He's the sheriff," J.J. said and then emptied his glass. He immediately caught the eye of the bartender and waved his finger in the air signifying another round.

"Anybody else?" asked Dostal.

"Yeah, there were more, but I will need to go again to get more information."

"Will you?" Conrad requested. "We'll pay you. Handsomely."

Teddy smiled at that prospect. "Thank you." He was actually having fun being a spy, and he didn't want to tell them, but he would have done it for free. It was a rush.

"Here's something odd..." Teddy said. "A couple of guys got in my way when I left. I thought they wanted to fight at first, but then they invited me to their Sons of Temperance meeting next week."

"Sons of what?" Conrad asked, his temper right at the surface.

"Sons of Temperance. They said they take care of things that need done that Mrs. Armstrong can't do."

No one spoke for a moment. Teddy took a quick drink of his beer. Conrad smiled at the sight of him drinking.

The three brewers stared at each other for a moment, contemplating their rapidly changing world.

"Well. Hmm...that's how it's going to be then?" Dostal said. "We need our own force."

Conrad and John nodded in agreement.

"Yes, we need men willing to do what needs done and no one wants to talk about," Conrad said. "Men loyal to our way."

"Let's start small. Each brewery put in two men. Six should be enough for now," J.J. decided. "But we must all three of us agree before we send them out on a task. We must be united in this. Our fates will be the same as the stakes go up with each hand."

"Sure. I have two guys I can give," Conrad offered.

"Agreed," Dostal said. "One hundred percent off the books. We pay these men in cash or beer trade. No records."

"Agreed," J.J. said.

Conrad nodded. "Agreed."

"What else do you know?" J.J. asked, turning his attention back to Teddy.

"Nothing until I go to the next meeting," Teddy said. "And I can't drink in public anymore. If they caught me, it would be all over."

"Drink up here. It's private and it's on the house," Dostal said. "It's not as lively as downstairs, but it is a fine place to drink an Erlanger."

"Oh please." J.J. rolled his eyes. "Are you trying to kill our drinking Methodist? I'll bring a fine stash of Englert beer up here for him."

"I also met a girl," Teddy said.

"A girl? What?" J.J. asked.

"Her name is Matilda," Teddy said with just a bit too much wistfulness in his voice.

"Jesus, Mary, and Joseph! We didn't say nothing about a girl!" J.J. stated with an edge.

"Matilda what?" Conrad snapped. "Get your head together! You're not there to meet girls."

"Matilda Dunlap."

"Oh, Stephen Dunlap's daughter. I know her, she's a beautiful girl." Dostal shook his head. "He's no friend of brewers."

"You better watch it. You don't want to get messed up with some Methodist girl," J.J. warned.

"I am a Methodist," Teddy said.

"Yeah but not a normal one."

"I just saw her. It's not like we're getting married!"

"That's how it starts." Conrad took a swig of his brew. "It's innocent enough at first."

"And before you know it that pretty little gal will be leading you around by the nostril," J.J. said with a laugh.

"You all have wives!" Teddy protested.

J.J. feigned outrage. "God rest her soul, I do not! At least not this side of heaven."

"You stay away from that girl if you know what's best for you," Dostal cautioned.

"You all are worse than my mother. If you were my age and single what would you do?"

Silence filled the table as the older men pondered the question.

"A good Catholic girl is one thing. A good Methodist girl is entirely different." Conrad laughed and all the brewers joined in.

Teddy frowned and took a healthy swallow of his brew. He realized quickly he wasn't going to win an endorsement from his bosses.

"The guy named Joe said the meeting was at his cabin down by the river near the old Gilbert Store. I don't know where that is," Teddy added.

"I can draw you a map. There are only a few old cabins down there. It's easy to find. Did he give you any idea what they were planning?" asked J.J.

"No. That's what the meeting is about I think."

By Tuesday, Teddy was already dreading Thursday. Wednesday his stomach was off the entire day. Thursday morning, he jumped awake before dawn drenched in a cold sweat.

"How did I get myself into this?" he asked himself out loud. "I just wanted to get my medical degree, go back to Minnesota or somewhere suitable, marry, raise some kids, live a nice life. Now I'm a damn spy!" He ran his hand through his hair and swung his feet to the cold floor.

He thought of all the money Louis Englert had given his mother. How much he'd given to him. He knew he'd be out there on a wagon loading hops or ice right now without that opportunity. After his dad died in the war, without the money from his friend in Iowa, his mother would have lost everything.

He thought of his mother. By this time, she'd be up and cooking breakfast for his younger brothers and sisters. The ham she was frying was because of Englert money and the bond his father had with Louis. His father had paid for it with his life. Louis had honored it with his money. He'd be damned if he let them down now.

He stood resolute and dressed for the day. He was excited for his hands-on training with Dr. Clapp. Today they were going to make an entire day of calls upon patients in their homes and he was excited to see what it would bring. He decided to put tonight's mission out of his mind.

The brewers had filled Dr. Clapp in on the special nature of Teddy's evening requirements, so he offered the use of his carriage. Dr. Clapp was indebted to the northside as much as anyone. His life and practice were made up entirely within this community. He was one of them. He lived it and breathed it. He birthed their children, set their bones, stitched their wounds, and ultimately closed their eyes as he shook hands with Father Edmonds.

He loved the people he cared for. Teddy could see it in everything Dr. Clapp did. It was not a job to him, it was a calling, and he knew he was at home. He often talked about Dr. Peck and the Sisters of Mercy who had first planted the dream of a special hospital, a Catholic hospital. Dr. Clapp's dream was to see it a reality, and thanks to men like Englert, Graf, and Dostal, it was going to happen. It was his dream to build on what they'd started.

Teddy wondered where he fit in all of that. Was he supposed to stay here and help realize Dr. Clapp's dream? What about this girl, Matilda?

He sat alone in the carriage as the sun was setting to the west and painting the cold day with a brilliant display of orange, yellow, and red on its way down.

What would Matilda think of his subterfuge? Her father definitely wouldn't condone it. What was he doing here? He grabbed the reins to give them a flick. He had to tell J.J. he just couldn't do it.

Suddenly, Joe Lund stood before the carriage grabbing the reins where they attach to the bit. "Nice carriage," he said with a wry smile.

"It's Doctor Clapp's. He let me borrow it."

"I told you not to tell anyone about meeting us," Joe snapped.

"No, you told me to come alone."

Joe thought back and realized technically Teddy was right. "Did you tell him?"

"I told him I needed to go out for a few hours and see the countryside. Get some fresh air."

"Did he believe that?"

"Oh yes. I did need to clear my head after examining the inner workings of the bowels of a deceased patient. My job was to list the last meal from visual evidence obtained from inspection of the cavity."

Joe made a horrible face as Richard stepped up. "That sounds disgusting. Come on inside. Richard will take care of your rig in the stable there."

Richard walked the horse and buggy off toward the barn. It was a building of unknown origin whose demise appeared imminent. The roof was sagging and several of the corral poles were down.

"Is it safe?" Teddy asked. "I do need to return both horse and carriage to Doctor Clapp."

"It's safe. Not used to the low side of town, huh Doc?"

"I'm here to learn what the Sons of Temperance do, and I don't have all night. Contrary to some, I have other duties that require my attention."

"Come on." Joe walked away toward the cabin. Several horses stood tied to the rails near the "stable." Joe disappeared into the cabin as another horse cantered into the yard, skidding to a halt. The rider leapt to the ground and tied his horse to the rail.

He was a man of great size and his grizzly beard was as dark as his penetrating gaze. He marched straight to Teddy and stared into him for a moment, sizing him up.

"Who might you be?" the man finally asked, his voice deep and slow.

"I'm Doctor Miller, or Teddy, if you prefer."

The man laughed. "I'm Cody," he said and walked right past Teddy into the cabin. Teddy followed, and Richard was right behind him.

A glorious fire roared in the massive stone hearth at one end of the simple cabin. A stove stood in one corner surrounded by shelves with a small table making it a kitchen of sorts, and a ladder led up to a loft that covered about half of the single peak cabin.

Three men stood by the fire while two others sat in chairs facing the warmth. They all turned to stare at the new person in the room.

Joe stepped to the center of the room and motioned to Teddy. "This is Theodore Miller. He is a Methodist and teetotaler from Minnesota and is a doctor working with Doctor Clapp, of all people. He may be one of us. What do you think, boys?"

They all stared.

The crazy bearded fellow from outside named Cody stepped in close and poked Teddy in the chest. "Well, Doc, it's good to know you." His words slurred just a bit and he sauntered over and took a seat by the fire. Teddy turned his head with a quizzical look on his face due to the fact that Cody appeared slightly impaired. No one else seemed to care.

"Our time has come, fellas. Mrs. Armstrong is getting ready to take on the brewers. She will need us more than ever. Are you ready to do battle?" he yelled.

"Yes, yes, battle, battle, battle!" the others shouted.

"I'll be in touch with you when the time is right. We're going to make things tough for these brewers, but for now they must not know who we are. We will slip in and slip out. We'll infiltrate their saloons. They'll think we are one of them, and yet we will be reporting back to Mrs. Armstrong and the Women of Temperance. Are you ready to do your duty?"

The gathered men yelled some version of, "Yes! Joe, we're ready!"

Teddy carefully slipped to the outer wall of the cabin, taking in the scene. Joe noticed him fading to the back and motioned him forward. Teddy had no choice but to step into the middle. He was obviously uncomfortable.

"Doc, the Sons of Temperance are ready for whatever is needed. We will be there."

Teddy was trying not to laugh. He knew any number of men who hauled ice for a living who would wreck these men in a matter of moments. They thought themselves tough, though in reality were the furthest thing from it. Joe nodded to Richard, who immediately went outside.

"I have received word that our great desire of a dry Johnson County could be coming soon. They are going to ban drinking at the next city council meeting. The ladies have asked us to be present in case anything gets unruly."

Just then Richard returned carrying a small keg of beer. It was undeniably marked on the side of the keg and it read Union Brewery.

Teddy imagined Conrad was going to be furious when he told him this.

Joe uncorked it and it began to flow, they filled every cup and the boys drank it down. Joe slammed back his entire cup, letting the overflow run down his thin beard.

He handed a cup to Teddy. Was this a test simply to see if he'd fail?

Teddy glanced at Joe. "Aren't we the Sons of Temperance? Why are we drinking beer?"

"Theodore, we must prepare to go undercover. God sees our exception. We must be accustomed to drinking beer. If we were not, the experienced beer men would know we were false. So drink up, but don't tell Vernice!"

Teddy took the cup of beer and swallowed a hearty drink. "For the glory of God!"

"Amen, brother!" Joe hollered, hoisting his mug in the air.

After a couple more beers, Teddy realized that he had witnessed the full extent of the meeting. He grabbed his coat. "Joe, thanks for having me to your meeting. I have to be going. I have studying to do, and I don't want my house lady to see me come in too late."

Joe stood face-to-face with Teddy. "Can we trust you, Doc?"

"Of course. With what?"

"Our training. No one must know."

Teddy smiled slightly with his eyes and nodded. "Your secret is safe with me. May I come again sometime if you have another meeting?"

Joe nodded. "We'll be in touch. If you hear anything about the brewers from Doctor Clapp or anything, let me know right away."

"You want me to spy on them?"

"Call it listening if that's better. Just let me know what you hear. Can you do that?"

Teddy shrugged. "Yes, I guess." He stepped out into the ice-cold night, climbed in the carriage, and was off toward home. The ground was a sheet of gleaming white snow illuminated by an almost full moon and clear sky full of stars. His breath came in visible puffs of smoke and he could hear the river gurgle off to the west. Shivering against the chill, he was glad he did not have far to go.

Teddy chuckled a bit, thinking about the Sons of Temperance drinking beer and talking tough as he pulled into the carriage house behind his boarding house. He put the horse up and retreated to his room.

He read his anatomy book for an hour until his eyes grew heavy. He turned out the lantern and noticed the moonlight streaming in his window. He didn't think of the Sons of Temperance, Dr. Clapp, or the brewers, he only imagined Matilda in the moonlight.

**6**

CONRAD picked up a cloth and used it to grab the metal pot from the stove, pouring himself a steaming cup of coffee. He leaned on the bar while Max finished placing the glassware back on its shelves after a good washing. Conrad appreciated the method to Max's madness. He was a meticulous man. He ordered each cup in rows of perfect symmetry. His plates were stacked in exactly equal piles. That kind of pride in one's work brought a smile to Conrad's face.

"Max, we're putting together a secret group of fellas," Conrad said.

"Who's we?"

"J.J., Dostal, and me."

Max raised an eyebrow and poured himself a cup of coffee. "What's this secret group of fellas to do?"

Conrad took a solid drink and wiped the coffee from his mustached lip with the back of his hand. "They will do things that may need doing, that nobody wants done in the light of day. That sort of thing, if you know what I mean?"

Max frowned. "Really? It's coming to that?"

"Yep, it is."

"Well that's too bad. You guys really are the Beer Mafia now."

"Stop it. We have to do something."

"I knew we had trouble the minute I saw those temperance hags marching right down our street, the main one wagging her finger in your face like that. Don't they know the northside is ours? We aren't bothering anybody, but they aren't going to leave well enough alone," Max said, his voice filled with frustration.

"No, they are not going to leave it alone. Sounds like they think they're going to get the sale of liquor outlawed entirely in the state legislature this coming session."

"They can't do that. America is freedom! They can't just say we can't brew beer anymore, can they?"

"They think they can do just that," Conrad said with a tense look to his face. "That's why we need a group of fellas. Teamsters, we're gonna call them, to do whatever might need doing. The Methodists already have a group of young thugs they call the Sons of Temperance."

"Seriously, I thought they were against violence?" Max asked.

"They are, so I don't know how they're doing it, but they are. Maybe Methodists have some kind of confession? I don't know. No matter what, we have to be ready. Who do you think we should put forth to represent the Union Brewery? We need two guys."

"Let me think. Jimmy O'Connor; he's as tough as they come. A true Saint Pat's Irishman," Max said with a favorable nod.

"He's working the ice and driving mostly?"

"Yes, that's him. Good lad. Ah yes, and how about Tom Bontrager?"

Conrad smiled. "Yeah, he's the right sort. He's strong and not to be trifled with."

"Faithful as the day is long to the Union and to you, sir, as well. Not a day goes by he doesn't tell me how thankful he is working for you. I've seen him toss bags of hops that usually takes two men, throws them like they were a pillow."

"Will you see them later today?"

"Of course, I see them every day. They come for the beer and a meal."

"When they get here send them down to the caves. Let them go down in the back and cross under the street so no one sees. Be discreet." Conrad removed his pocket watch and glanced at it. "Send them to meet me at five."

"Will do, Mister G."

"Thanks, Max."

CONRAD Graf stood alone in the cave. Gallon upon gallon of Graf's Golden Brew filled the casks all around him. The dank smell of beer filled his senses. Several lanterns loaded with whale oil lit the room in an amber light, bouncing off the walls in a beautiful dancing motion. No matter what sort of man you were, being alone in the caves usually caused a certain level of jumpiness.

The darkness, the shadows, and the caverns full of the unseen amplified every sound, but tonight Conrad felt a peace. A peace like he was right at home and whatever spirit, malevolent or otherwise, would have to suffer his presence and not the other way around.

Conrad saw a light coming from the tunnel that led to the Public House. Their voices carried and bounced off the round bricked ceilings. The two men entered the entrance to the main caves to find their boss sitting at a table with beers for all. They approached and without a word both lifted their glasses. Conrad lifted his as well.

"Thank you, Mister G! May God bless all your endeavors," Jimmy O'Connor said.

"Amen," Tom Bontrager added, enjoying a sip of his beer.

Jimmy O'Connor tipped his glass and took a solid swill. "Good to the last golden drop, sir!"

"It is." Conrad laughed. "It is indeed."

Tom Bontrager took another drink. "What are we doing here, sir?"

"Thanks for asking, Tom. Here it is."

Jimmy raised his hand to pause Conrad's message. It was obvious he'd already had a few brews. "Mister G, I want to say that I was sorry to hear of Simeon's passing."

"Thank you, Jimmy. He was great man and founded this brewery. He built these very caves." Conrad waved his hand around.

"What can we do for you, Mister G?" Tom asked.

"Did you see the protest march through the northside from these Ladies of Temperance?"

"Yes, Mister G, we saw that. An absolute travesty of justice." Jimmy nodded. "An abomination!"

"Well, that's not the only group they have. They have a group of young thugs set to do their bidding," Conrad stated.

"What do you mean?"

"I mean we're starting our own force, if you will. Two men from each brewery to begin with. A group of six men."

"What will they do?" Jimmy asked.

"Anything we see fit."

Jimmy glanced at Tom Bontrager. "Are you asking us to do it?"

"I am, Jimmy. If you say no, I'll not think less of you, but this will have to remain a secret conversation. Understand?"

"I can keep a secret, Mister G," Jimmy said.

"What will we have to do?" Tom asked.

"Not sure, Tom, but it could get a little chippy. There could be a use for tough men like yourselves. Men who, shall we say, know their way around a scuffle?"

Jimmy laughed. "You need fighters. Count me in. Is there pay?"

"Yes, of course, but not on the books. You can take your pay in cash or in credits for beer, good at any of the brew pubs on Market Street."

"Free beer? I've been in fights for a lot less than that!" Jimmy grinned. "Count me in."

"How about you, Tom?"

Tom nodded. "If we get sideways to the law are you going to have our backs? I can't afford no lawyer or no doctor."

"Yes, Tom, if it came to that, all the owners of the three breweries would provide you a lawyer and Doctor Clapp is here when you need him. We're each putting in two men. You'd be representing the Union."

"Then count me in," Tom said with a somber tone. "Anything for you, Mister G. You've been good to me."

The two men nodded their agreement, and Conrad said, "Let's keep our plans between us for now, agreed?"

"Yes, boss," Jimmy said and shook Conrad's hand.

"Yes, Mister G." Tommy did the same.

"If I need you, I'll have Max get word to you and I'll let you know who the other members of our Teamster group are once I know who they are. Thank you, fellas." Conrad stood. "Now let's go up top and have a beer together."

"Grand idea, sir." Jimmy stood and followed Conrad back through the tunnel under the street to the Public House.

CONRAD slid his paperwork into the right-hand drawer of his desk. The sun had risen, and the street outside was a buzz of activity. He stood to make his rounds as a light knock came against his door.

"Come," he said. The door opened, and it was one of J.J.'s boys they called Mickey. He was a good sort of kid and did a lot of errands for J.J.

He had a paper in his hand and extended to Conrad. "From Mister Englert, sir."

Conrad took the paper from the boy. "Thank you, Mickey." He flipped him a coin, spinning it through the air.

The young man caught it and grinned. "Thank you, sir," he said, and he was back out the door.

Conrad opened the note. It simply read: *Noon at Dostal's Second Floor. J.J.*

He tucked the note into his vest and continued about his business. He inspected the latest mix. It looked good. Real good. He clasped Hans on the shoulder. "Good batch."

Conrad continued on about his business. Good help made his work easy. Most of his employees had been with him a long time. Some had been with the brewery since the beginning and they loved it as if it was their own.

Conrad crossed Market Street and briskly made his way up the steps to his office. He could hear voices before he opened the door. A wide smile grew across his face when he found the room full of his family. "Well hello, what brings you boys here today?"

His two boys both ran to their father. Simeon was five and as lively as they come. Otto, the younger, was three and lived to find mischief. Conrad bent over and greeted them with a hug. He stood up and caught the gaze of his wife and said, "We needed some fresh air, you could say."

Conrad focused his attention back on the boys. "Have you two been fighting again?"

They both straightened up. "No, sir," Simeon said, glancing at his shoes.

"Not fighting, he just keeps pushing me," said Otto.

"Oh really?" Conrad said. "And what did you do?"

Otto looked away mumbling, "I kicked him."

Conrad couldn't help but laugh and stared into his wife Anna's blue eyes. "You boys better straighten up. When I get home, I'm going to ask your mama how you behaved, and she better tell me you were little angels."

Both boys glanced up at their mother.

"Understand me?" Conrad added in as stern a tone as he could muster.

"Yes, sir," they said in unison.

"Anna, maybe you should take them to Bushnagle's Ice Cream Shoppe?"

The boys immediately started screaming and running around the room. "Yes, ice cream!"

"It's too cold for ice cream," Anna said with a roll of her eyes at Conrad.

"It's never too cold for ice cream, is it boys?"

They obviously agreed with their father.

"You're incorrigible. Ice cream? They should be getting a switch with the morning I've had, and you give them treats!"

"That's why you love me." Conrad gave her a hug as well. She shook her head and smiled at him as he sat on the edge of his desk.

"I've been weepy, also," Anna said looking down.

"Weepy?"

"I keep thinking of Father and it just comes over me." Anna wiped away a single tear.

"It's not been long. You'll miss him forever. He was a good father to you."

"And you," she said.

"And me," Conrad echoed.

"Come have ice cream with us," she pleaded.

"I'm on my way to meet Dostal and J.J."

"That sounds serious."

"We are working together to stop this woman and her prohibition nonsense."

"I've never seen anything like that march in the streets. Have they no shame?"

"Not all women can be as wonderful as you."

Anna blushed. "Stop it."

Conrad pulled his watch from his pocket. "I must be going."

Anna snapped the boys to attention. "Let's go, boys. Ice cream time!"

They walked out the front doors on the northeast corner of the massive building her father had built. It was full of his memory. She'd grown up at the brewery. Conrad watched Anna walk off holding the boys' hands. He smiled at his little family and made his way toward the Great Western.

He entered the Second Floor Club to find J.J. and Dostal at the big round table by the windows. He noticed they had been joined by Robert Byington. The men stood and shook Conrad's hand as he found his seat.

"Robert, good to see you," Conrad said. "Can you help us?"

"I hope so, but this woman is a zealot. She will not quit."

"I have news from Teddy," J.J. said. "He went to the Sons of Temperance meeting as planned."

"What's the word?" Dostal asked.

"He said it was peculiar."

"Peculiar?" Conrad wrinkled his brow. "How so?"

"He said they were mostly younger men than him. The leader appears to be this Joe Lund. They basically talked about prohibition and how they were ready for a fight. The peculiar part is they brought in a barrel of lager and drank it!" J.J. laughed.

"What?" Dostal scoffed. "I thought they were teetotalers?"

"He said they were drinking it so they could infiltrate our saloons and not appear too temperant. So they could fit in with our fellas."

"Surely you are joking," Conrad said.

"No sir. He did hear something though, and that's one of the reasons I asked Robert to join us," J.J. said. "He said they are going to bring an ordinance to the next city council meeting outlawing the sale of liquor within city limits."

"That's ridiculous." Conrad shook his head. "They don't have the votes."

"I know. The only two votes they'll get are Schell and Cozine," J.J. said. "It makes no sense. I guess Andrew Maine is behind it and he's having Schell bring it forward."

"Maine and Schell may be bringing this forward, but we all know it's Vernice behind this," Robert said.

"Good point. I bet she's planning another show. She'll get more stories in the paper talking about her cause. She's trying to build support, trying to turn the community against us," Conrad said.

"We can send people with signs just as easy as she can," J.J. said.

"Yes," Conrad said. "I have my two men for our squad. Jimmy O'Connor and Tom Bontrager."

"Those are good men," J.J. said. "My two are Frank Weber and Gunnar Schmidt."

"Mine," said Dostal, "are Ed Dvorak and Krystof Kolar."

"Good. Should we have a meeting with them all to make sure they know each other and what our plan is for the meeting?" Conrad asked.

Dostal nodded. "Yes, let's meet."

"We can do it in my caves," Conrad offered. "I'll treat you to some real beer."

J.J. laughed. "Fine, tomorrow evening. In Graf's cave."

"Come in the back door off the alley," Conrad said. "I'll be there to let you in."

"I'll not be there," Robert said coyly. "That way I don't have to deny knowing anything."

Dostal laughed and hit his friend on the shoulder. "Know anything about what? We're just a few friends meeting in a secret cave under the cover of darkness to discuss our nefarious plans."

"I thought it was easy for you to lie," J.J. chided.

"Why is that?"

"You are a lawyer."

The brewers all laughed and took drinks of their beers.

Robert Byington didn't laugh. "Some lawyers lie better than others. I prefer to stay out of the confessional as much as possible. The Beer Mafia must be keeping Father Edmonds busy for hours on end with all the penance you deserve."

Dostal laughed and waved to the bartender for another round. "I shudder at the penance I deserve!"

"Father Edmonds is a saint," J.J. said, raising his glass. The other men raised theirs as well. "To Father Edmonds, may God bless his soul."

CONRAD was sitting at his desk reading the paper while he waited for the boys to show up. His office door was open. He folded his paper and stood when he heard them coming. Jimmy and Tom sauntered in after a short stop at The Public House.

"Mister G, how are you this fine, cold night?" Jimmy asked.

"Well, Jimmy, well. How are you?"

"Grand, sir. Looking forward to our meeting."

"I want you and Tom to go down to the cave. Get the lanterns going and set up enough chairs around the table for nine of us. You'll have to take four chairs down the elevator—I think there are only five down there already."

"Yes, sir." Tom turned to go about his task.

"I'll wait for the others and meet you down there." Conrad made his way to the back door. He opened it to see the others just arriving. "Hello boys, come on inside."

Once they were all inside, Conrad pulled the door shut and latched it behind them. "Follow me."

It took two trips of the elevator to ferry everyone down. They each found a seat around the wooden table and glassware full of the famed Pilsner, Graf's Golden Brew. Dostal and J.J. looked around the cave. They both had been there before, but it had been a long time. The brewers didn't usually invite the competition into the private recesses of the enterprise.

Conrad noticed them surreptitiously counting barrels. "Come on, have a beer," he said, interrupting their reconnaissance.

"Did Simeon build this cave?" J.J. asked.

"Yes. And Geiger. It's the oldest one."

"It's fine work." Dostal admired the arch work of bricks laid by a craftsman.

The three brewers each took a beer but did not sit, instead standing to face their crew.

"Welcome, men. Thanks for coming," Conrad said.

"Thank you for taking on this cause," Dostal added. "We need you boys."

"These are strained times. Our very way of life is under attack," J.J. picked up. "I assume you saw the march or heard about it?"

All of the men seated at the table nodded affirmation.

"Vernice Armstrong is the leader of the temperance movement in Johnson County and she is out to burn us to the ground. She wants nothing short of eliminating us altogether. They have some support around the community."

"Not on the northside," Jimmy O'Connor said.

Conrad smiled. "No, not much on the northside, but we can't take her lightly. She's got friends in politics. She's got friends on the council and she's financed well."

"I heard a story of some woman in Kansas who marched right into a saloon with a hatchet and smashed it to pieces," Jimmy said incredulously.

"Hopefully it won't come to that. We have brought you lads together because we know they have a group of fellas they call the Sons of Temperance. They haven't done anything yet, but after the march, we want to be ready. We're not going to just let a bunch of teetotalers destroy our businesses and take away our jobs, our way of life," Dostal stated.

"No, no!" the men shouted, pounding their fists on the table.

Dostal raised his arm and waited for them to calm down. "For now, we want you to keep our little group to yourselves."

Frank Weber raised his arm. "We need a name. They have a name—we need one too."

"How about Sons of Beer!" Jimmy O'Connor cracked loudly, his voice full of laughter. Everyone joined in the guffaw and shared a drink. Tom Bontrager was standing and refilling their mugs.

Conrad glanced at Dostal and J.J., and they shared a grin.

"I tink we be called Da Sons a'Da Bitches!" Gunnar Schmidt quipped in his heavily accented English. Everyone roared in raucous laughter at that.

J.J. waited until their laughter had subsided. He could see they were losing control of the meeting. "Okay, lads, you ready for your first job?"

"Yes sir!" Jimmy shouted.

"We need you to gather some of the other boys. As many as you can get to come to the next City Council meeting. We want you to bring signs so we can oppose whatever the Ladies of Temperance have in mind," J.J. explained.

"We know they plan to try to ban beer in Iowa City," Conrad told them.

"No!" the group of beer men shouted.

"That's their plan, but we won't let it happen, will we?"

"No, no!"

"We want you to wave the signs and make our presence known at the meeting. No fighting and no trouble. Whatever you do will be on us. Only signs and marching for now. You can tell the men that every man who comes to the meeting will get one free beer when it's done."

"Yes, yes, a free beer!" The rowdy men were excited.

"Compliments of the Great Western of course," Conrad said, flashing a grin at Dostal.

"One free beer at any of the saloons!" Dostal shouted above the din.

"One more round and we'll be on our way," Conrad said. "Thank you...you sons of da bitches!"

Laughter filled the cave and the beer flowed. The cave was warm, and it felt good to be needed. The men were more than friends, they were like a brotherhood.

**7**

VERNICE Armstrong handed a one-page document to A.E. Maine. He shook his head and placed his wire rimmed glasses on the end of his nose, slightly tipping his head back to focus through the lenses.

"Give me a minute before you say anything," Andrew said.

Vernice straightened her skirt and turned her head to look out the windows at the Old Capitol. "It's short," she said.

Mr. Maine raised his index finger without comment. When he finished, he lay the paper on his desk before him.

"Well?" Vernice pressed.

"Well, I think you could have been a lawyer," Andrew said with a voice devoid of emotion.

"My father was a lawyer and not afraid of teaching his daughter. I'd be happy just to be allowed to vote once," Vernice snapped.

"Why don't you fight for that? It would make more sense than this...this prohibitory nonsense."

"Nonsense? Is it nonsense when half of our men are led astray by the evil one? By this spirit we brew amongst us in cauldrons of deceit?"

Andrew raised an eyebrow. "Cauldrons of deceit?"

"And worse," Vernice spat. "This *prohibitory nonsense* is a cause of the ages. It's a scourge."

"It's as good a cause as any," Mr. Maine said, sounding defeated.

"That's right."

"I'm just afraid it's a lost cause."

"Doing what's right is right no matter what. Is the document acceptable?"

"Yes, it's perfectly adequate and will be voted down even if it wasn't."

Vernice shot to her feet with a look of disgust on her face. "You might as well go have a drink as confident as you are!"

"Vernice, you don't have to talk like that. You know I'm on your side."

"I'll see you later at the meeting." She marched out of his office, her feet snapping a cadence all the way down the stairs.

Mr. Maine carried the document to the front office and handed it to his secretary, who sat mildly in her chair as if nothing had happened.

"Please make ten copies of this document as soon as you can for tonight's meeting."

"Yes sir."

"Thank you, Libby." He went back to his office, closing the door behind him.

Joe Lund was waiting for Vernice at the bottom of the steps. He was leaning against the building looking down Washington Street where the sun hung low in the winter sky.

She paused near him and stared toward the setting sun, smoke emanating from her mouth as she whispered just loud enough for Joe to hear, "Be at City Hall at six. We will be stirring the pot. I'm not sure what is required of you tonight, just be there and watching. Understand?"

"God's will be done," he said.

"Quite right, God's will. Bless you, Joe, and guide your path as we face the darkness of our city." She patted Joe on the shoulder and walked in front of him on her way north toward the Methodist church. She had a lot to do to be ready for tonight.

JIMMY O'Connor stood on a chair in The Public House, looking out at his friends. He wasn't nervous, and he loved everyone in the room like they were family.

"Down your beer, fellas. It's time to head to the meeting. If you count yourself as a Northsider then you're coming along. These teetotalers are out to take our beer away. Are we gonna let them do that?"

"Hell *no!*" they yelled.

"Mister G promised a free beer to everyone who comes to the meeting. Just be there, no fighting. Show up and show our support for Graf's Golden Brew. We won't let them take it away!"

"No, no!" the crowd yelled. The more Jimmy spoke the angrier the mob got.

"Let's go. To City Hall!" Jimmy hopped down and pushed his way through the crowd. They followed him like he was the pied piper. Tom Bontrager carried three signs they'd made up. Jimmy was the orator. Tom knew he was there for what needed done that didn't involve talking. He was fine with that. He knew his place.

As they made their way down Linn Street, they were joined by two other mobs. One from the Great Western led by Ed Dvorak, and another from the City Pub led by Gunnar Schmidt. They were easily a hundred strong once the groups combined, waving signs and shouting in solidarity.

As they passed St. Mary's, Father Edmonds stood on the step watching the mob pass. They didn't notice him bow his head and say a fervent Hail Mary. Not the kind of Hail Mary that everyone says while at mass, a *real* prayer. The kind that you sincerely hope God actually hears, not a ritual you do for those around you.

When he was done, he kissed his rosary. The rosary was a gift from Father Mazzuchelli, and made of opal. It was one of his most prized possessions and was deeply sacred to him. He put the rosary back inside his shirt and followed the mob. They were his friends. Their fate would be his fate, unless he could intervene and let God's light shine upon the dire circumstances.

Vernice Armstrong grabbed a sign and began her silent march south down Dubuque Street. She was followed by a throng of fifty or more fervent devotees. They had many signs and marched with a resolute will, a gift from God. They could hear a mob chanting a block south on Linn Street, "We want beer! We want beer!"

Most of the marchers were afraid. The other march had been unopposed. Vernice had led the way and victory was assured, but not this time. Victory was not assured, and an enemy had risen against them. The fear that threatened to stop their mission also strengthened their resolve as they turned east onto Washington Street toward the brand-new City Hall.

The last one had burned to the ground in '81 and the new one was bigger and better, even housing the headquarters for the Fire Brigade in the back, as well as providing offices for the mayor, the sheriff, and the other city agencies. It was good to have them all under one roof at their new home on the corner of Linn and Washington.

The city fathers had no idea what kind of outrage was marching their way. The five-member City Council found their seats in the front of the main meeting room that could fit a hundred people standing.

Usually about four people came to the Council meetings beyond the members themselves to complain about some wrong that had been done. Almost none of the world at large cared about their boring meetings. Tonight, it appeared that the entire town cared, and they were coming to be heard.

The two opposing groups met in the street in front of the municipality. They instantly began shouting at one another.

The brewer's group chanted, "We want beer, we want beer!"

The prohibition group shouted, "No beer, Prohibition now! No beer, Prohibition now!"

They began pushing and shoving and devolving into a general mob of mayhem.

*Bam!* A gunshot rang out through the cold night.

Literally everyone froze, startled by the unmistakable sound of a twelve-gauge shotgun.

A man stood on the top step of the brand-new City Hall building. His dark hair spilled out from under his badged cap and he wore a plain uniform with a shiny silver star upon his chest. Everyone knew him to be Sheriff John Coldren, a normally mild-mannered sort, but he looked all business at the moment.

"Disperse or be peaceable!" he yelled. "I'm not kidding, disperse or act respectable!" He shouted at the top of his lungs with a shotgun in his hands and a Navy Colt on his hip ready to enforce his words. He looked like a man not to be crossed.

Both sides of the crowd grumbled and fell into a murmuring silence. No one wanted to face that shotgun. The two parties pushed and pulled their way into the building sharing icy glares and a few sharp elbows.

Coldren stood near the doors counting until the room was a good ten people past capacity. He raised his arms, still holding the shotgun in his right hand. "That's it, folks. That's all I can let in."

The people who remained outside stood in separate camps talking amongst themselves.

John Englert slammed the gavel down once and hard. It did call people to order for the most part.

"We will not tolerate outbreaks from either side, but we feel it's valuable to let the citizens of our fair city experience the gift of democracy on a local level," J.J. said loudly. "If you want to be heard, you must raise your hand. When I call on you, you must stand and say your piece. Secretary Easley, please take roll as I call the January 1882, Iowa City Council meeting to order."

J.J. slammed the gavel once more.

A young man no one had noticed sat at a table off to the side taking notes. He stood and read the names of the members, writing on his note pad as he went. Each man replied after his name was called.

"J.J. Englert."

"Here."

"Forrest Peck."

"Here."

"John Schell."

"Here."

"William Cozine."

"Here."

"Robert Byington."

"Here."

"All present and recorded. You may begin, sir," the secretary said, and took his seat.

"We have one complaint and two orders of business to attend to. I'm sure most of you are here for one reason, you will have to suffer the meeting's usual business or be off with you. Patience is a virtue. Let's hear the complaint."

An elderly man limped his way to the center of the room. He faced the council like it was an inquisition. "My name is Robert Farley. I've lived here more than twenty years. I raised my children on Dodge Street and worked for the state school as a teacher. Many of you know me. I'm here to say we have to do something about the youth racing their horses up and down Dodge Street. They spin the corners, nearly tipping their carriages, screaming and a laughing all the while.

"I had a fine Labrador dog, Bess. She could hunt with the best of them." He paused his monologue to wipe his eye.

J.J. glanced at the other council members. They had nothing to do but wait patiently.

"One of these youngsters with no care at all ran her down and killed her in the street right in front of my house. The cursed devil didn't even stop. Just left her to die in the street. Something must be done to slow down the carriages in town."

"Mister Farley, I'm sorry for the loss of your good dog. I'm sure she is irreplaceable. Did you take this to the sheriff?" J.J. asked with real empathy in his voice.

"Yes, sir. He told me there was nothing he could do. So I'm asking that you do something."

J.J. looked at his fellow councilors. "The sheriff may be right. I'm not sure what we can do that will improve upon youngsters with poor parentage. Life will have to teach them the hard way, I'm afraid."

"You could make it illegal to go faster than a trot inside the city limits," Farley snapped.

The crowd chuckled behind him.

"Laugh if you want. It won't be funny when the next time some rowdy kid runs his wagon over someone's child instead of a dog!"

Forrest Peck had salt and pepper hair and a fine beard groomed to a point. He was respected as a fair-dealing banker, even if he was also known as a friend of the brewers and member of St. Patrick's. "That's enough laughing. Mister Farley is quite right. My wife and daughter were nearly run over last week when a buggy sped away without a care. The council will take this under consideration. Thank you for stating your case, Mister Farley. Anything else?"

"No, sir. Thank you." Farley returned to his seat.

"Doctor Cozine has a report to give about the new medical building," J.J. said.

Dr. Cozine stood and read a few words. He was a slender man with wire rimmed glasses and a quiet voice. He spoke as loudly as he could muster, but those in the back strained to hear. "The new medical building will be completed sometime this summer. It is progressing nicely but has been slowed by winter weather. The cold and persistent snow has been a hindrance to progress. The building will be a fine addition to our state and will house the premier teaching facilities for medicine in the entire Midwest. Please continue to take care when walking near the project. Thank you."

He took his seat and nodded for J.J. to continue.

"Order of business number one. There has been a request from the Barnum and Bailey Circus for a permit to use Church Park as a location for their tented menagerie this September. Due to the substantial public nuisance we will hear any complaints now."

No one stood from the crowd to complain. Justice Schell motioned to J.J. and was granted the right to speak.

"I'm all for this, as Cedar Rapids and Davenport have both been stops in recent years past. It's been a long while since they came here. If we were to say no to them, they'll simply go to one of our neighboring towns. I'm glad to see them visit the best town west of the Mississippi."

That statement caused an uproar of cheering and agreement from both sides of the audience.

"Great commerce will follow the circus event for our merchants, hotels, and restaurants. Barnum is known far and wide. This event will provide a joy filled time for residents, but our medical professionals, law enforcement, and fire brigade will need to prepare for heightened services as the town will be filled to capacity."

"All true, John," J.J. allowed. "Is it true they have an actual African elephant they're bringing from England?"

John handed a flyer to J.J. He turned it to the crowd and stood so all could see. It had the image of a large gray elephant in the center and in big letters across the top it read *Jumbo, The Giant African Elephant.*

"Very exciting indeed. People will come from far and wide to see a live elephant. Any more discussion?" No one spoke. "Then I call the council to vote. All in favor of approving the permit and scheduling the event say aye."

All five of the councilors said, "Aye."

"Opposed, nay," J.J. said, followed by a moment of silence. "Motion carries. We will inform the Barnum people to make their plans and the public will be informed well in advance of the dates. Our businessmen and city government should prepare for a memorable event! Once in a lifetime, really. It's a great opportunity for us."

The crowd clapped in approval.

"In the spirit of agreement and harmonious accord, that brings us to our final piece of business. Justice Schell?" J.J. gave him a sideways glance.

John Schell stood and took a deep breath, facing the crowd. "I am presenting for a vote of the council a city ordinance to forbid the brewing, sale, and consumption of alcohol within the Iowa City limits."

The crowd erupted in shouts. "No! No!"

J.J. stood and smiled at his compatriots, letting them shout for a moment more, then raised his hand to silence them. "No more outbursts like that. Justice Schell has a right to speak."

"That's right, let him speak!" someone yelled from the prohibitory side of the room.

"Please continue," J.J. said.

"The brewing of beer in our town center, though a thing natural in other cultures and countries, is contrary to our way of life."

"No, it's not!" someone shouted.

J.J. slammed his gavel loudly. "I'll remove you if you can't hold your tongue!"

"Thank you, Mister Englert," Mr. Schell said with genuine appreciation, knowing what side J.J. Englert was on.

"Prohibition is coming to Iowa. Maine and Kansas have already done it and Iowa will follow suit, but we believe that Iowa City being known as a leader in thought and way should lead the state by doing what is right in the sight of the Lord and ban the spirits of our own accord in advance of an edict from Des Moines. The ordinance would allow ninety days for the brewers and saloons to comply. Thank you, J.J."

"Discussion?" J.J. put it to the crowd.

Vernice Armstrong and Conrad Graf marched to the front of the room. Conrad beat her to the front and turned to face the crowd. Vernice stood patiently to the side.

"I am obviously against this ridiculous ordinance. How can it even be legal? The entire town of Iowa City is beholden to the blessing of the northside breweries. We provide much more than beer. We provide jobs, lots of jobs. We provide commerce that employs other trades. Ice men, stable hands, blacksmiths, teamsters, farmers, carpenters, clothiers, and even doctors, bankers, and lawyers all depend on the success of our breweries.

"Voting for this ordinance is like voting to cut off your own head. It's utter nonsense!" Conrad spoke with a deep voice thundering with confidence. "My father-in-law, Simeon Hotz, may he rest in peace, founded my brewery, and I will pass it on to my son when he is a man. No ordinance will stop me." Conrad proudly walked back to his seat.

Vernice stepped into the center spot. She was obviously nervous; Conrad was a tough act to follow.

When a man in the back yelled, "We want beer!" Sheriff Coldren escorted him out the back door amidst clapping from his friends and boos from his opponents.

Vernice waited until the room quieted down.

"Prohibition is coming," she said. "It will pass the legislature this spring for the second time. An amendment to the Iowa Constitution will make it the law of the land. All in Iowa will submit to this and the angels in Heaven will rejoice when the pubs and saloons see their men who have been led astray return to their forlorn families.

"We have the chance to pass this self-governance and lead Iowa, as we are its heart and soul. The capitol that still graces our campus and keeps watch over the Iowa River calls us to a higher place. I implore you to pass this ordinance. Do not keep an abomination like these breweries and bars open simply in the name of commerce. We are better than that." Her friends all clapped as she walked back to her seat while hisses and boos erupted from the other side.

"Any other discussion?"

Mr. Dunleavy stood from his seat as if he was going to make his way to the front, but J.J. continued as if he didn't see him.

"I call for a vote on the prohibitory ordinance. All those in favor of the ordinance say aye."

Councilors John Schell and Dr. Cozine said, "Aye."

"All those opposed to the ordinance say nay."

Councilors Englert, Peck, and Byington loudly said, "Nay!"

"The nays have it. The ordinance is voted down and this meeting is adjourned."

"No!" Vernice snapped around. She hadn't even found her seat and the ordinance was shot down. Many on her side shouted beside her. Some held their heads in hopeless defeat.

The brewer's side was cheering loudly as they made their way out of the chambers, some chanting, "We want beer! We want beer!"

The night air was clear and cold as the groups dispersed into the darkness, friends heading to their favorite pub for their free beer and others walking home or climbing in carriages.

J.J. followed the crowd out the front door. Secretary Easley would see to the room. Suddenly, Vernice stepped in front of him, the Swafford brothers right behind and Dunleavy off to one side, "You'll pay for this!"

"Stop it. This was theatre! You knew we had the votes."

"You'll pay for your wicked ways."

J.J. shook his head. "You can't think you will shut us down? It's folly!"

"Prohibition is coming whether you want it to or not. Mark my words, your day is coming!" Vernice was so angry her cheeks were red, and she stabbed her finger in his face as she spoke.

"Vernice, go home. Go home and have a drink with your husband."

"What did you say?" she snarled.

"Nothing, just go home," J.J. said.

Frank Weber appeared from nowhere and stepped between J.J. and Vernice. "Step back, ma'am."

She stared at him with contempt. "Who's this? One of your Teamsters?"

"Vernice, it doesn't have to be like this. We could do a benefit together and raise money for the orphans of our town. I'll donate first. We could make it a better place together," J.J. suggested.

"Are you offering me a bribe?"

"No, I'm serious. We should work together because the breweries are not going anywhere."

"You can't buy me with your beer or blood money!"

"You know that's not what I meant."

"Your days are numbered. The beer mafia's days are numbered. God will bring you down!" she shouted.

"My God wouldn't do that. Good night, Vernice," J.J. said and walked out the door with Frank following along right behind.

As soon as they were out of earshot, J.J. slapped Frank on the shoulder. "Thanks for coming back for me. She's crazy."

Frank nodded. "Teetotalers are angry. Beer makes people happy." They moved down Linn Street and in a few minutes were back on the northside. It felt like home.

Laughing and talking loudly, Jimmy O'Connor and a few of the lads made their way back to the Union Public House to claim their free beer and maybe another one before heading home. They passed St. Mary's and Jimmy stopped at the entrance to the alley between the church and the brewery.

The alley led to the back entrance of the brewery compound near the stables and the icehouse. "I gotta take a leak," Jimmy said, trotting off into the alley. "I'll see you inside." The group continued on. The lights were just up ahead less than half a block and the free brew was calling.

Jimmy was going about his business when he heard movement in the darkness off to his left and his instinct took over. He spun toward the way he had come and burst forward in a sprint toward the lighted street in an attempt to get back to his friends.

A sharp pain to the face ripped through the night. He never saw it coming. He heard a crunching sound and his feet were over his head. Struggling to maintain his wits, he hit the ground hard, landing flat on his back. He glimpsed the stars overhead.

Jimmy could feel blood streaming down his face and he knew his nose was broken. All he could do was cover his head and ball up against the kicks that were coming fast from all sides. He never saw an attacker. One hit his ear hard, causing a ringing sound. Another hit the small of his back, then his stomach. The kicks just kept coming. He felt himself fading and thankfully the kicking stopped as suddenly as it began.

"Stop, he's had enough! Let's go!"

He rolled onto his stomach still covering his head when a voice whispered in his ear, "You think because your masters voted that ordinance down this is over? Well, you're wrong. It's just starting. You brewers better go away. No one wants you here anymore. This was just a warning. Your time is up. The Sons of Temperance are always watching. Turn from your wicked ways."

Jimmy's eyes were swelling shut but he stole a glance. All he saw were a few figures running west down the alley into the darkness.

With his one good ear, Jimmy could hear them laughing. He struggled to his feet and was happily surprised that he could stand and was able to walk. With each step, a sharp pain ripped up his right leg and into his back, and his left hand was out of sorts.

Jimmy stumbled onto Linn Street and turned north. He could see the lights of the Public House. Why was the street empty? Did no one see him? He needed help fast.

No one was out. He could hear the laughter and see the saloon was full of happy people. Just a few more steps and he'd be there.

It felt like he floated up the steps to the door into the Public House. Later, he had no idea how he made it up those steps other than angels helping him along.

When he pushed open the door several men gasped.

"Jimmy!"

Both Max and Conrad heard the call and ran to Jimmy. They laid him down. Max handed them several towels for Conrad to wipe his face and attempt to clean him up as best he could. Jimmy's face looked a wreck. One eye was totally shut, and several cuts were bleeding. His nose was swollen and bent off to one side.

"Who did this to you, Jimmy?" Conrad asked.

Max poured a small sip of water into his gaping mouth. "Who was it, Jimmy?"

"I don't know..." Jimmy faded into darkness.

"Get the wagon!" Conrad shouted.

Two Union stable hands ran out of the building about their task. In minutes they had Jimmy loaded and on his way to Dr. Clapp's house.

The wagon slid to a stop and Conrad ran to the door. A lantern was burning inside. Dr. Clapp opened the door just as Conrad reached the first step. "What is it?"

"It's Jimmy. He's beat up pretty bad."

"How bad?"

Conrad's face looked panicked. "Bad, Doc, bad."

"Let me grab my coat. Let's go to the hospital. I have more there." Dr. Clapp disappeared into his home. The lantern inside went dark and Dr. Clapp trotted toward the wagon with Conrad, climbing into the shotgun seat. Tom Bontrager sat in the back holding Jimmy, who lay crumpled in his lap covered in blood.

The Sisters of Mercy hospital wasn't far. Conrad and Tom put one of Jimmy's arms around each shoulder and carried him in while Dr. Clapp lit several lanterns and prepared the room. They laid Jimmy on the exam table.

"Tom, can you go get Teddy?" Dr. Clapp asked. "I need his help."

"Yes, Doc." He immediately left the room and disappeared in the wagon. His boarding house was only a block away.

Dr. Clapp inspected Jimmy's face to first address the cuts and plug his nose to bring the bleeding to a stop. He then moved onto gently feeling for broken ribs.

"Is he going to make it, Doc?" Conrad asked.

"I hope so. He's hurt bad that's for sure. Concussion or internal injuries are unknown for now, but we'll do all we can, you know that. Who did it to him?"

"He didn't see. I guess he was in the alley between St. Mary's and the Union."

The sound of the wagon outside was followed by Teddy bursting through the door and immediately going to work to help Dr. Clapp.

"Doctor Miller, please begin cleaning and prepare for stitching of the head wounds," Dr. Clapp ordered.

Teddy jumped to the task with no complaint. Conrad could tell the young man was good at what he was doing, and Dr. Clapp obviously trusted him.

"Conrad, please go wait in the front room. We'll be out when we're done if you want to wait. Does he have anyone you need to notify?"

"He's just got us. I think he has a sister in Davenport. I'll let her know." Conrad walked into the front room where he found Tom waiting patiently.

"How's he doing?" Tom asked.

"I don't know," Conrad said with a shake of his head.

"I should have been with him."

"You can't blame yourself, Tom. This isn't your fault. Did he fight with anyone recently?"

"No, he's always filled with laughter. Everyone likes Jimmy," Tom said. "But he's as tough as they come. We shouldn't have left him."

"He was right in our backyard. You can't take the blame, Tom. The blame is mine. It's a message to me and J.J. and Dostal. I know it."

"What are we going to do?"

"We have to find out who it was. Then we'll send a message of our own."

"Send me," Tom said.

Conrad clasped his shoulder. "I will, but for now we need Doctor Clapp to work his magic. I'll wait here. Go tell the boys back at the Public House not to do anything rash. Tell them Jimmy will be okay."

"Will he?"

"You said he was tough as they come."

"He is."

"He'll be making us laugh and sharing a brew with us in no time."

**8**

DR. Clapp leaned in close since Jimmy appeared to be attempting to speak. The words were unintelligible.

"Prepare some morphine, he's waking up," Dr. Clapp said. Teddy selected a brown bottle from the cabinet on the side wall.

Jimmy took a loud breath and attempted to sit up, his arms flailing about. Dr. Clapp gently grabbed a hold of him and forced him to lie back. "Jimmy, you're hurt. We're here to help. Lie back."

Dr. Clapp nodded to Teddy, who slipped the needle into his arm and injected the morphine. Jimmy almost instantly relaxed as the liquid hit his bloodstream.

"Sons of Temperance," he whispered as his eyes closed.

The two doctors continued their work into the night.

Dr. Clapp tapped Conrad on his knee to rouse him from where he sat asleep in the chair in the front room.

He rubbed his eyes and focused in on Dr. Clapp. "How is he?"

"He's beat up, but he'll live. He's going to have a couple of new scars. A nasty one over his left eye, and his nose was busted up good. It will heal, but it's as straight as I could make it. Good thing he doesn't make his living by his good looks."

"That's good news," Conrad said.

"He's got a couple of broken ribs, and his left wrist is sprained pretty badly. He's going to be black and blue all over. They kicked him while he was down."

"How many? Did he say who did it?"

Dr. Clapp leaned back in his chair, obviously hesitant to tell Conrad.

"What is it, Doc?"

"He only said one thing. Sons of Temperance."

Conrad's face tightened into a simmering anger. "Son of a bitch!" he swore bitterly as he stood. "Thanks, Doc. Let me know what I owe you."

"I'm not done with him yet. I'm not sure what it will run you. I know where to find you, but you can't pay me in beer!" Dr. Clapp grinned.

"I owe you, Doc. Thanks."

"No problem. I had a good helper. I like this kid Englert sent me."

Conrad nodded. "He's a good one."

The next morning Conrad sent a message to J.J. and Dostal calling for a meeting in the caves that night. News of Jimmy's assault spread like wildfire around town.

After making his rounds, Conrad stood talking to Max in the Public House as was his custom. Max nodded toward the door over Conrad's shoulder. He turned to see Sheriff Coldren being followed by the young constable he'd met at the Hess murder.

"Would you like a beer, John?" Conrad asked.

"You know I don't, Conrad," Sheriff Coldren said with a voice that sounded all business. "This is Deputy Parrot. We've a few questions to ask you."

Conrad nodded to Parrot. "Yes, we've met. What questions?"

"We're looking into what happened to your man Jimmy O'Connor. He got walloped pretty good."

"You can say that again. It's not safe to walk the streets anymore." Conrad was bristling at the questions already. "What are you doing about it?"

"We talked to Doctor Clapp. He said Jimmy will survive, thankfully, but has not regained much consciousness."

"They kicked him while he was down, John. What are you going to do about this?"

"That's why we're here. We'd like to arrest whoever did this. What do you know about it?"

"Nothing that you don't know. Jimmy steps into the alley and bang, they jumped him."

"How many was it?"

"I don't know, but more than one according to the doc."

"What else have you heard?"

Conrad stared into the sheriff's eyes for a moment and shook his head. "I don't know anything."

The sheriff stared right back at Conrad. "Conrad, you know everything that goes on in the northside. Why won't you tell me?"

"I'm telling you if I knew who did this, we wouldn't be talking here now, would we?"

"Let the law handle this," the sheriff warned.

"Thanks for stopping by, Sheriff. I'll be sure to let you know anything I find out. Good day, John, I have a lot to attend to."

Coldren and Parrot made their way to the door.

"Hey, John?" Conrad called out. Deputy Parrot held the knob while Coldren turned back toward the beer men. "Which side were you on at the council meeting?"

Coldren smiled. "I don't get to be on a side. I just enforce the law."

"Some laws would be hard to enforce," Conrad said. "These Methodists are crazy if they think they're going to stop us from brewing beer. My recipe is from my great-great-grandfather in Bavaria. Grafs have been cooking it for hundreds of years."

"We're not in Bavaria," Sheriff Coldren said as he walked out. "Let me know if you hear anything about Jimmy."

After they were gone Conrad flung his metal coffee cup viciously across the room, slamming it into the bar, spraying the coffee everywhere. "Damn him! We're all going to choose a side in this."

"If he's not for us, he's against us," Max said, sliding a beer across the bar to Conrad.

"Thank you, Max."

"It's the best beer this side of the Mississippi."

Conrad took a solid drink, filling his bushy mustache with foam. "Best pilsner this side of the Atlantic!"

TEDDY Miller left his room and stepped out briskly on his way into the hospital to meet Dr. Clapp. The air was clear and crisp with brilliantly bright sunlight dancing among the crystal-white snow clinging to the trees.

A speeding covered carriage stopped abruptly and the door opened. "Get in!" Joe Lund hollered.

Teddy hesitated after what had happened to Jimmy.

"Come on!"

"I can't. I'm on my way to work," Teddy protested.

"We'll drop you off. Get in!"

Teddy glanced each direction up and down the street and stepped into the carriage. Richard was driving, and they were off.

"Is he going to live?" Joe asked.

"Who?"

"You know, that Teamster O'Connor who got beat up."

"Why? Did you do it?"

"It's time to let these beer men know we mean business," Joe said.

"This kind of *business* isn't good for anyone," Teddy said.

"I thought you were on our side, Theodore?"

"I am, but he's beat up pretty bad. I'm not sure that is the way to go. Does Vernice know what you did?"

"Mrs. Armstrong doesn't need to know everything, but as long as it pushes our cause forward, she will be supportive."

"Maybe," Teddy said uncomfortably. "I don't think she'd support violence."

"Let me worry about that. Have you heard anything? Are they going to retaliate? Do they know who did it or who we are?"

"I haven't heard anything. I mostly have been working to try to save Mister O'Connor from a life of disfigurement and misery. Please let me out."

"If you hear anything, let me know. I'm working at Hanson's Hardware store on College Street. You can find me there most days."

"I didn't know you had a job other than mischief," Teddy stated.

"Of course I have a job. I'm not doctor smart like you, but I work for my money like everyone else."

The carriage came to a halt and Joe put his hand on the latch. He looked right at Teddy. "Be sure to warn us if you hear anything."

"Yes, I will." Teddy pushed out the door and stepped down into the street. Without a look back at the carriage, Teddy marched straight into Dr. Clapp's office. Despite his cool exterior, his mind was racing. How had he gotten into this mess?

His convictions were not against drinking a beer, but he definitely was not going to be a part of beating anyone. He decided to focus on finishing his education. That's what he was here for.

When he entered Jimmy's room, he found Dr. Clapp sitting in the corner reading his notes while Jimmy was sitting up, gingerly feeding himself some soup with his good hand. His other one hung in a sling.

"Well good morning, sir. It's good to see you eating," Teddy said.

Dr. Clapp smiled. "Yes, he's turned the corner."

"Don't give me no more of that morphine. I've got a headache and it makes me foggy," Jimmy said.

"That could be from your wounds as well. You have a concussion," Dr. Clapp said. "But we can be sure to use it sparingly."

"I don't want it. My sweet ma got stuck on it back in Ireland and I don't want nothing to do with it."

"Once it wears off, your pain will be substantial with the ribs and your internal bruising," Teddy argued. "A few small doses would be normal for a man with your injuries."

"I'd rather have a lick or two of a strong Irish Whiskey to get me through the pain."

"We'll let you go in the morning if you continue to improve and then your pain management is up to you, how's that?" Dr. Clapp said. "A man can get just as 'stuck' on whiskey as morphine."

"I'm Irish, we drink whiskey from the teat," Jimmy laughed, sending pain ripping through his ribs and he grimaced.

A light rap on the door preceded it opening. A small elderly woman who was obviously a nun signified by her black garb stepped in. "Doctor Clapp, Sheriff Coldren and a Deputy Parrot are here to talk to the patient."

Dr. Clapp scowled and removed his glasses. "Thank you, Sister Delores."

"They're in the front room," Sister Delores said.

"I'll tell them to leave," Dr. Clapp said, looking at Jimmy.

"No, I can talk to them. It's alright," Jimmy said.

"Just for a short time. If I'm letting you go home, I want you to rest most of this day." Dr. Clapp stepped out and returned with Coldren and Parrot.

"Good to see you awake, Jimmy. Took quite a beating it looks like?" Sheriff Coldren noticed Jimmy's left eye swollen almost completely shut, with black, blue, and yellow hues on his entire face, not to mention his nose looked to be a crooked disaster.

"Yeah, I guess I fell down pretty hard." Jimmy grimaced.

Coldren glanced at Parrot. "It looks like somebody knocked you down and then kicked you while you were on the ground."

"I'm glad to have grown up with a brother, may he rest in peace, who taught me how to take a licking."

"We're trying to find out who did this to you. Anything you can tell us?" Coldren asked.

"No, sir. I went into the alley to see a man about a horse and heard a noise and then the lights went out."

"You didn't see anybody?"

"No, sir. Wish I did." Jimmy handed is empty soup bowl to Teddy, who was standing quietly to the side.

"Hear anyone talking or anything that could help us?"

"Nothing that would help."

"Do you know anyone who would want to hurt you personally, Jimmy? Someone you had a beef with, you know what I mean?"

"No. I'm a fairly happy-go-lucky sort. I don't make too many enemies." Jimmy forced a smile.

"Well, you may have one now or someone you work for may have one?"

Silence filled the room. Jimmy was calculating through his foggy brain what they were after. "You think it was some of those teetotalers bucking the breweries who did this because I work for Mister G?"

"We don't know anything. We're trying to figure it out. We don't put up with this sort of thing in our town," Coldren said.

"God, I hope not. I'd be embarrassed to have my ass handed to me like this by a bunch of Methodists." Jimmy chuckled until his ribs hurt. He put his hand on them in response to the pain.

"That's enough, gentlemen," Dr. Clapp said. "My patient needs rest."

"If you think of anything that could help us, you let us know," Sheriff Coldren said and the two lawmen exited, closing the door behind them.

"Lie back," Teddy said. "How are you feeling?"

"It does hurt a bit, maybe just a half dose of the morphine to help me sleep?"

Teddy went about preparing it.

"Your face is going to mend up just fine," said Dr. Clapp. "Your nose may not quite be how it once was."

"That's alright. I've got too many ladies after me as it is. Thanks for doing this, Doc."

"Do you remember anything else from the attack? Anything you didn't say to the officers?" Dr. Clapp asked.

Jimmy didn't answer at first and then whispered, "Sons of Temperance."

"Yes. You said that in your delirium."

Teddy administered the morphine.

Jimmy closed his eyes. "No need to tell those cops. The northside will take care of them."

Conrad lit all the lanterns and set out some glasses and a loaf of sliced bread from the bakery. It smelled delicious, so he ate a piece and sipped a glass of golden lager while he waited.

He could hear them coming through the passage and see the light of their lanterns flickering on the round top caverns.

J.J. and Dostal were in front with the crew following along. "Hey there," J.J. called out.

"Come on in. Thanks for coming," Conrad said as the group made themselves at home.

"Max let us in the back of the Public House and no one saw us make our way down. That worked well, but I think I can reopen the tunnel under Linn Street from one of my old caves to yours. Hasn't been used in years. I just found the map to it," Dostal added. "Ole Simeon and my dad put it in, just in case someone had to borrow a cup of sugar!"

"I'd love to see that map," Conrad said.

"I'll bring it to our next meeting at Dostal's for lunch."

Conrad got right down to business. "Good. You may have guessed why I called the meeting."

"Jimmy, of course," Dostal said.

"What are we gonna do about it?" Tom Bontrager demanded. He was obviously ready for whatever his orders were.

"Do you know who did it?" J.J. asked.

Conrad nodded. "It was those Sons of Temperance bastards Teddy's been looking into. At least that is what Jimmy said."

"Let's pay them in kind." Frank Weber sneered. "With interest!" He slammed his fist on the table, knocking over the bread bowl.

His compatriots hooted their agreement. They wanted blood and the sound of it echoed amongst the kegs of fermenting beer.

"We don't even know who the whole group is yet, but we do know the leader and where his cabin is," Dostal said.

"Let's burn the cabin and beat that sombitch, like they did Jimmy!" Ed Dvorak said with an edge to his voice that left no doubt he was serious.

"Teddy just found out they did do this thing. Jimmy said it right to him. He stopped by the brewery and told me all about it." J.J. shook his head. "These sons of whatever paid him a visit trying to find out what we know and what we're going to do. They think Teddy is a spy for them. He said the leader, this Joe Lund, works at Hanson's Hardware on College Street."

"I know it," Ed Dvorak said. "We'll pay him a visit."

"Hold on a minute, boys. Let's talk it through," Dostal suggested. "The cops are looking into this. We could give them some time and see if they arrest these jackwagons."

"He's right," Conrad admitted. "So far, it's them that's spilled blood. If we go off half-cocked here, that won't be good."

"Those cops won't figure this out," Tom snarled.

"Maybe if we gave them some clues," Conrad said. "I want to figure out who this Joe fella is. Is he being financed by anyone we know, or who's his family? How long has he been in town? What's got him so riled up against us?"

"He's probably Vernice's bastard," Gunnar Schmidt said with a laugh that everyone joined in.

"Vernice doesn't have any children, thank the Lord in Heaven. Her husband and his partner keep a print shop. You know it, Armstrong's Print & Binding on Burlington. He does a fine job. He did the flyers for our Oktoberfest last year. That was before I knew his wife wanted to bury us. The rumor is Mister Armstrong isn't too fond of Vernice. He's more inclined to work long hours with his partner in the business and they are more than just in business together," Conrad said.

An extended pause fell over the group.

Krystof Kolar bent over laughing. "Who *would* be fond of Vernice?"

"I'd take the business partner too!" Frank added, laughing all the more.

Everyone burst into hysterics until they finally pulled themselves together.

"Is that true?" J.J. ran his fingers through his hair. "I had not heard that."

Conrad furrowed his brow. "Is that why she's so darn angry all the time?"

"Well, it's not our fault her life is miserable. No reason to take it out on us," Dostal growled. "We're just providing a product to willing buyers. What's more American than that?"

"Are we agreed then? No action until we see what the cops come up with?" Conrad pressed.

"Yes," said J.J.

Dostal nodded. "Yes."

"I'd rather settle this right now," Tom countered.

"We know, Tom. And you'll get your chance to do that. That's why we wanted you on this crew," Conrad explained. "Just give it a little time or it will look like a retaliation and bring more heat down on us. Understand?"

"We should also plan for some kind of 'Fall Fest' or something to coincide with that circus coming to town. They're going to be set up a block away in Church Park. There will be hundreds, if not thousands, of people in town to see that giant elephant," J.J. said. "And what are they going to want to do?"

"Drink beer!" Frank Weber exclaimed.

"That's right, Frank. And they don't sell it at the circus, but they do at the three breweries less than a block away!" J.J. grinned.

"My lord, it's good to know someone on the City Council I guess," Dostal said with a laugh, patting J.J. on the back. "We'll make a fortune that weekend!"

"Definitely. 'Fall Fest' it is! Can we close the streets to only foot traffic and have all our beers for sale in tents or something right on the street?" Conrad posed. "Maybe have food from the neighborhood for sale?"

"An old-fashioned street party like Oktoberfest in the old country? Sounds great." Dostal raised his hand. "Count the Great Western in!"

J.J. threw up both hands. "Count us all in!"

JOE glanced to the front of the store when he heard the tiny bell jingle signifying someone had entered. Dread flooded him when he saw it was Vernice Armstrong.

He placed his broom against the wall and walked behind the counter. She was clearly not happy.

Her furrowed brow and pursed lips made him feel like he was a child again. She reminded him of his mother.

"Good morning, Vernice," he said. "Coffee is on sale."

"Is it?" she said with confused look.

"On sale? Yes, it is."

"Is it a nice day?"

"Well, it is sunny."

"I don't care about the sun. I care about doing what's right and I care about prohibition," she said with conviction. "I care about the three breweries right in the middle of our town churning out gallon after gallon of death every day!"

"Yes, ma'am. I couldn't agree more."

"Do you want to tell me anything?" she said, focusing her blue eyes intently on Joe.

It was more than he could stand. "N-no, wh-what do you mean?" he stammered and looked away.

"I mean, why did Sheriff Coldren just visit me about some brewer named Jimmy who nearly got beat to death in the alley behind the church?"

"Um, I don't know why he would visit you."

"Because this happened on the very night we were defeated by the city council. The very night our ordinance to outlaw the sale of liquor in our city lost out. That's why! It looks like someone on our side didn't take it very well and took it out on a brewer!" She was shouting now. Joe was glad no one else was around. "Some brewer everyone seems to love and a good friend of Conrad Graf. Do you get my meaning?"

"I don't know."

Vernice stabbed a finger in his face. "Don't you lie to me! I know you did it. Don't ever do something like that again without my approval, understand?"

"Um...I...uh—"

"*Understand?* I call the shots here."

Joe mustered his courage and answered, "Yes, I understand." His loathing remained just below the surface.

"Good. It makes us all look bad. What you do makes the Ladies of Temperance look bad, do you understand? Did anyone see you?"

"No."

She shook her head. "You are not smart. You're just not. Do you think anything happens on the northside these mafia men don't know about?"

"I guess not," Joe mumbled.

"You guess not? That's why I do the thinking for this group and you don't."

Joe could feel anger building in his heart. His father used to talk down to him this way until he finally made him go away for good.

"I understand," he said. "Nothing like that will happen again."

"Has your brother heard anything?"

"No. He's mostly up in Solon now. I have another person on the inside with them, a doctor working with Doctor Clapp. He's on our side. It's like they are just going about business as usual. Like the brewers don't care about us at all. That's why I did what I did. They need to know we mean business."

"They'll care soon enough. The legislature votes next month on the prohibitory amendment and I don't want anything happening between now and then to hurt our cause. You just leave it alone for now, understand?"

"I will," Joe said. The little bell jingled and a mother with two small children in tow entered. "Good morning, ma'am," Joe said.

"I'll take a pound," Vernice snapped.

Joe stared. "A pound?"

"Of coffee. It's on sale, right?"

"Yes, ma'am, on sale."

Joe scooped the aromatic beans into a small bag, placing it on the scale. Vernice slid her money across the counter. Joe opened the register and gave her the change.

"Have a good day, sir," she said with a smile, but her eyes told a different story.

"Good day to you as well, ma'am," he said.

Vernice pushed her way out the door.

THE cold days of January slid by like water under the frozen Iowa River. Children raced sleds down the hill behind the old capitol on sunny afternoons, but only for a short while. The cold bit viciously at any exposed skin, driving even hearty Midwesterners indoors around a warm fire.

9

DOSTAL walked over to Ed Dvorak, who had recently been moved to special assistant to the bar of the Second Floor Club. Mr. Dostal leaned in and whispered his orders. Ed began pouring beers and sent the request to the kitchen. John returned to his seat with his VIPs.

"Gentlemen, thank you for coming," Dostal said as Ed placed a glass of Erlanger in front of each man. "My friends will be joining us soon, and I will tell you that we are in this together. The fate of the Great Western Brewery will be the same as the Union or the City Brewery. We must fight together now to prevail."

Conrad and J.J. were escorted to the table. Every man stood as any real man would. No one would shake a hand sitting down and be counted as trustworthy.

Dostal made the introductions as a good host. "Conrad and J.J., I think you know Congressman Lucas and Congressman Wolfe. Sadly, Senator Shrader declined our invitation for lunch over a beer."

Everyone laughed since Senator John Shrader was a Republican and that forced him to be for prohibition or risk the wrath of his party. In the shadow of the old capitol and a town built on beer, that was a tough position to hold.

"Take a seat, my friends," Dostal said.

Conrad snickered. "The funny part is, we deliver a keg to Shrader's house once a week."

Laughter ensued.

"The Republicans in Des Moines are not making it easy for their people. He has to drink behind closed doors."

"I don't think Shrader will run again. He's had enough of the games," Edward Lucas said.

"I'm not surprised. I'm tired of it and I'm not a politician," Conrad stated.

"I'm not running again either," Lewis Wolfe said. "My wife is pregnant with our fourth and this term will be my last. I need to tend to my business. One of you fellas should think of running for my seat."

"Very interesting idea to think about," J.J. said. "I can tell you I'm not running, but I can think of a couple who might. Thanks for the warning."

"Who are you thinking?" Lucas asked.

"Maybe Moses Bloom? He's got the gift of an orator and I know he likes politics," J.J. said.

Lucas nodded. "He'd be good."

"What can you tell us about this prohibitory amendment?" Dostal asked.

"It's going to pass," Lucas said. "Nothing you or me can do to stop it. They have the votes."

Silence filled the table with that realization.

Ed interrupted the somber news, delivering sizzling steaks to the table. The aroma was an olfactory dream triggering saliva to flow and bellies to growl.

"My, my, Dostal, that smells good! You have a great kitchen," Lewis said.

"And a great brewery I intend to keep open for many years." Dostal cut off a chunk of red meat, tossing it in his mouth. "What are we to do about these teetotalers?"

"We're cooked if it's going to pass," Conrad said.

Congressman Lucas leaned in. "After it passes the legislature it will go to a statewide vote of the people. All amendments to the Constitution must pass the legislature twice, two sessions in a row. They then must be voted on by the people. If it passes the statewide popular vote it will finally become law. Right now, it's unclear how that vote will turn out. It depends on the local mood at the time what happens with that vote," Lucas explained. "Most people I've talked to think it would pass a statewide vote by the people."

"Well, if they outlaw my brewery, I'll burn it to the ground before I let them have it or watch it founder," Dostal promised.

Lucas glanced at Lewis Wolfe. "I can promise we are both on your side, but it's going to be a rough few years here, and to be honest, I don't know how it will end."

"I can tell you how it will end," Conrad said. "We will win. This is crazy. America is freedom. If the state laws make beer illegal, we shall sell even more of it. You don't understand human nature."

"I assure you I understand human nature, Conrad," Edward Lucas said. "I was in the 'Hornets' Nest' at Shiloh. I watched all my friends die and then I slept with their corpses through the long night, only to be imprisoned the following morning. I know what men are capable of. After I got my freedom, I decided to do all I could for my friends and my state the rest of my life. That's why I serve."

"No one doubts your loyalty to the state or the nation. Serving is great, but you said yourself you can't stop this travesty," Dostal snapped. "You said they're going to outlaw our entire business! What are we to do?"

Lucas looked at his food and slowly sawed his meat as he spoke. "You should plan accordingly with the knowledge we've just given you. I don't know what your other business ventures are, but diversifying might be an option."

The table fell silent.

"Diversifying?" Conrad asked, exasperated. "There's no stopping this?"

"We are calling this monstrosity the *Republican Amendment*. They are birthing this horror. Let them suckle it." Wolfe smiled.

"It's coming for sure, but I believe it will be an albatross around the Republicans' necks. They may have the votes, but any state that enacts a law that forty-five percent or more of its populous vehemently doesn't want is going to find it almost impossible to enforce," Congressman Lucas added.

"You're saying to defy the law?" Conrad asked.

"I'm saying what would law enforcement do if you simply refused to stop producing?" Lucas said.

"They'd force our hand. Lock us up maybe?" Dostal said.

"I'd rather go to jail than give in to this," said Conrad.

"Also, it could be challenged in the courts. There will almost certainly be a challenge to the amendment in court after it passes, and before enforcement starts. Mark my words," Congressman Wolfe said with a nod of his head, "a successful challenge would nullify the entire amendment and all the votes will be for naught."

"I like that," J.J. said. "How do we do that?"

"An opportunity will present itself, not to worry. I've met with the brewers in Davenport, Cedar Rapids, Burlington, and Marshalltown as well. If this all comes to pass as I've told you it will, one of you will be asked to press the issue in court all the way to the Iowa Supreme Court. It's the only way. An amendment can't be easily removed. The next legislature, even if it has a new majority, would be hard pressed to repeal an amendment. The court will be our way," Lucas said.

"I hope you're wrong and it doesn't come to that," Conrad said. "I don't trust the courts."

"I don't trust politicians," Congressman Lucas said with a laugh.

FEBRUARY came in clear and cold. Iowa was covered in a lingering blanket of white. Trees devoid of leaves stood as stark reminders of warmer days both gone and those to come. Bald eagles soared up and down the river searching for an easy meal.

Everything was harder in Iowa during a snowy winter. Wagons were difficult to pull, machinery invariably broke more often, and people were getting grumpy for lack of outdoor enjoyment.

The pubs of the northside were one of the few happy respites for the hearty Iowa folk who called it home.

Conrad sat in his office reading the news, as was his ritual. He always read the *Iowa City Post* for his local news and since the trouble started with the temperance zealots, he had taken to reading the *Iowa State Register* to gauge the statewide mood as best he could. He felt it was important to stay informed.

He folded his copy of the *Post* and laid it on his desk. Nothing much of interest in it this particular day. Conrad looked out his window. "The calm before the storm," he whispered. He wished he could go talk to his father-in-law. Conrad was surprised how much he missed his guiding hand since his passing.

THE little bell jingled at Hanson's Store. Joe glanced up as he handed a small package to an elderly woman. "There you go, ma'am," he said, and she ambled her way out the door.

"Can I help you, sir?" Joe asked the newcomer.

"I'm not sure," the man said.

"What are you looking for? I know everything in here."

"Do you have anything that is good for cuts?"

"Sure do." Joe reached into the display wall behind the counter, pulling out a small container with a metal lid. He turned to find the man standing at the counter staring rather intently into his eyes.

"Is that all?" Joe asked.

"Do you have anything for a broken nose?"

Joe was trying to ignore an uncomfortable feeling that was settling into the exchange. "I think you might need a doctor for something like that."

"How about headaches. Got anything for that?"

"We have laudanum."

"You see, my friend got hit on the head one night and he's been getting headaches ever since."

"That's too bad. How did he get hit on the head?"

The big man smiled and stepped even closer to the counter. Joe took an immediate step back, increasing the distance between them. "That's the funniest thing. He was just walking one night in a dark alley and someone whacked him. Who would do something like that?"

"I-I don't know," Joe stammered, "but the laudanum might help him sleep."

"It might at that."

Joe set a small bottle of it on the counter.

The man picked it up and looked at it. "Horrible stuff. My ma got hooked on it."

"I'm sorry to hear that. It should be used sparingly," Joe said.

"Not much choice after some cowards put the boots to you while you're down and crack your ribs. Terrible, don't you think?"

"Will that be all?" Joe said nervously. He wished someone else would walk in.

"Oh, I'm not buying any of this stuff."

"Then what do you want?" Joe asked.

"I'd like to do for you what you did for my friend, and I will when the time is right."

"What do you mean? I don't know your friend."

"My friend's name is Jimmy." Joe's stomach sank. "Jimmy O'Connor. He's a fine Irishman and a good man. I came in here to let you know two things. One, I know who you are. And two, I know where you live."

"Who are you? I don't know what you think I've done, but—"

"My name is Tom Bontrager, and I'll see you again sometime." Tom made his way to the door. He glanced back at Joe, who stood motionless. "You may not see me though. Good day to you, sir."

Tom walked down the street smiling. It had been two weeks since Jimmy had gotten beat up. The cops had found out nothing and the case was already forgotten. While Mr. G had made him promise not to do anything, nobody had made him promise not to talk to Joe Lund. That's all he had done, just a little chat. He hoped that store keep would be looking over his shoulder.

FEBRUARY 1882 was a month to be forgotten. Not because it was so horrible or catastrophic, but because it was so normal. Nothing happened at all other than regular life, and that was just fine with Conrad Graf.

He stepped out of the icehouse into the alley between the brewery and the two churches standing like defiant twins on opposing corners of the same block. Kicking each other as sisters from the same mother but clamoring for dominance. St. Mary's to the east and the Methodists to the west.

Conrad was shocked how warm it was. He closed his eyes and turned his face to the sun for a moment. It felt warm on his cheeks and he wiped sweat from his brow. The warmth of the sun was a welcome change after coming out of the icehouse. It felt good to work a little and get the blood pumping after so much time at his desk. He spotted Teddy walking down the alley straight toward him.

"Well hello, my friend," Conrad said.

"Hello to you as well, Mister Graf. How are you on this fine day?"

The warm temperatures were bringing out the best in everyone. The snow had melted, and mud ruled the day.

"It wasn't too many years past when a warm spell like this meant blood," Conrad said.

"Ah yes, the legend of the 'Indian Summer,'" Teddy said with a nod.

Conrad shook his head. "No legend if your scalp is the one that's lifted. The old Chiefs Keokuk and Poweshiek ruled this land not too long ago and they were terrifying to behold. They're trying to find a way for us to live together rather than killing each other all the time like they're doing further out west. I remember when I first came here, things were a bit more spirited. Now all we have to worry about are Methodists."

"I'm a Methodist!"

"I'm sure we could entice Father Edmonds to convert you to the true light of the Lord and the love of Mary," Conrad laughed. He was in a fine mood.

"My dear mother would die an unholy death if I became a Catholic."

"Well at least you're a wet-Methodist. That's the kind I can get along with."

Teddy laughed heartily and lifted a thick book to show Conrad. "I'm off to enjoy the fine weather and study the intricacies of the human heart with this fine book, a gift from Doctor Clapp. He's going to test me on it tomorrow, so I best be at it."

Conrad laughed. "Ah yes, the intricacies of the human heart. You can study till the cows come home, but it will all be for nothing when you fall for a fine lady."

Teddy nodded. "That could be true."

"It most certainly is true. You could memorize that whole book and one look from the right woman and you'll forget your own name." Conrad slapped Teddy on the shoulder. "A mischievous glance from the wrong woman has led many a man astray. So you'd better be on your best till you know which woman it is."

"I think I'll stick to my book learning for now," Teddy said.

"Very wise, lad. Books and beer, two things you can trust. Leave all that love nonsense until you've got yourself a trade," Conrad said with a nod of his head.

"Yes sir, I'll keep that in my mind." Teddy continued on down the alley and turned left onto Dubuque Street and then right onto Iowa Avenue, which led him straight west toward the old capitol building.

It took his breath away every time he saw it. Iowa Avenue had been designed to mirror Washington, D.C. when Iowa City was still the capitol of Iowa and the architect's effect was stunning indeed.

The split street had grass in the middle, running from the east edge of town straight west, culminating in the capitol building. At one time the governor's mansion had been planned to be built at the easternmost point, the mansion on one end, the old capitol on the other. When the capitol was moved to Des Moines, the governor's mansion was never built.

Teddy continued through campus and down the slope, finding a place to sit on Madison Street that the students enjoyed during the summer because it overlooked the river. He found a good spot against a tree and cracked his book open, enjoying the moment. Cardinals flitted amongst the trees, their red feathers so striking you couldn't help but watch them go about their business. Chunks of the ice layer were noisily breaking free in the frozen river as it was thawing in the unseasonably warm weather.

Teddy removed his outer jacket. The afternoon sun was intense, and with no wind it was comfortable in a light shirt. He continued his reading, not wanting to disappoint Dr. Clapp.

He was several paragraphs into the aorta when he heard a voice.

"Teddy." He was so focused on his book it felt like it was from some other world for a moment. "Teddy?" it came again, a sweet female voice calling out his name.

Teddy snapped to attention and looked up from his book to find himself staring straight into Matilda's eyes. He was now awake, mesmerized by her beauty. Her friend giggled.

"Teddy, this is my friend, Miss Cora Wilson."

"Miss Wilson, I'm happy to meet you," Teddy said, standing and politely bowing his head. "I am Theodore Miller, but you may call me Teddy."

"Are you studying?" Matilda asked, pointing pointed at the large book in his hand.

"Yes, the human heart," Teddy said with a smile.

"Are you a doctor?" Cora asked.

"Yes, sort of. Once I finish my residency with Doctor Clapp and pass my test I will be considered fully credentialed."

"Doctor Clapp? He's the brewer's doctor, isn't he?" Cora asked with a bit of contempt in her voice.

"He is a resident of the northside yes, but he is a brilliant doctor. I'm lucky to be studying under him."

"We're taking a walk on the river trail. Would you care to escort us?" Matilda asked.

"I could join you, I suppose," Teddy said, the idea of reading about ventricles flying right out the window in the face of spending time with a couple of young ladies on a warm day.

Teddy put his outer jacket back on rather than carry it, collected his book, and they were off walking down the trail.

"So, your studies are going well?" Matilda asked.

"Oh yes. Doctor Clapp is very fond of me and has even mentioned that Iowa City always has room for another good doctor."

Matilda placed her hand innocuously upon his arm. Teddy's every sense was suddenly focused upon the very spot where she was touching him.

"You are considering setting up your practice here?" Matilda asked, obviously excited about that prospect.

"Perhaps. It is a fine town, and growing every day. It's full of intellectual people and the setting is lovely," Teddy said. "It's a great place to raise a family."

Cora stared. Matilda gasped, and stopped as if he'd just proposed. Teddy had no idea what he was getting himself into with his words.

Teddy noticed they were aghast. "Well, it is a fine place for children, isn't it?"

Matilda gathered herself. "Why yes, it is. Fine educational opportunities."

"How many children do you want, Teddy?" Cora asked with a wink at Matilda, her voice full of spite.

"I don't know about that. I'd have to be married first and I'm sure my wife would have a superior opinion about such things, as she would have to do the birthing of the babies," Teddy said.

"That's very kind of you, Teddy," Cora said, giggling, "to consider your wife's opinion superior."

"Kind?"

"Most men see women as a brood mare whose opinion matters not," Cora explained. Matilda shot her a cold look, but she knew Cora wouldn't stop.

"I'm not most men then, I guess. My mother was educated and taught me to love learning whether male or female. I wouldn't be a doctor today if not for her. She'd have been a fine doctor in her own right," Teddy said.

Cora raised an eyebrow. "You think a woman could be a doctor?"

"It's simply a matter of time until women are admitted into all the worlds that are availed presently to men."

"Oh my, Teddy. You would let a woman *vote*?" Matilda asked.

"Of course. A woman has the same amount of reason as a man, even if she is incapable of lifting a heavy log or fighting off an attacker. Her mind is every bit the equal to a man's. Some might even argue *superior*."

Cora stole a glance at Matilda, and they shared a knowing moment. Matilda had never seen a young man like Teddy and both of the women knew she was falling head-first.

A black carriage pulled up beside them and the door opened. It was Matilda's father.

"Matilda, come now. I need to take you home. Cora's mother is looking for her."

The two girls politely bowed to Teddy.

"I hope to see you soon," Matilda said. "Thanks for being our escort."

"It was eye opening," Cora laughed.

They both climbed into the carriage and were gone. Teddy watched as his heart drove away. He knew he would go anywhere Matilda wanted him to go as long as he could be with her.

"HAVE you seen this?" J.J. slammed a newspaper down on the table.

"I saw it," Conrad said.

"What is it?" Dostal asked.

"Last week's *Knoxville State Journal*. They attack us for being German, they attack us for drinking beer, and now for speaking our native tongue!" J.J. handed it to Dostal. "Read it."

Dostal had rarely seen J.J. so riled. He picked the paper up. *"The convention was not only un-American, it was anti-American, alien in its principles, practices, and purposes, it speaks the tongue of the alien. It is the Iowa wing of the army of the Goths and Vandals, whose business it is to destroy the civilization of America and substitute therefore the barbarism of the beer houses and communistic clubs of Hamburg,"* he read aloud, then glanced up.

"Vandals? Destroy America with our beer houses?" J.J. said. "Keep going, there's more."

*"The Germans come from the pot-houses of vice to teach us purer morals, from the domain of despotism to teach us the principles of liberty. Was the Magna Carta written in German? Was the Declaration of Independence written in German? Did the men who emptied the tea into Boston Harbor take council in German? For many years German immigrants were of a character which deserves, and always receives, a welcome. But for thirty-five years we have been receiving the vile with the good. They have been introducing principles and customs repugnant to the American people, destructive of law, order, and morality and ruinous to the family and nation,"* Dostal read. He laid the paper down and took a sip of his beer.

"That is what they think of us." J.J. waved his hand as he announced the statement.

"You Germans sound awful," Dostal said, attempting humor.

"Very funny. These fanatical preachers are stirring up anger and slandering our very race. Beer brewing has been in America since the Puritans landed from England. What do you suppose they drank?" Conrad asked rhetorically. "Beer!"

"There are more Germans arriving every day. Three new families just this week rented houses from me. They think they will put us down and call us foreigners, call us communists. They will lose. I'm as American as any baby born on American soil. They call our customs repugnant just because we brew beer like our forefathers from Bavaria. Is that any different than the blacksmith who brought his trade with him from the old country?" J.J. was pontificating loud enough for the entire room to hear.

"You should write a letter to the editor," Conrad suggested.

J.J. slammed his fist on the table. "I think I will. That's a grand idea. We could get it to run in the *Post*."

"You should send it to the *Register* and the *Staats Anzieger,* then the whole state would read it," Dostal said.

"These teetotalers aren't simply against the brewing of beer, they're against Germans! They say they are afraid we're going to destroy America, while they want to destroy our heritage, destroy who we are!" J.J. was on a roll.

Conrad stood. "I have to go, fellas. I'm shorthanded today and need to be getting back."

"Hire a couple of the new German lads who just came to town," J.J. suggested.

"I just might. Send them by my office in the morning. I'll be looking for that letter in the paper, J.J. We need your passionate words to spread over the state."

"I'll do it."

Dr. Clapp and Teddy appeared at the entrance to the Second Street Club. Dostal waved them over and they joined the brewers. After greetings and salutations, Ed pulled a couple more chairs to the table.

Once seated, Dr. Clapp spoke. "Thanks for having us, fellas. I trust you're all feeling well, or is this a business call?" He smiled and stroked his impressive beard that extended formidably off of each corner of his chin in separate, yet matching, growths.

"We are in fine health due to our splendid doctor," Conrad answered. "I personally want to thank both you and Teddy for all that you did for my man Jimmy."

"No thanks are necessary, Conrad. I'm glad he is improving. He took a real blow to the head, and with his other wounds it could have been worse."

"He is a good man and didn't deserve the treatment he was given."

"Has Coldren determined who might have perpetrated the deed?" Dr. Clapp asked.

Conrad glanced at Teddy. "No. Coldren knows nothing, but through my sources we know who did it."

"Are you keeping that information to yourself or sharing it with the law?" asked Dr. Clapp.

"All will work itself out. No need to involve the law in private matters."

"With times like these, I'm assured a steady flow of business," Dr. Clapp laughed. "J.J., what can we do to entice Doctor Miller to stay on in Iowa City once he's learned all that I know?"

"It would take a lifetime to learn all that you know, Doctor Clapp," Teddy said humbly.

"I think our chances of keeping Teddy have greatly increased since he's fallen for a young lady of our community, a Miss Matilda Dunlap, I believe," J.J. said, winking at Teddy.

"I haven't f-fallen for her. We, um, we just w-walked," Teddy stammered.

All the older men laughed as it was obvious that Teddy was smitten.

"I'm not convinced she's the one for Teddy. She's a teetotaler and a Methodist." Conrad laughed. "I think we could find him a fine Catholic Democrat and his life would be much more enjoyable!"

"What would be worse? A wet Methodist marrying a dry Methodist or a wet Methodist marrying a Catholic?" Dostal hypothesized.

"We need to find him a dry Catholic," J.J. said.

Each man hooted at that prospect.

"There is no such thing!" Conrad bellowed.

"Or maybe we could convert Teddy to the true way. Make a good Catholic out of him," Dr. Clapp said.

"I'll not convert." Teddy shook his head. "I could not break my mother's heart like that."

"Ah, Teddy, you're a good lad who loves his mother," Conrad said. "Well, Matilda the teetotaler it is then. May God bless you in your struggles."

**10**

FEBRUARY gave way to March and the days were soaring into the forties on a regular basis. All the snow had turned the world muddy. Small buds were starting to show a hint of green on the leafy trees and all around the signs of spring abounded.

Spring was full of hope in Iowa. The deep soil, black as night, promised to bring forth its bounty, and men who worked the land were getting their tools and tack ready to turn the soil and plant their seeds.

All the brewers owned property and had fields of hops, which grew well in Iowa soil. Most of the wheat was shipped in from Kansas. Sugar and all the other ingredients came by the trainload from all over the country. The train connected them to everything, and it had literally changed the world in a few short years. The small freight companies still managed a living hauling with wagons and horses in towns and even regionally, but everything moving long distances went by train.

The breweries owned many wagons for hauling and delivering both beer and ice. They had become so proficient at creating block ice necessary for the cooling of beer in the brewing process that they had begun selling the extra. They hauled it around town and to the neighboring communities, providing even more business opportunities both in the hauling and selling the ice.

DR. Clapp finished washing the blood from his hands while Teddy, his hands equally bloodied, waited his turn at the sink. The sound of a newborn squawking turned both their heads.

One of the nuns, Sister Lucile, was attending to the young mother as she attempted to get her baby to nurse for the first time.

The young mother looked spent. Her hair was sweaty, her face drained of energy, yet she glowed as if she was an angel. She noticed the doctors looking her way. She had lost all modesty and didn't attempt to cover herself.

"Thank you, Doctor Clapp. May God bless you," she said.

"And you, Irena, you've a fine young boy there. I can't wait to see him grow," Dr. Clapp said.

He left the room while Teddy finished washing his hands. Within a moment they were out in the night air. A large golden moon hung low to the east and the stars twinkled like diamonds strewn across the sea of darkness.

Dr. Clapp exhaled loudly, and his breath could be seen in the moonlight. "Join me for a beer at Louie's Pub?" he asked Teddy.

Dr. Clapp rarely socialized with Teddy outside of work, so he felt excited to accept. "Why yes, sir, that sounds like a great idea."

"Excellent." Dr. Clapp set off at a steady pace down the quiet street. A horse with a rider heading east passed by, filling the night with the distinct sound of shod hooves clicking upon the pavers. The pub was only a few short blocks from the Sisters of Mercy Hospital. They turned down Market Street where it met Gilbert Street. Baker's Hall was lit up with lantern light and the sound of men having a good time spilled out onto the street.

A new section of the building facing Market Street was under construction. The shape of the new building could be seen by the masonry underway.

"What's that place?" Teddy asked. "I've not been in there."

"That's Samuel Baker's place. He'll sell you dry goods and a beer. He's a good friend. You could call it fireman's hall and be close to right. Most of the fellas in there are part of the fire brigade. The new building will be a part of the new Alert Hose Company. The population is growing so fast we are doubling the number of firemen. The second floor has a couple of meeting halls and old Samuel lives upstairs. Always has, probably will until I visit him at his last."

The Great Western towered over the street to the north, while Englert's City Brewery stood tall in its own right to the south side of the street. Dr. Clapp stepped up the short step and into a well-lit room full of men standing and drinking beer.

A piano was being played off to the side of the hall, providing an entertaining ambiance.

Dr. Clapp made his way to the bar.

"How is Doctor Clapp this fine evening?" the bartender asked with a grin.

"Very well, George. How are you, sir?"

"Can't complain." George placed two beers on the bar in front of the doctors.

"Delivered a fine baby boy this day," Dr. Clapp said. He smiled in satisfaction from a job well done. Bringing a baby into the world was perhaps the most enjoyable part of being a doctor, when everything went well. So much of medicine focused on the horrible aspects of life. Delivering a baby and watching new life take its first breath was bound to bring hope to the most hardened doctor, and Dr. Clapp was no different.

"What baby is this?" George asked.

"Irena Novak. Ludvik Novak's wife. He drives a wagon for Great Western."

"Yes, I know Ludy. Good lad. A son?"

"A fine boy," Dr. Clapp announced.

"Drinks for the doctors on the house in honor of a fine young American." George slid Dr. Clapp's coin back across the bar to him.

"Thank you, sir." Dr. Clapp raised his glass and Teddy raised his as well. "To the boy Novak!" The two doctors toasted and enjoyed a hearty drink.

J.J. appeared through the crowd. "My friends! I'm glad to see you tonight. Welcome to Louie's Pub, the finest place you can drink a lager in Johnson County."

"That's quite a claim in Brewery Square," Dr. Clapp said.

"It is indeed, and I stand by it." J.J. laughed. "Will you join me in the back for a seat and some fine company?"

"Yes, we will," Dr. Clapp agreed.

They followed J.J. down a short hall that opened up into another room full of men drinking and talking loudly. The main difference was they were seated at tables. Some men were eating while others played cards.

"Welcome to what we call the Back Room. It's not as swanky as Dostal's Second Floor, but we like it," J.J. said with a wry grin. He led them to a table with two men already seated. J.J. offered the doctors the two empty seats. The other two men stood.

Teddy and the old man at the table stared intently at one another as if no one else was in the room. The old man looked spry even though he was obviously aged. His thin hair was mostly gray, and his bearded face was magnificent to behold. At his age, he appeared a man to be respected.

"Doctor Clapp, you already know everyone, but for Doctor Miller's sake, this is my partner and brother-in-law, Frank Rittenmeyer. He does all the *real* work around here." A strong man in his fifties shook Teddy's hand with a grip of steel. "And of course, you both know my father, Louis Englert."

Louis smiled at Teddy. "I was going to find my way home, but I'll stay for one more beer with the doctors." He sat back down.

"We delivered a fine baby boy today," Dr. Clapp crowed. "Doctor Miller was the lead and I merely watched."

Teddy smiled sheepishly. "Doctor Clapp is too kind. I feel good about the outcome, but Doctor Clapp did a little more than watch and I am grateful for each day I learn more."

"It's striking." Louis Englert's voice was low and raspy. He rarely spoke at social events, so everyone took notice and waited upon his words, leaning in against the noisy room. "You sound just like your father."

Teddy immediately struggled to hold back any public display of tears, but it was difficult. "Do I?" It was like a little boy asking a question, hoping for the answer.

Louis nodded with a steady gaze as if he was searching Teddy's face for signs of his father. "You look a little like him, but I imagine you take after your mother."

"Yes sir, I do."

"But your voice, it's uncanny. I will never forget the sound of your father's voice. He was a fine baritone and could regale us with a story or a song around the campfire." Louis paused, remembering. His lip quivered a bit. Every man at the table sat captive to his words. "I held your father as he passed from this world to the next."

"Yes, I know," Teddy said, his voice wobbly.

"That war...that war was bloody business. I lost many friends, but your father's voice, I'll never forget the sound of it. I hear it my dreams sometimes crying out my name. It haunts me. He saved my life before he died, and his last words were of you and your mother." Louis glanced at J.J., who rarely saw his father this emotional. "Your father, he said to me, take care of my boy and his mama. I promised him I always would, and I have tried."

Every man at the table was holding back their emotions.

His lip quivering, Teddy raised his glass. "To you, sir! I thank you. You have lived up to your promise, both to me and my mother. I would not be here studying with Doctor Clapp if not for you and your support. My father thanks you, as do I."

Any man at the table with an ounce of honor and a pinch of compassion wiped a tear away no matter how much they fought against it.

"It will never repay his sacrifice, but I'm glad you're here and doing well," Louis said. "He would be proud of you delivering a baby."

"He'll be a fine doctor someday very soon," Dr. Clapp said to Louis.

Louis raised his glass and waited for the others to join him. When all the glasses were high, he stood to his feet. "To my friend, Francis Miller, may he rest in peace."

"Amen," J.J. said while everyone took a solid drink to the honored man. Louis took more than one; he continued until he finished his entire beer. A little golden liquid ran down his grizzled beard when his glass was empty, and he slammed it to the table. "Gents, I'll be on my way. I'm too old to stay out with you young fellas. Good night." He shrugged into his coat and placed a dark cowboy styled hat with a colored leather band upon his head. Everyone watched in silence as he walked out.

When he was gone Teddy raised his glass again. "To Louis Englert, a great man."

"A legend," Frank added.

"And a fine father," J.J. said.

They all drank again. Every man continued until his mug was empty, not to be outdone by the master of the brewhouse. Another round was necessary to continue the evening right.

"Have you ever heard the story of Louis Englert?" Frank Rittenmeyer asked, leaning in over his brew. "J.J. not included of course."

J.J. laughed. "Yeah, I've heard it."

"Well I'm gonna tell it again," he said with a serious face. "Because few of us will ever fill a shoe like that."

J.J. motioned to the bartender for another round.

"Bavaria on the Rhine birthed him in 1810, and it took him thirty years to find his way to Iowa, passing through some tough places on his way here: New Orleans, and Cincinnati. He came here when it was still the new capitol and the Sac and Fox, the Mesquakis, still had a camp here. He built his home on the main trail into town, now Dubuque Street, and provided for travelers a saloon, a stage stop, and an inn. Then he started the first brewery in Iowa City. I daresay one of the first west of the Mississippi. He created it from nothing with his own hands and a dream from the old country. A dream to brew beer and raise a family free as you please in America. Nothing more. What could be a better life?"

Frank paused to take a hearty drink of his beer. "Old Louis is a hardworking man as ever there was, but smart, quick as a whip he is, and he enjoys the finer things. He has told me many a time about the opera houses he saw in New Orleans and his vision of building one here on the prairie. Even now J.J. talks about it, but the brewery was what he knew and that's what he built. The brewing of beer is a grand trade of old, and he learned its tricks from his father, who learned it from his father, and he's passed it on to his sons. It was what he knew, and he did it well.

"It's true. Louis Englert made a lot of money brewing beer, but do you know what mattered more?"

"No, what was it?" Teddy asked.

"What mattered more was his honor, that's what! He was not a young man when the war between the states broke out. He was a man of business, not a soldier. He'd left Germany to avoid becoming a conscript even, as he was not a fighting man. And at his age, no one would have expected him to serve. He was too old, a man in his late fifties, and a successful man at that.

"No one would expect him to do what he did. To shut down his brewery for two years. He literally closed it up for business and joined the Army. He joined the 37th Regiment Company D, the Graybeards. While they were mostly charged with guarding prisoners and kept from the terrible violence of the front lines, old Louis stole away and joined the fray of several battles. That is the type of man we are in the company of."

"Drink to that!" Frank shouted, and everyone drank as commanded. "A great man to be sure. He put his entire business on hold to serve a cause that mattered above all else, a united America and freedom for all, even the slaves.

"When Louis made his way from New Orleans to the Midwest, he saw firsthand how the black man was treated in the South. He grew up poor in Germany and they were treated poorly. If the Kaiser said jump, you jumped. The men with the money or the title had all the power, yet even after seeing that, he told me he never had seen anything like how the Africans were treated in the South, like animals.

"He said it was inhumane, and he vowed to do what he could to help bring that to an end, and that's what he did. How many men would do what he did?" Frank asked, each man hanging on every word.

"None," J.J. said. "He's a one-of-a-kind, he is."

"To Louis!" they each drank heartily.

"Mark my words, one day we'll build a music hall or an opera house in his name," J.J. said. "We've got to get all this temperance nonsense behind us, and I'll do it. I promise you."

Frank rolled his eyes. "Don't bring that up. I was having a fine time."

"Laugh all you want, but these crazy temperance hags mean business. We're going to lose the vote in Des Moines this week. That will send it to a statewide vote," J.J. said.

"Please, J.J. I can't hear it tonight. No politics," Frank said.

"Fine. You brew the beer, but this is what I do and it's not good. I deal with the politics, and believe me, they are coming after us. They mean to destroy us."

"I know, I just can't listen to it all the time," Frank said.

"Well, hide your head in the sand then, because I'm doing all I can to simply keep what we do *legal*. To keep my father's legacy alive."

"Did I mention that the Novaks had a fine baby boy today?" Dr. Clapp said.

J.J. smiled at Dr. Clapp and nodded. "Yes, a new life. I'll drink to that." He raised his glass. "Frank is right. Politics is making us all angry."

"Most people, democrat or republican, brewer or teetotaler, want to simply be left alone to prosper and love their families," Teddy said.

After a long pause J.J. said, "I don't doubt these Methodists love their children, but they most definitely won't leave us alone to prosper as we will. If they think they can take away my business and that I won't fight that to the death, they're crazy."

"All people are the same under the skin," Dr. Clapp said, taking another drink.

"I know you're right, but some people won't leave well enough alone. They've made it their goal to destroy me and everything my father built."

Frank wagged a finger. "I told you no politics."

"Frank, politics doesn't care if you don't care. We are watching politicians with the stroke of a pen and a yay or a nay simply decree that what we do is illegal and that all things German are anti-American. Does that make sense to you?"

"No, of course not."

"Did my father do what he did so that the business he started could be taken away by politicians and teetotalers?"

"No. I know you're right, J.J., but I'm just a brewer and that's all I'll ever be." Frank stood up. "I've got to head out. My wife is expecting, and I told her I'd be home."

"I'm sorry, Frank, but I want you to be a brewer the rest of your life. That's what I'm fighting for," J.J. said.

"I know, J.J." Frank slipped his jacket on his big shoulders.

"Tell my sister I love her," J.J. said. "I'll stop by in the next day or so to say hello."

"I will tell her. Goodnight, gents."

Teddy was becoming more and more uncomfortable with the political ranting. He wanted to be in his room studying until he fell asleep. He could sense he was falling between two great enemies, his benefactors whom he loved and the love that was his future, Matilda.

He had no idea how the two could be reconciled and it caused a sinking feeling in his stomach.

J.J. unrolled a piece of paper he pulled from his vest pocket and read aloud. "The vote will be this week. Most likely Thursday. You'll see it in the papers after that. Just wanted to give you a warning. We won't win. It will go to a statewide vote. God help us. E. Lucas." He paused and looked up. "I got this telegram from Lucas today."

"Well, we're in for a fight," Dr. Clapp said.

J.J. nodded curtly. "Looks that way."

Teddy stood. "I think I'll take my leave if you don't mind, Doctor Clapp. My boss is tough as they come and demands me rested and ready to go in the morning."

Dr. Clapp stood as well. "I'll go with you, Teddy. Your boss sounds like a hard one." He laughed. "I'm tired too."

"Thanks for all you do for the neighborhood, fellas," J.J. said. "I hope I didn't upset you too much with the talk of temperance."

"It takes more than that to upset me," Dr. Clapp said. "I can deliver a Methodist baby as well as a Catholic one, I don't have to pick a side. It's too bad about this temperance business. I wish it would all go away."

"It won't go away by wishing it, I'm sorry to say," J.J. said solemnly.

"I can't believe they actually did it," Dostal said.

Conrad took a sip of his beer and peered out the window. A light snow was falling. It was beautiful. "They told us this would happen. Lucas and Wolfe sat right here and predicted it."

"That doesn't mean I like it," Dostal said sternly.

"None of us like it," Conrad said. "They're here." Conrad nodded out the window at the black carriage that had just stopped in the street below. Dostal glanced down to see J.J. and Ed Lucas climbing out of it.

Dostal waved his bartender over. "Two more beers and a two more plates."

"Yes, sir," the man said with a nod.

"Thank you, Walt."

J.J. and Congressman Lucas made their way across the room that only had a few other patrons in the midafternoon. Congressman Lucas, ever the politician, stopped at each table to shake hands and say hello.

After salutations, Lucas and J.J. found their seats. Each man took a sip of their beer when Walt carefully placed it in front of them.

"How was the train?" Dostal asked.

Ed leaned back in his chair and ran his fingers through his thinning hair. "Fine, I even fell asleep a little. A true marvel of transportation. I was arguing on the house floor hours ago and now I am here to tell you face-to-face what's been done. I doubt I will take a carriage ever again. Amazing, is it not?"

"It is a modern marvel," J.J. conceded.

Conrad scowled. "Not all things modern are good. What happened? It passed."

"Yes, just like we knew it would," Lucas said.

"We should have greased the skids and switched some votes," Conrad snorted.

"That would not have been wise. The vote was mostly along party lines." Ed laughed. "There would have been too many skids to grease and the greasing is not easily done when the pious are involved."

"I've heard of the pious being greased as easily as the backslidden," Conrad retorted.

"That may be, but the votes are cast. Amendment 1 has passed stating that the sale, manufacture, and consumption of alcohol is prohibited in Iowa," Ed stated as a matter of fact.

Conrad raised his glass and took a big drink. He slammed his cup to the table. "Stop me," he said with angry edge to his voice.

J.J. and Dostal shook their heads and smiled at their friend.

"No one will stop you. Not yet. A statewide ballot is scheduled for June 27th. They can't enforce the law until it passes the statewide vote to the people."

"Will it pass that vote?" Dostal asked.

"Sadly, we think so," Lucas said. "The counties with the most Germans and the breweries will vote against it, of course. Dubuque, Scott, Des Moines, Wapello, Clayton, Plymouth, Lee, Johnson." The congressman pulled a small paper from his pocket and read from it. "And Jackson. Those are solid against. Solidly for the amendment are Emmet County, Winnebago, Dickinson, Clarke, Story, Cherokee, Buena Vista, Appanoose, Ringgold, and Calhoun. The rest are up for grabs."

"Linn County is not against? They have three breweries!" Conrad exclaimed. "What about Marshall County or Muscatine? They have to be against!"

"We'll see, but as near as we can tell it's going to pass," Lucas affirmed.

"Then what?" Dostal asked.

"Then they'll decide when it takes effect."

"I can tell you how the northside would vote, but beyond that who the hell knows? These damn temperance ladies are running rampant all across the state!" Conrad fumed. "Don't they have anything better to do?"

"I guess not," J.J. said.

"If anybody needed a drink it would be them."

"I've said that for years," Lucas laughed. "I've even shared a beer or two in a back room with some of my teetotaling friends, only to watch them rail against the evils of alcohol the very next morning on the house floor."

"I hate politicians," Conrad said.

"You've hurt my feelings," Congressman Lucas said, then grinned. "But I forgive you. If anyone had call to hate politicians, it would be the German Beer Mafia of Iowa City. Take heart, fellas, you're not out of business just yet and we've got a few tricks up our sleeves."

"I'm not even German," Dostal said. "I'm Bohemian."

The entire table paused for a moment before breaking into hysterical laughter.

CONRAD had just settled into his office after making his rounds when he heard it. He got a sinking feeling in his stomach, knowing it was Vernice up to her old tricks.

He walked out front and stood still on the corner of Linn and Market listening intently. He was right. He heard the sound of a disturbance on the opposite corner of the block. He shouldered his jacket on and headed south toward St. Mary's, the sound of chanting getting louder with each step. The street was full of people rubbernecking to see what the commotion was.

As he turned west onto Jefferson, he could see them. They had several wagons with people filled to capacity, each carrying signs and shouting.

"Victory! Victory! Down with all the breweries!"

Some of the signs read, "NO BEER!" Others said, "Temperance WINS!" The one that hit Conrad in the gut read, "Brewers Must GO!"

He could feel his blood boiling, his rage pushing him on. He reached the front of the crowd as they started marching, all the while chanting their victorious mantra. Vernice was marching right out in front carrying a sign as happy as she'd ever been. He was shaking with anger and wanted to charge after her, but a strong hand clasped his shoulder.

He turned fast and raised his fists. "No, boss, let them go." It was Tom Bontrager and he looked straight into Conrad's eyes, sharing his frustration.

Conrad nodded to his friend and stomped away from the crowd, turning back to the business he loved. He could hear them marching further away down Iowa Avenue and Clinton Street, reveling in their victory. His mind was wild with thoughts of retribution and his eyes cast glances about left and right. Tom followed right behind, quiet and faithful as ever.

Conrad paused and glanced over his shoulder, listening and judging where the march was at that moment. When he turned back, he ran full force into a big man dressed in black. The man took a solid step back but did not fall when most men would have with such a blow.

"Watch it!" Conrad yelled before he realized it was Father Edmonds.

"You weren't looking, Conrad," Father Edmonds said as Conrad fumbled for words in embarrassment.

"I'm sorry, Father, I wasn't..."

It was obvious that Conrad was upset, especially to a man who'd spent his life praying for people in times of need.

"Stop in to my office tomorrow. It's been too long since we just talked, and I will pray for you, Conrad," Father Edmonds, placing his hand on Conrad's shoulder and giving him a calming smile.

"I will, Father," Conrad promised.

Father Edmonds continued down the street, heading toward the sound of the march which was several blocks away but could still be heard.

"Let's go, Mister G," Tom said.

The two men walked at a much more normal pace back to the brewery.

Conrad paused in front of the door to the Union and looked at Tom, "Thanks, Tom. I'm not sure what I'd have done if you hadn't stopped me."

"It's okay, Mister G. This *no beer* stuff has everybody on edge." Tom tipped his bowler and gave a slight smile, "I'm always here to help."

"Thanks, Tom. You're a good friend."

"Did you know I started working here when I was only fifteen?"

"No, I didn't know that. I knew you worked for Simeon."

"Simeon gave me a job after my ma died. My father had left years earlier. My sister had died of scarlet fever. I didn't have anybody. Father Edmonds told me to go see Simeon. He gave me a job, but it was much more. He gave me a family. I became a man slinging ice, loading barrels, and working the caves. This is my home."

Conrad smiled. "Simeon was a good man."

"He sure was," Tom said. "We won't let them take the Union from us."

Conrad nodded. "No, we won't, Tom. Thanks for sharing that story with me. I never knew all of that. I'm glad you're part of the Union family."

After Conrad disappeared into the brewery, Tom headed back toward the distant sound of the march.

Out of nowhere, Jimmy was walking beside him. "Where you off to, Tom?"

"Just gonna go have a look," Tom said. "How are you feeling?"

"I'm tip-top," Jimmy said despite an obvious limp and a yellow hue to one eye that hadn't faded in weeks. Not to mention his nose had healed a little less than straight. "They'll be standing on the Old Cap steps giving their speeches and calling for our demise."

"Yep," Tom said as the Old Capitol came into view.

Jimmy was right with his prediction. A large crowd filled the campus centered on the capitol steps. The crowd cheered and waved its signs to support whoever was talking.

As they got close, they could see it was one of the Swafford brothers. They couldn't tell which one. The other Swafford stood next to his brother as well as Vernice and Senator Shrader.

Tom pointed off to one side where several men slouched under a large oak tree whispering to each other. "You see them?"

"Yes."

"That's them. They're the ones who did it to you. The Sons of Temperance."

"Sonsabitches!" Jimmy spat.

Tom put a hand to his shoulder to keep him from limping across Clinton Street and starting a fight.

"Not yet, Jimmy. Soon. We'll do it together. All of us Teamsters. We got your back."

"When?"

"How about tonight?" Tom grinned. "Is that soon enough?"

"Yeah, tonight sounds good."

"You see that one in the middle? He's the leader I guess," Tom said. "Joe Lund."

"He's mine," Jimmy said. All hint of his jocular personality had vanished.

# 11

DARKNESS settled over the Midwest cool and cloudy spring night. Flyers with pro-temperance statements littered the streets where the march had been. Jimmy and Tom stepped into Louie's and immediately locked eyes with Gunnar Schmidt standing with some friends across the room. Gunnar left his friends and made his way toward them.

"What's up, boys? What brings you to the southside of Market Street?" He laughed. It was obvious he'd had a few beers already.

"We're going out tonight to get a little payback for what these sons of whatever did to Jimmy, and their little march today putting it in our face they're gonna close us down. Want to come along?" Tom asked.

Gunnar grinned and nodded. "It's about time. Let me get my coat."

"Do you know where Frank is?"

"He took a load of ice up to Solon late. He won't be back tonight."

"Okay, let's stop over at Dostal's and see if Ed or Krystof want to join us," Jimmy said.

"Did the bosses set this up?" Gunnar asked.

Jimmy glanced at Tom. "Sometimes things gotta be done they can't be a part of."

"Count me in," Gunnar said with a crazy smile. He put on his coat and drained the last drop of his beer. "Let's go."

As they crossed the street to Dostal's, they ran into Krystof Kolar.

"Just the man we were looking for," Gunnar said.

"What's going on, fellas?"

"Where's Ed?" Tom asked.

"He's bartending upstairs all night," Krystof replied.

"Just us then," said Tom. "You want to go settle up for Jimmy with those sonsabitches that beat him?"

"Hell yeah. I was wondering what was taking the big boys so long to order it."

The other three men all chuckled and shared a glance.

Krystof frowned. "They didn't order it, did they?"

"If you don't want to go, we understand, but we've had enough with politics. They need to be taught a lesson that you can't just come to the northside and toss one of us like they did." Gunnar had raised his voice loud enough to cause Jimmy to look around to see if anyone heard. He didn't see anyone who could have overheard. "You in or out?"

Krystof nodded. "I'm in."

Tom set off toward the Union, ducking down the dark alley that led to the icehouses. The crew slapped each other's shoulders and cried out hoots of excitement as they trotted along thinking of what lay ahead. Tom maneuvered down the dark alley with ease. He knew it like the back of his hand. It was the very alley where Jimmy had taken his beating. Tom had a wagon ready to go. He jumped up into the driver's seat, Jimmy and Krystof hopped in back, and Gunnar climbed aboard next to Tom.

When everyone was ready, Tom slapped leather to a fine chestnut gelding. The animal was used to pulling wagons of ice, hops, and beer. A wagon with only a few men aboard was light work indeed. In a few minutes they crossed the tracks to the south and pulled up in a stand of trees not far from the old Gilbert landing.

Tom hopped down. He threw back the tarp to the front of the wagon uncovering a half a dozen axe handles with no axe heads attached. Every man grabbed one. They felt good in their hands. Tom handed each man a bandana and then tied his around his neck.

"What's the plan, Tom?" Gunnar whispered, his voice trembling with anticipation.

"They've got a cabin by the river just up ahead. They mostly hang around the cabin and drink," Tom said.

"Drink? You're pulling my good leg," Jimmy said.

"Yeah, they drink in secret down by the river."

"You've got to be kidding me," Jimmy scoffed. "Hypocrites!"

"It could be just the leader Joe in there all alone since it's his cabin. Or it could be half a dozen of them loafing about." Tom glanced at his crew. "We'll creep up and have a look, then decide what to do."

"I want that Joe bastard," Jimmy said with an edge to his voice, swinging the axe handle in his hand.

"None of them look too tough, no matter what they think, and we should have them caught surprised. Let's just give them what they gave Jimmy and be on our way. Agreed?" Tom said.

Everyone nodded. "Agreed."

"If all goes well, we'll meet back here at the wagon. If anything goes awry, make your way to the northside as best you can back to Brewery Square. Let's go." Tom led off into the night. A waning moon provided a little light as the big river gurgled off to the east. Tom held up fast next to an old barn and pointed at the cabin. Light was gently pouring forth from the single window, the golden hue of a lantern, and smoke lifted lazily from the chimney. Tom pulled his bandana up over his face. The others followed suit.

He sprinted across the open ground and pressed himself against the cabin with the others right behind. Tom eased a peek into the widow. Three men were inside sitting around a table drinking. He put up three fingers to his friends. One was definitely Joe Lund; he didn't know the other two. One was a skinny kid with long and flowing black hair, the other a fair fellow with thinning hair and some heft to his shoulders.

Tom nodded to his friends and stood up, facing the front door. He knocked three times. "Come in!" a voice yelled from inside. Tom waited.

With a creak of the latch, the door swung wide. Tom rushed in, which came as a great shock to all inside. The skinny lad at the table screamed at the sight of masked men barging violently in the cabin. Tom swung his axe handle horizontally, cracking Joe Lund hard on the shoulder with a wicked thump. Joe cried out as more masked men entered the room. The bigger man squared his shoulders and began swinging his fists with wide swipes. He went down when an axe handle caught the back of his head. Axe handles were swinging high and low. All three of men in the cabin were taking blows to the body and attempting to protect their heads.

The skinny, long-haired teen dove under the table. Gunnar kicked the table hard, sending it flying across the room, shattering the lantern and igniting the oil in a blast of fire. The skinny boy jumped up and charged toward Gunnar, but collapsed in a pile when one hit to the ear sent his eyes rolling back into his head. He was out cold.

The fire leapt up the wall and jumped to a stack of blankets, significantly growing in size. Still holding his axe handle, Jimmy put the boots to Joe, who was down on the floor. Jimmy kicked him solidly in the head, splitting his cheek open and sending blood streaming down his face. The other man was down in the corner thanks to Krystof and his axe handle.

The fire was obviously out of hand. "Let's go!" Tom yelled.

The four men fled, running a safe distance, full of adrenaline and excitement. They stopped next to the wagon and looked back. Flames were pouring out of the cabin window and smoke billowed into the night sky through a hole in the roof.

The sound of fire alarm and men shouting could be heard in all directions since the fire was easily noticed.

"We should go drag those fellas out," Jimmy said. "We didn't want to burn them!"

The siren of a fire wagon on its way wailed its way straight toward them.

"We have to go!" Tom hopped into the wagon slapped the leads. The other men jumped in the back in a hurry as the big chestnut exploded into a canter east away from the fire. Tom kept his head down as they passed the Close Mansion. Every other horse or wagon they met was going toward the fire to help. They fled. The boys in the back of the wagon laid flat to not be seen.

Tom didn't stop until he was all the way to Hickory Hill. "Hop out," he said to his compatriots. "We can't be seen together. Meet at my place tomorrow after dark. Come in the back. Don't talk about this to anyone! Got it? Not even the bosses!"

"Got it."

The men disappeared into the darkness like creatures of the night. Tom gathered himself and slowly trotted the gelding back toward Brewery Square as if nothing was amiss. The whole town was focused upon the bright flames and smoke wafting from the cabin down by the river.

Horses, men, and brigades with pump wagons all launched into action. Nothing hit a small town on the prairie worse than a fire raging out of control. No one noticed Tom put the wagon away and turn out the chestnut gelding into the small corral.

The fire raged on into the night and the cabin was a complete loss. The proximity to the river helped the fire brigades keep control of the blaze and they managed to contain it to the single building. After the roof collapsed the firemen mostly watched it burn. It wasn't long, and the fire began to dwindle. The men used their pumps to put it out, leaving nothing but a massive two-story stone fireplace and a pile of blackened timbers and ash.

The sun was rising in the east as the men from the firehouses returned to their roosts and set about the daunting task of cleaning and reorganizing their gear. They were tired, but they had to be prepared for the next fire that inevitably would come when they least expected it.

SHERIFF Coldren walked through the ashes as the sun was gently rising in the east. Fire Chief McGrath looked on. They knew each other well. Jim McGrath had been on fire brigades long before Coldren ever became sheriff and would likely still be pulling hoses after Coldren was gone.

"Jim," he said, "what do you think caused it?"

"The two fellas that went to the hospital said it was a lantern got knocked over," Chief McGrath replied. He lifted up an empty cask with the lettering *Union Brewery* stenciled across it. "Maybe this is why?"

"Who are they?"

"Joe Lund works at Hanson's Hardware. The other fella does odd jobs. Farmhand kind of stuff. Charlie Johnson is his name. They're both at Doctor Cozine's, not hurt too bad, banged up and minor burns," McGrath said. "But there's more."

"More?"

"Lund said there was some Indian kid that was with them, he didn't think made it out."

"Indian kid? No name?"

"No. It was odd. Johnson didn't say a word. Looked down mostly, pretty upset, I guess."

"Nobody else?" Coldren crouched and poked his knife at something that had caught his attention. It was a series of sticks shaped like a rib cage. He scraped his knife along the blackened bone, displaying the white calcium underneath. "Looks like ribs."

"We'll gather what we can of the remains," McGrath said.

"Not much left," the sheriff noted.

"It was pretty hot," said Chief McGrath.

"Whose cabin was this?" Coldren asked. "Lund?"

"No, he was renting it from one of the Tysons."

"Which one?"

Two men on matching black horses rode up to the sheriff. He knew them both as businessmen and property owners. The older was Isaiah Tyson and the younger his son, Karl. Isaiah had graying hair and a little extra around the middle. He brought his horse to a stop and shook his head at the debris.

"I guess you need another pump wagon. Didn't save my cabin, did you?"

"Did the best we could. Saved your old barn and no other buildings caught fire," McGrath said.

"Sheriff, what do you think happened?" Karl asked.

"Not sure. The survivors say it was an accident with a lantern, but I've yet to speak with them. Sadly, there's one here who didn't make it out. An Indian kid maybe?"

"Who made it out?" Tyson asked.

"Joe Lund and Charlie Johnson," Coldren answered.

"Lund is the one who rented it from me. He always paid on time. Shame to see it burn down. I'm out the rent."

Coldren furrowed his brow. "And a shame someone died in the fire."

"And that," Tyson conceded. "I can't be responsible for what my tenants do."

Coldren stared in disbelief. "I didn't say you were to blame. Just stating what I know."

"I've seen all I need to see. If you have any more questions, Sheriff, you can find me at my office on Gilbert. Good luck figuring it out." Tyson bounded off on his horse with his son following behind.

Coldren climbed down out of the remains of the cabin. "That's a shame about the boy. I lost my brother to a fire back east."

"It's a bad way to go."

Coldren pulled out his watch, glanced at the time, and placed it back in his pocket. He walked toward his horse tied to the barn. "If you find anything else, let me know."

"Will do," McGrath said.

Determined to get answers, Coldren rode straight to Dr. Cozine's office—a large home where he saw patients on the main floor and had living quarters upstairs. The sheriff entered the front room and found a seat.

Dr. Cozine appeared. "Hello, Sheriff, can I help you?"

"Are you treating the men from the fire?" Coldren asked.

"One of them. The other I stitched up a cut and let him go. Mister Johnson. I have Mister Lund back here."

"I need to speak with him about the fire if he's able."

"He's awake. Not hurt too bad. Come on back."

The wood floors under a fine carpet creaked at the weight of their steps. Sheriff Coldren was carrying his hat in his hand and his silver badge stood out in sharp contrast to his dark suit.

Dr. Cozine showed him into an exam room. Joe Lund sat reclining in a chair next to a table of instruments.

"Hello, Joe. I believe we've met once or twice." Sheriff Coldren had seen Joe at the Ladies of Temperance events. "I share your beliefs on temperance."

"Yes, I know you, Sheriff," Joe said.

"I am sure you know the cabin is gone. They saved the barn though."

"I heard that."

Dr. Cozine applied a piece of gauze to the freshly stitched cut on Joe's cheek.

"I'm glad, my horse was in there."

"How'd you get the cut?"

Joe looked down and didn't answer for a moment.

"Glad you're alright." Coldren stared straight at Joe. "And your friend?"

"Yeah, he's fine. We got lucky."

"Your other friend didn't make it out, I'm sorry to tell you," Coldren said.

Joe paused, reading the sheriff's face. "He wasn't really a friend. Just an Indian who ran away from the reservation. I gave him a place to stay and a meal."

"Bad luck for him." Coldren tucked a couple of fingers into his pocket.

"Bad luck, yes."

"Did you see him? Why didn't he make it out when both you and Mister Johnson did?"

Joe shook his head. "It was the brewers that done it."

"Brewers? What do you mean?"

Joe looked at Dr. Cozine, who sat quietly listening.

Joe frowned. "That fire was no accident. We were attacked."

Sheriff Coldren glanced at Dr. Cozine. "What happened, Joe?"

"They kicked the door open and yelled 'this is for Jimmy O'Connor!' Then they started kicking us and hitting us with axe handles. We tried to fight, but the lantern got smashed and the fire took off."

"Did you see who it was?"

"No, they had masks over their faces, but it was the brewers," Joe said. "I know it."

"Why would they come after you, Joe? Did you beat up Jimmy?"

Cozine blanched white as a sheet. Although he knew some of what the Sons of Temperance were up to and he was a sympathizer, he had no desire to be involved in any shenanigans.

Joe steadied his face to appear calm. "No, sir, I am a man of peaceful protest, but because they see me as part of the temperance movement, they hate me."

"What do you mean they hate you?"

"Well, that Tom Bontrager came to my store and threatened me, that's what I mean. I knew they thought I did that to their friend Jimmy, but I didn't. Look at me. I'm too small to do all that got done to him."

"More than one person did that to Jimmy," the sheriff said. "Why didn't you come to me after Tom threatened you? I could have helped."

"I trust in the Lord. It was not me who did that to that O'Connor fella, but the Lord's justice works in mysterious ways. Now they've killed an innocent kid just looking for a place to sleep."

Coldren stared at Joe. Something felt...off. "Did you see anything that could tell us who exactly set upon you at the cabin before we go blaming the whole northside?"

"I just know it was them. They even smelled like beer."

"That's not proof, Joe. Think hard and try to remember anything you can. What about an empty cask of Union beer found at the cabin...were you drinking it, Joe?"

Joe feigned shock. "Sheriff, I am a temperant man!"

"Oh, I know that, Joe. Still, there was beer there."

Joe shook his head and looked down. "I tried to stop him. It was the half-breed. He brought it and he'd drunk a lot of it. I prayed for him to stop, but you know how Indians can be with liquor."

"I know how white people can be with liquor too," Coldren said. "So, you weren't drinking, only the Indian kid was drinking?"

"That's right," Joe said.

"And someone accidentally knocked over the lantern?"

"No, sir, I told you, it was those brewers. That's how I got this cut and that's how the fire started. They killed that poor boy. That was no accident, they were beating us."

"Alright then, Joe. I'll go interview your friend Charlie and see what he remembers."

"Oh Charlie, he's not too bright."

"All the same, I need to know what he saw."

Joe appeared nervous. "Yes sir, talk to Charlie. He'll tell you the same thing I did. It was the brewers who done it."

"We can't indict everyone who smells like beer, Joe. Do you know where I can find Charlie?"

"No. He works for a couple farmers mostly down by Riverside. Amos Yoder, also east of Kalona, Hochstetler maybe? He only comes by my place a couple times a month."

Sheriff Coldren stood. "If you think of anything, come by the office and you let me know right away, Joe. We got a dead boy here. He deserves justice. What was his name?"

"We called him Chief. He said he was a grandson of Chief Poweshiek, but who knows if he was telling the truth? He was a half-breed."

"You already said he was half-breed, Joe. Do you have any idea about his family?"

"No, sir. You could ask the Indians on the reservation if they knew him, but he seemed to be all alone."

"Well that's a shame, to die alone like that."

"It sure is. Those brewers are the devil incarnate."

"The devil dances in unlikely places," Coldren said, sauntering out the door.

Charlie Johnson had packed all that he owned into his saddlebags and was twenty miles south, pushing his horse as hard as he dared. He had friends in St. Louis. He had to put some distance between himself and Iowa as fast as he could get it done. He glanced over his shoulder and kept moving.

He didn't know what Joe Lund was up to, but he knew he wanted no part of it. He couldn't get it out of his head...he'd never seen anything like it. As they stood watching the fire enveloping the cabin, they both knew the boy hadn't made it out. Then they saw the boy staggering into the doorway. Joe sprinted toward him, the heat from the flames intense.

Charlie stood motionless at Joe's bravery. His admiration turned to horror when Joe raised his right leg and kicked the boy in the chest, sending him flying back into the cabin. Joe turned and ran toward Charlie as the loft caved in, causing the fire to roar loudly and intensify.

"I guess Chief didn't make it out," Joe said. "What a terrible tragedy. Those brewers attacked us." A sick smile was plastered on his face, dried blood from a cut on his cheek.

"What brewers? We never saw who it was."

"Just do what I say, Charlie, or I'll tell them you hit me on the head, killed the boy, and lit the fire to cover it up."

Charlie was horrified. "What? I didn't do nothing!"

"Do what I say, Charlie."

"Okay, sure, Joe. Whatever you say, but I don't understand. We got attacked, um, by the um, brewers I guess?" Charlie said. "But why the boy?"

132

"He was nobody. He was a runaway from the reservation. A half-breed claiming he was Chief Poweshiek's grandson. He won't be missed." Joe stared at the raging flames with no emotion on his face.

"Wasn't he your friend?" Charlie asked, incredulous at what was unfolding.

"No more than you," Joe stated. "Don't tell them about the boy."

Charlie had never seen anyone so remorseless as he watched another human being burned alive. He looked over at Joe and he knew right then he was going to light out for Missouri at his first chance. He never wanted to see Joe Lund ever again and he had no desire to take the fall for murder.

CONRAD was in his office, prepared to hear about the temperance march and the passage of the amendment all day long. He was dreading it so much he thought about taking a wagon and going on the run to Tiffin for lumber just to get away from the brewery for the day.

He was pleasantly surprised that other news would consume the day. Not one person talked about the temperance march or the passage of the prohibitory amendment. The fire at the cabin was all anyone was talking about. News spread as well about the mysterious Indian boy who had died.

Some people thought they'd seen him about up to no good, begging around town for handouts. The most outrageous tale that spread was that the half-breed was actually the son of Congressman Lucas from an illicit affair with a Meskwaki consort. By the end of the day that rumor had been replaced and blame for the fire and the boy's death fell solidly on the northside.

Firsthand accounts from none other than Joe Lund turned rumor into conviction. He told anyone who would listen, "It was the brewers! They kicked open the door and beat us like dogs! *For Jimmy* they yelled as they beat the boy into submission, pouring oil over his body and laughing when they dropped the match!"

Joe continued living up every minute of his newfound notoriety. "The devil has set up home and the brewers are demons amongst us! They must go! Murderers!"

Joe never named a name, only repeating it was *the brewers* who'd attacked them. No one questioned him after what he'd been through. He continued to proclaim innocence when asked about any involvement in the Jimmy O'Connor beating.

"I had nothing to do with that. I'm a simple man for temperance and they attacked me for that reason alone, and killed an innocent boy seeking shelter and a meal."

On the heels of the amendment passing in Des Moines and the fire at the cabin, the grumblings against the brewers felt like a rising tide.

That afternoon, Mrs. Graf was walking Dubuque Street with her children and she found many a cold shoulder, where before smiles and welcome had been the norm. Women scowled right to her face as if she'd personally offended them. Her sons were young, but they noticed the outward displays of disdain.

"Mama, why did that man turn his back to you like that?" Simeon asked.

She smiled nervously. "He must have been busy."

"He didn't look busy, Mama. He looked mad."

"Let's go." Mrs. Graf hustled her children back to the northside. After she passed Church Park and St. Mary's she felt safe again, like she was home. She continued straight to the brewery and found Conrad standing in front of the main entrance enjoying the warm spring day.

He smiled and opened his arms, and the boys ran to him.

"What a nice surprise," he said, lifting them both up into his strong arms. He leaned over and gave Anna a kiss on the cheek. She was obviously upset.

"What is it?" he asked.

"You should see the way people are treating us," she snapped. "They turned their backs. One woman crossed the street because she saw us coming."

"Methodists?" Conrad said with a smile and set the boys on the ground.

"No, not just Methodists." She leaned in close to Conrad so the boys couldn't hear her whisper, "They're saying we killed that Indian boy! That you and the *Beer Mafia* are behind it."

"Ha! There's no beer mafia." Conrad sloughed it off. "We just brew like our fathers before us."

"Look me in the eyes and tell me you had nothing to do with that boy burning."

Conrad could tell she was serious, so he stared into his wife's eyes. "I had nothing to do with that."

"Then what is going on?"

"Since the amendment passed, these temperance zealots are emboldened, they are out for our heads. I don't know why this Joe Lund is saying what he's saying other than to paint us the villain."

"He is succeeding! People think the brewers were behind it. Do something, Conrad."

"I will. I'm meeting with J.J. and Dostal tonight to talk about it."

"Good." She exhaled loudly, convinced he'd heard her complaint. "Thank you."

"I'll be home late," Conrad said as she gathered the boys and started off toward home.

She blew him a kiss. "Do what you must, but fix this."

Shaking his head, Conrad turned and walked straight into the brewery.

*I'm not sure who is more terrifying, my wife or Vernice!*

He gripped the young boy who was sweeping the front room by the shoulder. He was a good kid who ran errands and did odd jobs. "Sammy, go tell Mister Dostal and Mister Englert I am calling a full meeting tonight. They'll know what I mean."

"Yes, Mister G," the boy said and immediately trotted off down the street, about his task.

CONRAD could hear voices in the caves as he lowered himself down the shaft. When he stepped off the elevator, everyone was already present and had served themselves a beer awaiting his arrival.

"Conrad!" J.J. hollered when he spotted him.

"J.J., give me a beer," Conrad said.

J.J. handed him the one he held and reached for another one on the table for himself.

"We've got trouble. Lots of trouble," Conrad started out.

Dostal harrumphed. "Tell me something I don't know."

"We have to deal with this amendment first off, but we have more immediate trouble with this Indian kid getting killed in the cabin fire, and the whole town blaming us for it." Conrad's voice grew louder as he spoke.

Silence fell throughout the cave. Conrad stared at his crew of men who all appeared suddenly very uncomfortable. "It's not like we had anything to do with that fire, did we?"

With more silence and downcast eyes from the crew the three owners got a sinking feeling in their stomachs and shared uneasy glances.

"Out with it! One of you tell us!" Dostal snarled, obviously angry.

The men stared at their beers until finally Tom Bontrager spoke up. "It was my idea. We only wanted a little payback for what they did to Jimmy."

"Payback?" J.J. said, shaking his head in disgust.

"It was me, Jimmy, Krystof, and Gunnar. Ed was bartending, and Frank was in Solon or something. We just wanted to beat that little Sons of Temperance asshole up a little bit. The lantern exploded. We didn't mean to kill the Indian kid."

"But you did," Conrad stated. "He's dead and they are blaming us for it, and rightly so."

"Why did the other two make it out and not take their friend with them?" Tom asked.

"I don't know," J.J. said. "Who knows? Maybe they panicked? Fire scares people."

"Did either of you order this?" Conrad asked the other two owners.

"No," J.J. said.

"No," Dostal said. "But it doesn't matter, these are our boys."

"I know. But damnit, fellas, how could you do this without talking to us?" Conrad shouted.

"We just wanted settle the score," Jimmy said quietly.

"It's settled now!" J.J. yelled. "And how do we look to the community now, huh? How are we supposed to win over these temperance ladies if they turn the town against us?"

"I'm sorry, boss," Gunnar said.

"We all are," Tom said. "It's my fault. It was my idea."

After a long silence Conrad took a drink and swallowed. "Did anybody see you? Has the sheriff come and talked to any of you?"

They all looked sideways at each other and shrugged.

"Nobody's come to me," Tom said. "We wore masks. There's no way Joe saw our faces. He's just saying it was us because he's guilty of beating Jimmy and he knows it was payback."

J.J. shook his head. "He's using it against us, but he doesn't have any proof."

"We have to shut him up," Dostal said.

"How?" Conrad asked.

"Not another fire," J.J. grinned. "I'll talk to McGrath about the fire, see if he knows anything that could help us."

"We need to talk to Teddy about this Joe Lund. Maybe he can get us some dirt on him?" Conrad suggested.

"I want to make it crystal clear for you fellas, anything you do reflects on all of us. Nothing else can happen like this without us ordering it or you are out of the group. Understand?" Dostal said sternly.

They all nodded.

"Tom? Understand?" Dostal pressed.

"Yes, I understand," Tom said.

"If anyone asks what the heck you were doing that night, friend or sheriff, you were all at Louie's drinking all night until you heard the sirens. Got it?" J.J. stated. "Frank was tending bar and I'll be sure he remembers all four of you were there."

"We understand," Tom said. "We were at your place all night."

"Good," Conrad said.

# 12

SHERIFF Coldren never questioned anybody on the northside. He never found any evidence other than Joe Lund's shaky word about the mysterious brewers he continued to blame. He knew more went on at that cabin than he was being told, but he couldn't confirm what it was.

Word of Charlie Johnson skipping town only added to the thought by Coldren that Lund was a little less than honest in his story. It did, however, make Johnson look guilty of something, otherwise why would he have skipped out?

Sheriff Coldren entered Hanson's Hardware store and found Joe working behind the counter. He waited patiently until a customer finished his business and left.

"Hello, Sheriff, what can I do for you?"

"Did you know Charlie Johnson has left town without ever talking to me?"

"Yes, I did hear that."

"Why would he do that?"

"I have no idea. Charlie always went his own way," Joe said.

"Why would he skip town right after your cabin fire and the death of the boy if he wasn't guilty of something?"

"Guilty of what, Sheriff?"

"I don't know, you tell me. Why would he run?"

"I told you what happened. Those brewers—"

"I know you told the whole town that the mysterious brewers, not one of whom you can name but they smelled like beer, beat you up and killed the boy in response to their friend Jimmy O'Connor getting beat. I've heard it, but why would Charlie take off if that was all true?"

"I don't speak for Charlie," Joe said nervously.

"So you said. Joe, if I come across Charlie, I'll be sure to let you know. I'd sure love to hear his side."

"Well, his side, um, would sound just like mine."

"Maybe so. I'm just curious by nature, I guess, and I don't see any reason for Charlie to run without something I don't yet know being in this story."

"I thought you were for temperance, Sheriff?" Joe said with a sideways glance.

"I am, but I'm more for truth and justice for all."

"The American way, right?" Joe said.

"It sure is, even for our German brothers who brew beer, right, Joe?"

"Brewing beer is illegal in Iowa now. I can't wait until they tell us to enforce the new amendment."

Coldren chuckled. "Yeah, I can't wait for that," he said, his voice laden with sarcasm.

"Sheriff, justice and the Lord will be on your side and now the whole town will be as well thanks to..."

"Thanks to what?" Coldren pressed.

"Nothing."

"Thanks to your fire? Is that what you were going to say?"

"Times are changing, Sheriff. The northside won't be ruled by the Beer Mafia forever."

"Instead the Sons of Temperance will rule, huh?"

Joe picked up his broom and starting sweeping. "Good day, Sheriff."

Coldren walked out without another word.


J.J. entered the side door to the mostly empty Bakers Corner Pub. He saw the man he was looking for and immediately made his way across the room.

"Chief, I'm looking for you," J.J. said.

"What'd I do now?" Fire Chief McGrath answered.

"A lot, according to your wife."

"She's getting surly in her age."

The bartender slid a beer in front of J.J. "We have beef stew as well."

"I'll take a bowl," J.J. said. "Thanks."

"It's good," the Chief said. "I just had some."

"You've heard what this Lund has been saying about that fire?" J.J. asked.

"I have. He's blaming that kid burning on the whole northside. Brewers be damned."

"Well, what do you think about that?"

"I don't get into politics."

"I don't want you to run for office, Jim, I just want to know about that fire."

"What about it?"

"Anything. So it was a lantern that started it?"

"Looked that way. Pretty common way to start a fire, especially if you're drunk."

"What are you talking about if you're drunk?"

"I found a partially burned cask of Graf's Golden Brew in the cabin. Somebody there had been partaking of the sweet nectar." McGrath took a sip of his beer.

"I don't think I'd go that far as to call Graf's beer nectar," J.J. laughed. "I thought those guys were teetotalers?"

"They are. That Lund is always hanging around with Vernice and her ilk."

"Then it's strange that they'd have beer, isn't it?"

"There's more teetotalers than you think take a little sip in the privacy of their own homes. These fellas might have been like that."

J.J. ate his soup in silence, thinking over what the chief had said.

"The new hose brigades will make the town much safer," McGrath told him. "I was happy we kept this to just the one cabin. A little wind and it could have been worse."

"I'm looking forward to it, Jim. Let me know if you guys need donations for anything." J.J. stood to go. "I'll buy the chief a beer," he said to the bartender, sliding a coin across the bar.

"Thanks, J.J."

"Thanks for all you do, Jim." J.J. turned to leave, excited to go to his weekly mafia lunch the next day at Dostal's and share his news.

CONRAD and Dostal were seated at the usual table for their regular meeting at the Second Floor Club when J.J. walked toward them, grinning from ear-to-ear.

"What is it? Dostal asked.

"Vernice is off the wagon?" Conrad cracked.

Dostal hit Conrad's shoulder and laughed out loud. "That would be grand."

"No, but good news, nonetheless. I talked to McGrath yesterday and found out the boys at the cabin, Lund, Anderson, and the Indian boy, were drunk. Just like Teddy told us. They hang out at that cabin and drink."

"An empty cask of Union Gold was found in the cabin." J.J. smiled. "I have a plan. While we can't prove anything, neither can Lund. We need to cast some doubt on his version of what happened."

"How do we do that?" Dostal asked.

"I have a couple of ideas. A two-part attack. One, we smear Lund's honesty, and two, we do good for the community. We each put in some money and create a fund to help any family who suffers loss from a fire. The message is that we take care of our friends and family. We take care of Iowa City, not just the northside."

"I like it," Conrad said. "We aren't going to offer to build Lund a new house, are we?"

"No, that cabin belonged to Tyson. He can afford to build his own cabin. We could pay for Lund's room at the St. James maybe? It could show we don't hold any grudges even with all he's been speaking against us. We're here to help anyone in need, not just northsiders. What do you think?"

"I like it," Dostal said. "How are you going to smear that little bastard?"

"Leave that to me." J.J. grinned. "I've got an idea. I'll tell you if it works. I plan to send the wrath of God down on him."

Conrad chuckled. "Okay. We trust you, but if you have the power to bring down the wrath of God, then why haven't we used that before?"

"It's metaphorically speaking, of course."

"Meta what?" Conrad asked.

Dostal slapped Conrad on the shoulder and laughed. "Just trust him!"

"Oh, I do," Conrad said. "No matter how he's speaking."

J.J. knocked on Teddy's door. It was late.

Teddy had already settled into his bed and was reading his medical homework, as was his routine. He was angry at the late intrusion. He held his breath and intended to feign sleep, but the visitor was persistent.

"Teddy! Let me in! It's J.J., are you awake in there?"

Teddy exhaled loudly when he heard it was J.J. Anyone else he would ignore, but he owed the Englerts a debt he could not repay. His feet touched the cold wooden floor and he carried his small lantern to the door, opening it just a crack.

J.J. pushed it open and let himself in. "Thanks. I'm sorry to call so late."

"It's okay, J.J. What can I do for you?"

"I need you to deliver a message."

"What kind of message? To whom?"

"Vernice." J.J. held out a simple white envelope.

Teddy took it in his hand and looked at it. "What's it say?"

"A message for Vernice is all you need to know."

"What if she asks who gave it to me?"

J.J. smiled at his cleverness. "Just say it was from *someone who knows*. Can you do it tomorrow?"

"Yes, I will see her tomorrow night at the meeting."

"What meeting?"

"Our regular Wednesday night meeting, nothing special."

"You have a meeting every Wednesday night?"

"Yes."

"What do you do?"

"Sing songs, pray for the demise of the breweries, eat cupcakes, and drink soda."

J.J. snorted. "Seriously?"

"Seriously. Mattie is also there." Teddy blushed.

"Who's Mattie?"

"Matilda Dunlap. Remember?"

"Oh yes, I remember the teetotaler who has won Teddy's heart."

"Don't joke. I think I love her," Teddy said boldly.

"Oh my. Love?"

Teddy nodded.

"I'm sorry I joked. You're serious? Love?"

"Yes. I want to marry her."

J.J. laughed out loud and smacked Teddy on the shoulder. "That's wonderful! Does she know about this?"

Teddy grimaced. "No."

"Poor Teddy. Does she share your affections at least?"

"Yes...at least I think so. I catch her looking at me. Occasionally she touches my hand," Teddy said, innocent as a schoolboy.

"They are a strict family from what I know of them. Methodists, of course, and very proper. Have you talked to the father yet?"

"No!"

"You'd better talk to him first if you want to ever have a chance with her. It's the only way."

"What should I say?"

J.J. couldn't help but laugh. "You're supposed to be one of the smartest people I know."

"What's that mean?"

"Nothing. Just march in there and say, 'I want to speak with you sir, alone.'"

"Really?"

"Yes, really. Tell him you plan to be a doctor real soon and you'll make a fine living and will be able to provide well for a family. Then say, 'sir, I love your daughter and I want your permission and blessing to ask her to marry me.'"

Teddy looked sick to his stomach. "What if he says no?"

"Then you go tell her that her dad is a jackass and that to marry you she has to elope with you and become a brewer's bride. We can have your wedding at my house." J.J. laughed.

"That's not funny."

"It is funny. Her father will say yes. You're going to be a *doctor* for God's sake and you genuinely love his daughter. He'll say yes. I promise."

"Okay, I'll do it."

"But not until after you give that letter to Vernice. I predict right now that if you marry this teetotaler, you'll be sneaking lunch with me and Conrad just to have a beer once in a while."

"If she says yes, I'll never have another beer," Teddy said with a wispy sound to his voice.

J.J. put his face in his hand. "Oh, dear God help me. Young love. I wouldn't make promises like that, but to each his own."

"What's that supposed to mean?"

"Nothing. I'll see you in a couple years and we'll talk, probably over a beer."

"You're a cynic, J.J. I didn't know that about you."

"Nah, not a cynic, just a realist. You go talk to that gal's father. I can't wait to hear how it goes. The first scandal would be inviting me to your wedding."

"I can't worry about that. I just know she's the one."

"Then by all means, go for it. You only live once."

"Thank you, J.J."

J.J. turned to go. "I'm sorry to have disturbed you tonight. Thanks for delivering my letter."

"Anything for you, J.J."

He walked to the door, opening it. J.J. glanced back. "You haven't heard from Lund lately, have you?"

"No. Not since Jimmy."

"Did you hear anything about this cabin fire?"

"Nothing other than Joe telling everyone that you're the devil and you all killed that Indian boy with your evil beer."

"I'd be careful around him. He's not all he seems."

Teddy nodded. "I know. I'm careful, but he doesn't involve me."

"That's good. Good night, Teddy."

"Good night, J.J."

THE Wednesday meeting was jubilant. Victory was almost at hand. The brewers were finally on the run. The amendment had passed and was on its way to the people for a final statewide vote, and that was looking more promising every day. Iowa City, of all places, appeared to be turning on the brewers.

No Methodist would have believed it a year earlier. The three brewers controlled the town and its inhabitants both with their intoxicants and with their money, a very powerful combination. When Vernice first began to pray for the brewers to fall, no one believed it was possible.

She didn't believe it was possible either, without God. She prodded her friends to believe that God's will would be done in their midst. The breweries would fall like Jericho's wall if God willed it. If no one else believed, Vernice definitely did, and that was enough.

Victory was at hand. Songs had been sung, benedictions vehemently stated. Now it was time for lemonade and sweet treats. No young Methodist would admit it, but the only reason they wanted to come to the Wednesday night meeting was to socialize. Their passion for temperance became a fine excuse to meet. Teens and youths alike found time for approved social interaction with their peers a precious commodity.

Teddy made a beeline for Vernice. He had to accomplish his task quickly since he'd already spotted Matilda toward the back of the room.

He stepped in front of the pastor and bowed slightly to Vernice.

"How may I help you, Teddy?"

"I have a message for you," he said, handing her the note.

She took the envelope and Teddy was immediately off in search of Matilda.

"Thank you, Teddy," she called after him, then noticed no writing on the envelope. "Who is it from?"

"I was told to tell you that it's from *a person who knows*. That's all. Please excuse me?" Matilda's father was moving them toward the door.

Vernice was the least of his concerns. Suddenly he was face-to-face with Matilda. He caught his breath. Her beauty deeply affected his ability to act like a normal human being.

He didn't notice Vernice quietly reading her message. Her stomach flipped and her heart sank. She scanned the room, her eyes going back and forth. She didn't see Joe Lund anywhere. She put the note in her coat pocket; she'd find him tomorrow.

Teddy was beside himself. Mr. Dunlap had agreed to let him walk Matilda home. He'd taken the carriage on ahead, leaving them precious time alone to talk as they walked. Lanterns were lit, and the moon was out, bathing the cool evening in a subtle light, while stars glittered above. Love was in the air.

Teddy felt like he was going to throw up. "Mattie, I've decided to talk to your father, if it's alright with you?"

She smiled with her mouth, though even more with her eyes. Teddy was enthralled with her every move. "Talk to Father about what?" she asked coyly.

"A-About you, of c-course," he stammered. "I'm going to ask for your hand. Would you give it?"

Matilda squealed and tossed her arms around his neck. She was a foot shorter than he was and her arms pulled him down toward her. Before he knew what was happening his mouth was on hers, wet and warm, his mind and soul leaping, as well as other parts of his anatomy.

She pushed away and stared at him. Her face was flushed and she giggled at her own excitement. While she knew she'd be in trouble if anyone saw them kissing like that, she didn't care.

Teddy dropped to one knee. He literally felt drunk though he'd not had a drop of alcohol. "Matilda, will you marry me?"

She squealed again. "Yes, Teddy, I'll marry you!" She tossed her arms around him, pulling him close and they were kissing again even more deeply and passionately than before. Teddy then remembered they were on a public street and as they pulled apart, he glanced both ways. No one was around, for which Teddy was thankful.

They kept strolling toward Mattie's home, her hand on his arm. Once they were at the house, Mattie pulled Teddy behind the barn and they were kissing again. Teddy never wanted it to end. She was both sweet and hungry. He'd never experienced anything like it, and he wanted more of it. Suddenly a horse in the barn kicked the stall with a loud smack. It startled both of them and they jumped apart as if they'd been discovered. Their guilt turned to smiles and muted laughter as if they were giddy with pent up desire.

"Come call tomorrow and talk to my father," Matilda said. "He will approve, but you must ask him."

"I will. Tomorrow it is," Teddy said with nervous confidence.

She stepped in close and gave him one last kiss and then she was gone like the mist of a cool morning lingering and glorious, then suddenly gone. He could still taste her on his lips.

VERNICE entered Hanson's Hardware with a scowl on her face. Joe Lund jumped and imagined slipping out the back into the alley to avoid her. He had taken two steps when her voice pierced his soul.

"Joe, where are you off to?"

"Nowhere, Vernice. Nice to see you. Can I help you find something?"

"I've already found it." She stared at him and her face did not hide her disapproval.

"What's wrong?" he asked.

"I've come into knowledge that you have a problem."

"A problem?"

"Yes. You are living three lives. One for me, one for the world, and one hidden from view."

Joe glanced at the floor. "What?"

"You have been drinking, haven't you, Joe?"

"Um, I-I—"

"Admit your sin before God and He will forgive you."

"Why are you saying this, Vernice? I am a faithful servant, a Son of Temperance."

"While you've been blaming the brewers for the cabin fire, you partake in their sin. A cask of beer was found at your cabin. Do you deny it was yours?" She stared into his eyes.

He glanced away. Her gaze was too much for him. He thought about blaming the Indian as he had been doing, but she would see right through that. "I do not deny it."

"Good. You are to blame as much as the brewers for the fire and the death of that Indian boy. Your hidden sin and hypocrisy lit the match and brought death down upon us."

"But the Lord has used the fire to turn the town against the brewers," Joe pleaded.

"We will not win our victory on lies. Our Lord will have His way and the brewers will fall, but not built on the impure, do you understand?"

"What must I do?" Joe asked, looking defeated.

"I cannot trust you and our mission is very important. I have spoken with Senator Shrader. He needs help in Des Moines. You will be his page. He is a devout man with a strong will to serve the Lord and our state. You will learn from him and be away from Iowa City for a time. When the legislative session ends, you can return," she waved her hand around the room, "to this. Hopefully you will have turned from your wicked ways."

"I will, Vernice."

"Senator Shrader will be the judge of that. His testimony will be the proof."

"Yes, ma'am."

"Never speak of that fire again. Never tell the story unless you name yourself co-conspirator with the brewers. Understand?"

"I understand," Joe said with a little edge of resentment sneaking into his voice. If she only knew the beer was the least of it. If she knew the blood on his hands, she'd surely cast him out forever.

"Your train leaves at one. Go pack your things."

"What about the store?"

"I'll tell Mister Hanson, you go pack."

Joe removed the apron over his head and laid it on the counter. He walked past Vernice and out the front door in silence. He turned down Clinton Street, heading toward the St. James Hotel that faced the Old Capitol on the corner of Iowa Avenue.

He smiled as he passed the desk clerk and climbed the stairs to the third floor. His room was small, and the one window faced the alley rather than the beauty of the campus. He couldn't afford a room like that. His anger simmering, he filled his small bag with all that he owned.

*Damn Vernice! So high and mighty!*

He stopped by the store on his way to the train station. Mr. Hanson was behind the counter.

"Good luck in Des Moines, Joe," he said.

"Thank you, Mister Hanson," Joe said, surprised he was so excited for him to leave.

"It's quite an honor to be asked to serve a senator," Mr. Hanson said.

"Oh, um, yes, it is an honor."

"You've got a job here when you get back, don't you worry."

"Thank you, sir. I'll be off now."

Mr. Hanson motioned him to come to the counter. He opened the register and removed two coins, placing them in Joe's hand. "A little traveling money."

Joe was in shock. What had Vernice told him? Mr. Hanson had always been indifferent to him, now he felt like a supporter, a friend even.

"Thank you again." Joe left the store, smiling all the way to the station. He noticed Sheriff Coldren walking toward him. They nodded as they passed each other. A few steps later Joe peeked over his shoulder to see Sheriff Coldren was watching him walk away.

Joe walked a little faster. When he reached the station, he glanced back again in time to see Sheriff Coldren turn and continue on about his business.

Relieved, Joe gave the Ticketmaster his ticket and climbed aboard the train. He found a window seat, as anxious for the ride as a kid at a carnival. The whistle sounded, and the train lurched forward slowly at first, then faster. He spotted the charred remains of his old cabin and the spire of a chimney just before they passed over the river and left Iowa City behind.

In a month, the cabin fire was forgotten, and news of the Foundation for Fire Victims was all that people remembered. The endowment began with significant donations from the northside, specifically from the Dostal, Englert, and Graf families. Other well-to-do families followed suit and the fund grew fat. Its blessing would be open to all who suffered from a fire in Johnson County. The fund was approved by Catholic and Methodist alike, and for a moment the two groups actually agreed upon something.

Articles ran in local and state papers, in both English and German, praising the community leadership and benevolence of the brewers. The Foundation was decried as *ahead of its time* and the founders were showered with praise for their forward thinking and love of their fellow citizens and community.

Mrs. Graf walked the street with her head held high and found herself greeted with a smile at every turn.

# 13

MARCHES both for and against the prohibitory amendment filled the month of June. Every citizen knew of the special vote and everyone had an opinion, openly sharing it at ad nauseum. Most people just wanted it to be over so everyone would stop talking and arguing about it.

June 27, 1882, brought all the speechmaking and pontificating to an end. Ballot boxes were sent to each precinct and polling places were set up in the district firehose houses. The ballots were attended to by a delegate from each party, Democrat and Republican, and overseen by a sworn commissioner, usually the fire marshal from that precinct or his deputy.

Conrad promised a free beer to any man who voted against the amendment, as did the other brewers, which meant voter turnout on the northside was strong and jovial. Conrad and J.J. entered Bakers Hose House #1 and cast their votes to cheers from happy onlookers, hopeful the amendment would go down and fall into the dustbin of bad ideas.

The polls closed, and each precinct tallied their votes prior to delivering it to the city council, who sat waiting in their hall. They were instructed to tally the votes for the city, combine them with county-wide votes, and wire them all to Des Moines forthwith. Then the actual ballots would be locked in their official box and sent to Des Moines via train for recount and certification.

As the precinct's tallies were read aloud, it became obvious only a few precincts had wholeheartedly supported the amendment. The votes in Iowa City were more than two-to-one against the amendment.

J.J. stood to read the totals. "We have the certified totals from Iowa City and Johnson County. The amendment is defeated with 899 votes against the prohibitory amendment and 411 votes for the amendment!"

Cheering erupted as the crowd was heavily laden with brewers and their supporters. Vernice and her acolytes slipped out the back in defeat. They sent the totals on to Des Moines, a brief and happy moment for the northside.

News of totals from other counties began to arrive in Iowa City and they bode a very different outcome. Des Moines and Polk counties had supported the amendment, but the blow came heavy when news that Linn County had upheld the amendment. Although Cedar Rapids had brewers and a strong Bohemian contingency, even that didn't turn the vote against the amendment.

As the statewide tallies came in, the predictions had been right, and the prohibitory amendment passed.

Conrad sat at his desk looking at the newspapers laid out before him dated June 28, 1882. The *Iowa State Register* title read *Temperance Amendment Passes – Iowa Goes Dry.* He stared in disbelief at a New York Times newspaper dated June 29th that read, *Temperance Victory In Iowa – The Prohibitory Amendment Carried By An Overwhelming Majority.*

He felt utterly defeated. "Why would anyone in New York care about what we do out here?" he muttered after reading the *Times* article.

J.J. opened his office door and sat in the chair opposite Conrad's desk, noting the papers. "Are you torturing yourself?" he asked.

"Why?"

"Don't read that junk," J.J. said.

"We're sunk."

"Oh no we're not. Do you not remember Lucas telling us this would happen?"

"I guess," Conrad said, defeated.

"He sat right up there in Dostal's Second Floor and said the courts are how we'll defeat this amendment, not the votes. Remember?"

"Yes, I remember. How are the courts going to undo an amendment voted on twice by the legislature and passed by the people?"

"That is a politician's problem, not yours."

"We have to do something," Conrad said.

"I am."

"What are you doing?"

"I am going to head out north of town and check on the progress of our second icehouse. Come with me and see it. It will be twice as big as the one we have here. If you need ice, let me know. I'm happy to sell to my friends."

Conrad made a strange face. "You're not bothered by this? You're just business as usual?"

"It bothers me, but I am a man of business. That's what I know, and the stronger my business is, the harder it will be for them to come after us."

Conrad sat back in his chair. "You are quite the ray of sunshine today. I prefer to sulk at least one more day, thank you very much, while my fellow citizens vote to take away my children's inheritance."

J.J. stood. "Fine then. I'll come back tomorrow and tell you about my idea for the Fall Fest when the circus comes to town."

"Fall Fest?"

"Yes, remember? We'll be making money hand over fist. People will come from miles around to see that African elephant that is touring with Barnum and they'll all need food and beer. Who better to provide what the people want than us?"

"Sounds good, if we're even allowed to sell beer then," Conrad continued his dejected mood.

"I'll come back tomorrow when my happy entrepreneurial friend will have returned."

"I can't promise that."

"Then I'll see you at the weekly lunch at Dostal's. Be prepared for good news."

"Get out of here. You're driving me crazy!" Conrad said with a slight smile.

J.J. gave Conrad a tip of the hat and exited. Conrad smiled and shook his head. He couldn't help it, J.J. had improved his spirits.

J.J. was talking to a couple of his employees in front of his brewery when he noticed Conrad walking toward him on his way to their weekly meeting. He finished his business and stepped in beside Conrad, matching him step for step.

"Are you in a better state of mind?" J.J. asked.

"I don't know," Conrad grumbled.

"I told you to be ready for good news."

Conrad gave him a sideways glance "What? The temperance hacks have decided to leave me and my business alone?"

"You'll have to wait till we're upstairs," J.J. said.

They ducked inside the Great Western and headed up the steps to Dostal's club. Conrad waved at Ed, who was tending bar, as they crossed the room.

Dostal was reading a newspaper with his back to the windows and did not see them enter.

"Nothing good in there," Conrad said.

Dostal put the paper down. "Not at all."

"It's all in who you know, fellas," J.J. quipped.

"He's been like this all week," Conrad said, pointing his thumb at J.J. "You'd think things were going splendidly."

"The glass is half full either way. I just choose to add ice and take a drink. I have good news for you both."

"I'm ready," Conrad said.

"First, you both already know that our foundation is a huge success. I am actually stunned by the number of people who have donated to the cause, some with very large gifts, rivaling ours. What started as a public relations stunt is actually going to benefit our community for years to come."

"My wife is happier, I'll tell you that," Conrad stated. "That's worth the amount I gave no matter who we help."

The other men smiled knowingly.

"Also, I've received word that our troublesome Mister Lund has left town."

"What? Where did he go?" Dostal asked.

"He is working in Des Moines for our good Senator Shrader at least until the session is done. I heard it was Vernice's doing. She did it to shut him up and to work on his sinful drinking habit away from the eyes of our community." J.J. smiled as if he knew much more.

"Well, this is good news," Conrad said. "How'd did she find out about his habit I wonder?"

"The Lord works in mysterious ways. Oh, there's more. I've not even told you the good news yet."

"Whatever could it be?" Conrad said sarcastically.

"I missed you guys at the council meeting, they are so poorly attended," he said with a grin extending ear-to-ear. "Byington and I decided to fine any business in defiance of the Amendment, and low and behold, it passed the council. Along party lines, but it passed just the same. I told you it's all in who you know, boys."

"What do you mean a fine?" Conrad asked.

"The council agreed to charge a fine of fifty dollars per month for a business that continues to operate an establishment that manufactures, sells, or allows consumption of alcohol."

Dostal and Conrad stared in disbelief.

"Don't you get it? For fifty dollars a month you can go on business as usual!"

"How can that be with the amendment?" Dostal asked.

"How will Des Moines enforce the amendment?" J.J. shot back.

Silence lingered at the table.

"That's right, no one knows how a county who simply fines a saloon or a brewer rather than forcing them to close would be treated." J.J. smiled at his cleverness. "It could be years before they figure out how to address it."

Smiles slowly grew across Conrad and Dostal's faces.

J.J. lit a cigar and leaned back in his chair with a confident nod. "You owe me."

"How can you keep the sheriff from enforcing the amendment?" Conrad asked.

"I've been expecting to see him any day at my office with papers." Dostal said. "Or handcuffs."

"The sheriff is an elected official and serves at the county's behest. Our county voted down the amendment solidly. We don't want it here. The council has agreed to fine brewers and pubs. It might be a temporary fix, but it's a fix, nonetheless. I heard that Davenport has instituted fines of fifty dollar a month for a brewery just like us but some pubs are giving 'free beer' if a patron buys mum."

"What's mum?" Conrad asked.

"Mum's the word. It's nothing. It's a subterfuge. It's why we give free food to anyone buying beer in our pubs. Basically, it's a switch. Someone says, 'I'd like to order mum' they're not ordering beer. They aren't selling beer and then they're not in defiance."

"I can't believe that would work." Dostal said.

"In Johnson County, as long as you pay the fine, you'll be left to your business. Don't let the papers fool you, this is not a popular amendment and will be difficult to enforce."

"Thank you, J.J. I'm sorry I ever doubted you." Conrad raised his glass. "Can we appoint you to the council for life?"

"Can I make a donation to your re-election fund?" Dostal added.

"Yes, you may do so at any time!"

Conrad laughed. "Maybe we are the beer mafia after all!"

"Maybe so," J.J. conceded.

Conrad snickered. "This is going to infuriate Vernice."

"What *doesn't* infuriate Vernice?" J.J. asked. "There's nothing she can do other than march in the streets."

"We need to find her a new hobby," said Conrad.

"Quite right. I was thinking of naming her executive director of our foundation," J.J. said.

The group went silent as the idea settled in the minds of the other men.

"Are you serious?" Dostal asked.

J.J. nodded. "Absolutely."

"She would answer to the board controlled by us?" Conrad asked.

"Of course, we could find ways to work together for the betterment of the community. Maybe we'll even forge a new friendship, but mostly this project will keep her busy."

Dostal shook his head. "Dear God, J.J. you are an eternal optimist. I'll never be that woman's friend."

"You scare me." Conrad leaned back with his own cigar, a fragrant haze filling the immediate area.

"I thought it was a brilliant idea," J.J. added.

"We're not saying it isn't brilliant. We're just a little stunned at your audacity," Dostal said.

"I'm not sure what will be more shocking. That we put a woman in charge of so much money or that we put our most ardent enemy in a place of power?"

Dostal continued shaking his head and smiling. "This is by far your craziest idea yet."

"I like it," Conrad said. "Do you think she'll do it?"

"I have no idea, worth a try."


Teddy was used as courier once again as the brewers' only logical connection to Vernice.

"Another note?" she asked when Teddy handed it to her on Wednesday night. "What now?"

"This one is from the brewers. Open it, you'll see," Teddy said.

"Is that who sent the first one?"

Teddy stared ahead and offered no response, afraid any answer would betray the truth.

She looked at Teddy with a pitiful face. "I'm sorry you must consort with those men. How much longer on your residency?"

"Only till the end of this year," Teddy said.

"Congratulations on your recent engagement to Miss Matilda." She smiled. "You make a lovely couple."

Teddy grinned. "Yes, thank you."

"I hope that means you will be opening your own office here and starting your family?"

"Yes, ma'am. It remains to be worked out, but that is our plan."

"Splendid. Never enough good doctors with the right type of thinking like you."

"Yes, I suppose."

Vernice opened her letter and quickly read it. "Oh my, Teddy, have you read this?"

"No, but J.J. told me they wanted to meet with you."

"Do you know what for?"

"I believe it is something with the new foundation."

"You may tell them I will meet as requested."

"Really? I'm surprised you would meet them," Teddy said.

"I do not fear my enemies. My Lord will guide my steps in the lion's den."

"You are a brave woman."

"Thank you, Teddy. My strength is in the Lord. I would like you to attend the meeting with me since the brewers are fond of using you as our go between."

"Of course, Mrs. Armstrong. I'd be happy to."

Teddy was hoping his job as spy was coming to an end. With his impending marriage to Matilda, he wanted to move on from political activism and settle down as a proper husband, focusing on his business and family.


Vernice walked into the State Bank like she owned it. It was a well-respected bank and widely known to do business with both brewer and teetotaler. She was accompanied by Teddy on one side and John Swafford on the other.

The secretary was expecting her and stood upon her entry. "Right this way, Mrs. Armstrong. They're expecting you."

"I'm sure they are," she huffed.

Vernice marched on, her jaw set as if she was ready for a fight. The young lady opened an office door down a long hallway. Vernice quickly surveyed the room to see the three men she least liked in the world and the bank president, Jim Maxwell.

The president stood. "Welcome, Mrs. Armstrong, please take a seat."

She sat at the far end of the rectangular shaped table. Teddy sat to her left and Swafford to her right.

"Thank you for coming," J.J. said.

"I cannot endure pleasantries with you, please get to why you've invited me. I'm not enjoying the company," Vernice said with an edge.

Conrad could not hide his loathing as he stared at her.

J.J. laughed. He was in his element. "I understand it is an unlikely meeting under our *circumstances.*"

"You mean the circumstances where the lawful state has outlawed your breweries and pubs from operating and yet day and night you continue to brew and sell beer to ensnare the masses, as if the laws don't apply to you in defiance of the laws of both man and God?"

"Vernice, please," J.J. said.

"And the circumstance where you have used your power and position on the council to create a loophole to keep your dens of evil open for business? Well, your day's coming, let me tell you! You will not be able to bend the sheriff forever to your will."

Her voice was rising as fast as Conrad's blood pressure. Clenching both his fists and his teeth, he felt like he shouldn't have come.

J.J. raised his hand to stop her. "Mrs. Armstrong, we're not here about any of that."

"Why *are* we here?" John Swafford asked.

"No one knows why *you're* here, you no-good bootlicker," Conrad snapped. "We didn't invite you!"

Swafford jumped to his feet, his face full of rage. Conrad leapt to his feet as well, sending his chair flying backwards.

"Graf, your days are numbered in this town!" Swafford shouted, spit flying from his mouth.

"Oh really? Bring it on!" Conrad stood with feet spread shoulder width apart, his fists ready.

The bank president turned a previously unseen shade of gray.

"No!" J.J.'s voice thundered over it all. "You two sit down!"

The men froze under J.J.'s command. Swafford eased back into his seat as Conrad put his chair back on its feet and sat as well. They continued to glare at each other with simmering hatred.

"Mrs. Armstrong, despite our differences in politics and religion, we want to offer you a position," J.J. said.

"A position?"

"Yes. I assume you've heard of the new Foundation for Fire Victims?"

"Yes, I've heard of it, and even though I know it is a hypocritical ploy on your part, I'm sure the people of Iowa City will benefit from it."

"We genuinely hope so. And to prove it even more, we are extending the olive branch and offering you the job of Executive Director of the Foundation," J.J. said.

Vernice glanced at both Teddy and Swafford in the ensuing uneasy silence. "Well, I am surprised, I cannot lie. Why on earth would you do that when you know I detest everything about you?"

"It's not about us, it's about helping the citizens of our community. We are all three on the foundation board of directors, but we cannot run this foundation with our current duties."

"If you would close your breweries you would have more time to do God's work," Vernice said.

J.J. smiled. She was quite an adversary. "That idea aside, we would like you to be in charge of the foundation."

"Who else is on the board?"

"Chalmer Close and Charles Berryhill."

Vernice nodded curtly. "Chalmer is a good man."

"He is," J.J. said.

"Charles is a northsider," she said with skepticism.

"Charles goes his own way and was very generous to the cause."

"What would I do?"

"You would identify the families who need the money, then disperse it to them, irrespective of political party, temperant or not, Catholic or Methodist. The money is to be used strictly to help any family in need in our midst. We would trust you entirely to handle the funds, which are quite considerable."

"How much?"

"We have more than ten thousand dollars on account with Mister Maxwell and more coming in. The board would meet quarterly, or as needed, to approve any disbursement over two hundred dollars. Otherwise, you would be free to do God's good work with the money," J.J. said.

"Why not Father Edmonds? He's your man at St. Mary's. He could do this *good work* and we could have avoided each other's company."

"He's busy as well, building several new churches in the outlying communities. He could not do it justice."

"I will not be bought. I will not stop trying to end your brewing businesses."

"We didn't think anything of the sort. We simply thought we could agree that we love our town and this money could be used to help, no matter teetotaler or brewer, don't you agree?"

Vernice was speechless for one of the few times in her life.

"They're trying to trick you, Vernice. They're liars!" Swafford snapped.

Conrad jumped to his feet. "You call me a liar again and this won't end well for you!" Conrad's veins were pulsing, and his face was red.

"Stop it, John!" Vernice scolded her lawyer.

"I will take the position as long as you realize it changes nothing about my position as the leader of the Women's Christian Temperance Union. That must be clear, and the minute it is not, I will resign."

"Understood," J.J. said. "This should be seen by the community as a way for us to do good work, together. Maybe even heal some of the division."

"I'm all for helping the community and using your money to do it, as I believe the wealth of the wicked is laid up for the righteous. But make no mistake, the division in our community will end when your breweries close."

Conrad was doing all he could to restrain his anger and Dostal was sick to his stomach at her unwavering desire to destroy them. He wondered if they could get rid of her somehow. He imagined Gunnar and Tom could put her in the river and no one would ever see her again.

"Very well then, we agree. We can announce it in the next papers. You can meet with prospective recipients here at the bank any time you wish," J.J. said.

"I have a suggestion," Vernice said.

"What's that?" Dostal asked.

"Change the name of the foundation."

"To what?"

"How about the Foundation for Victims of Tragedy? Then it wouldn't have to just be for fires. I know of a family who recently had their father die, leaving them with no man to provide. The husband fell in the river fishing at night and drowned."

"Yes, I heard about that. A new family down by the squatter's cabins?"

"Some say he was drunk," Vernice said with a condemning look to the brewers.

"That is a great idea, Vernice. We will vote to change the name at the next board meeting to the Foundation for Victims of Tragedy. Determine an amount that might help them get back on their feet and then ask Jim for a draw on the account. You can deliver the money on the behalf of the foundation."

"You trust me to do that?"

"Should we not trust you?" J.J. said. "We will conduct a yearly audit to be sure funds are accounted for."

"You can trust me," Vernice said. "Thank you for the honor of this position, despite our, what did you call it? *Circumstances*?"

"Yes, circumstances. Thank you as well, Vernice. We will expect a report from you at the board meetings," J.J. said.

"Very well," Vernice said.

Everyone stood. "Good day," J.J. said.

Teddy and Swafford followed Vernice out. After she was gone, everyone exhaled in relief.

"I hate that damn Swafford," Conrad seethed. "He's a dandy."

"I don't think he loves you either," J.J said.

"I can't believe I just witnessed that," said Jim Maxwell. "I'd never believed it if I hadn't seen it. You have a gift, J.J."

**14**

THE Fall Fest tents went up on the last Wednesday in September all along Market and Linn Streets. The weather was perfect. Clear skies, warm days, and cool nights. It was the kind of weather people dream of for an outdoor event. The two-block area north of Church Park had been blocked off to horse and wagon travel in preparation for Fall Fest. The entire town was a buzz of excitement. While the northside had put on "Fests" in the past, none presented itself quite like this.

For weeks, couriers had been spreading promotional flyers throughout the county and every town within a days' ride of Iowa City. Not one citizen had failed to see them, and everyone knew that a once in a lifetime opportunity was at hand.

*P.T. Barnum's Greatest Show on Earth & The Great*
*London Circus featuring The Giant African Elephant JUMBO!*

The northside brewers had combined this momentous occasion with a four-day event they named Fall Fest starting on Wednesday and ending Saturday night, culminating with the main event, *The Greatest Show on Earth*.

Fall Fest consisted of rows of tents set up throughout the northside lining Market and Linn Streets. Vendors of all sorts brought tents and set up shop. Many of the vendors maintained full retail stores in town, while others had come from far and wide to ply their wares. German and Bohemian foods filled the air with delicious smells. The tents were full of candies, housewares, vegetables, dried meats, the latest fashions, and of course, beer.

Each brewery had its own tent showcasing their special brand of beer, and in the center of it all a stage had been erected to allow for music and entertainment to begin each day at four and continue into the evening.

By Thursday, the fest was in full swing with carriages and wagons coming from as far as Grinnell, Muscatine, and Dubuque, rolling into town one after the other. The train from Des Moines was filled to capacity with each stop. Every room at the St. James was taken as well as all the bed and breakfasts with a room for let. Tents sprouted up all along the river and on campus in the shadow of the golden-domed capitol.

The festival was a boon for anyone with a product to sell or service to provide. Laughter filled the air and the festive atmosphere was palpable. Children ran amok as all schools had been let out. Nothing remained normal about this week and it would be fondly remembered for years to come.

Dostal waved the wagon to a halt on the north side of the brewery. The driver smiled widely at Dostal as he hopped into the back and tossed off the tarp.

Dostal stepped up to inspect the goods. The wagon was filled with wooden crates labeled Lake Michigan Glassworks—Chicago Illinois.

The driver pried open a crate and carefully fished through the packaging. He removed a large mug of clear glass with a strong handle. He handed it to Dostal, who smiled with appreciation as he admired it.

"That's a thing of beauty!" he said to his driver.

"It sure is, boss."

"Did you get them all?"

"Yes, sir, we did. Five hundred in all. They tossed in an extra crate of twenty to cover any breakage."

"Very good. Thanks, Pete. You drivers take one for yourselves free of charge and have a grand time at the fest."

"Thank you, sir, we will!" The driver was elated.

Dostal marched straight toward the stage set in the intersection of Linn and Market, forming the heart of Brewery Square. Conrad and J.J. were talking in the middle of the growing morning crowd.

"What is it?" J.J. said as he approached and could see his obvious excitement.

Dostal held up the prize. The mug was all of ten inches tall and made of thick glass. "They came. I was worried they wouldn't make it, but they came. Look."

162

He handed the mug to J.J. and they all stood admiring it.

"They are nice," Conrad said. "And heavy." Conrad handed it to J.J.

J.J. hefted it in his hand. "Very nice."

"We have five hundred of them as we hoped. We'll sell them at one booth for a set fee and then people can fill it with their first beer for free and refills for a nickel at any of our tents for the duration of the fest. I've made a sign saying, 'Buy a JUMBO Mug Here!' Get it? Jumbo? Like the elephant?"

"Oh, that's well done, Dostal." J.J. grinned.

"And we split the money evenly from the sale of the mugs, correct?" Dostal asked.

Conrad smirked. "Sounds good, but since my beer is the best, I should take a larger cut."

"Equal shares," J.J. growled.

"I was just kidding you," Conrad said with a chuckle.

J.J. looked around at the growing crowd. "This is going to be great."

"It's looking pretty good, J.J. I must say, you had a good idea with this. All people can talk about is this elephant, Jumbo. The town is filling to the brim."

Thursday was filled with music, dancing, and brews, making the northside feel like a little slice of Germany. While the Bohemians and Irish were not to be outdone, the atmosphere was overwhelmingly German. One could easily forget they were in the center of Iowa and not somewhere in Bavaria.

Thursday night the railcars began to arrive one after another and the excitement began to build. Little kids, teens, and adults were all anxious to sneak a peek at the bright red train cars full of untold wonders and odd curiosities.

Friday morning by first light, covered wagons were taking trip after trip from the train depot to Church Park. Eyes widened as the massive three mast tent rose from the ground, literally covering the entire block. Around midday, several wagonloads of the menagerie rolled down Clinton Street, creating an unplanned parade. The sidewalks filled with gawkers as sounds unknown filled the prairie.

A massive roar followed by several chortles made onlookers speculate on the nature of the creature that could produce a sound like that. A green wagon pulled by eight golden draft horses with white manes and bobbed tails brought up the rear of the parade. A long gray snout wiggled its way from behind the loose hanging curtain as if it was an arm with a mind of its own. Several witnesses cried out in astonishment.

As if on cue, Jumbo's entire head protruded forth from the opening. He raised his trunk and bugled the call of the lone African Elephant in the entire state. The sound left people cheering and running to the ticket booths. No one could see the cause of Jumbo's massive call to the Sahara.

An elephant handler inside the wagon carefully stabbed Jumbo with a spear just behind his front leg. He'd done it many times before, so the spot was sensitive. The handler was careful to only penetrate the two-inch-thick hide enough to elicit the elephant's cry, though not cause a bleeding episode.

"Good boy, good Jumbo," the handler said as the sounds of the bugle echoed over the Iowa River. He placed a bucket of Jumbo's "special" biscuits in front of him. Jumbo immediately set about devouring them one at a time, picking them up carefully with his trunk and delivering them to his mouth as fast as he could.

The wagon disappeared into the tent of the menageries. The handler jumped down from the wagon as the crew unhitched the team of horses, sending them back to the train for a few more loads. The tent was hopping with activity. Each person had a task, and everyone went about it without difficulty. They were a well-oiled machine at this point. This show was the one hundred and twelfth show of a one hundred and thirty show tour.

They'd started in New York mid-March and would finish in Pennsylvania in three more weeks, in mid-October. Everyone, even Jumbo, was tired, but the end was near. A new town every day meant taking up and setting down the tents and all the necessities that went with it had become second nature. The towns ran together. It was Iowa City now, the day after that, Rock Island, and then Quincy, Illinois, and on and on. It didn't matter where they were, it was a job.

The handler left the tent in Church Park and noticed an ongoing festival in the streets just past the towering steeple of a massive Catholic Church. He began walking toward the street party with his task in mind. When he passed the great brick behemoth, he whispered aloud to himself the name stenciled onto the glass above the stunning arched door. St. Mary's Catholic Church.

Out of habits from his youth, he tapped his forehead, his heart, and then each shoulder forming the sign of the cross. He thought of his faithful mother, always penitent. He shook the memory out of his head and walked toward the music, smiling at the gaiety of the gathering. They would make a killing at this show. This town knew how to draw the crowds and it was obvious that Mr. Barnum was not the only entrepreneur in these parts.

The man noticed the large building to his left that was brightly labeled "Union Brewery." He entered the main door and found a pretty young blonde woman sitting at a desk.

Her voice thick with a German accent, she said, "Hello sir. All beer is available in the tent only for Fall Fest."

"Thank you, ma'am. I am with the circus, and I am in need of whiskey." He slightly bowed, his long, dark locks falling over his face.

The woman at the desk smiled at him as he was very handsome. She could not place his accent, but it was obvious English was a second language. She caught her breath when he stepped closer, staring right into her. She blushed and returned his gaze.

"Um, whiskey hmm... We brew beer, but let me ask Mister G." She stood and turned to go when Conrad appeared in the doorway. She jumped back, nearly running right into him.

"Oh, excuse me! Mister G, this man here..." she turned to the dark man in the lobby but didn't know his name to introduce him.

"Francisco," he said, fixing his gaze on Conrad.

"...is looking for whiskey," she finished.

"There are a couple of kiosks selling it outside," said Conrad. "A fine scotch whiskey at MacGregor's and an Irish favorite at O'Brien's."

"Very good. I would like to purchase several cases of the scotch whiskey. Could you facilitate this, and have it delivered to the Menagerie Tent as soon as it is possible?" Francisco handed Conrad several paper bills. "I trust this will be enough?"

Conrad took the money. "You could probably buy out his entire stock with that much. Let me go see what he's got with him. He could get you some more if you give him some time. Bates is his name. He cooks it out east of North Liberty somewhere. I've actually never been there, he keeps it private."

"We are only here for one day and then we move on to the next town, but I will buy all he can sell me."

Conrad made a strange face. "What are you going to do with all that whiskey? We have all the beer you can drink in our caves."

"I love beer myself, but one of my co-workers loves the whiskey above all else. Actually, he couldn't perform without it," Francisco said.

"Really? I hope it's not the trapeze guy or the lion tamer!" Conrad laughed.

"No, it is the star of our show."

"Not possible. I know Barnum is a teetotaler."

"Not Barnum, Jumbo."

"The elephant drinks whiskey?" Conrad was incredulous.

Francisco laughed. "Several gallons a day. He's quite large, you know. If he doesn't get his whiskey, he becomes quite unruly and we couldn't control him otherwise."

"You're kidding me. You keep the elephant drunk?"

"He was given whiskey on the trip over from England and since then he's become fairly addicted, which means I must keep a solid stock of whiskey. Scotch is his favorite."

"Oh really? He has a favorite? This is too much. No one will believe me when I tell them. How do you give it to him, in a bucket?"

"Sometimes, but he prefers to eat biscuits soaked in it. We make them by the hundreds."

Conrad laughed out loud. "Whiskey biscuits! Now I've heard it all. Barnum the teetotaler is making his fortune off of a drunk elephant!"

Francisco grinned. "Yes."

"There really is a sucker born every minute."

They shared a laugh.

"I'll have the whiskey sent over as soon as they can," said Conrad. "You are welcome to come have a beer with me and my friends if you get time later tonight."

"Thank you, sir, but it will be very late before we are ready for tomorrow's show."

"The festival will continue on into the night. Look me up if you get free." Conrad offered his hand. "Conrad Graf. This is my brewery. Welcome to Iowa City."

"Thank you, sir. Enjoy the show." Francisco bowed slightly, took a step back, and left the building.

Conrad's receptionist stood motionless watching him walk away.

"Are you alright?" Conrad asked

She blinked twice and regained her composure. "Yes, Mister G." She sat back down at her desk while Conrad went off to see the whiskey man.

A large white tent sat proudly on the corner of Dubuque and Jefferson Streets with the massive stone masterpiece that was the United Methodist Church behind it. The streets were packed with the festival, and with the arrival of the circus the energy was electric. Vernice stood defiantly watching as person after person strolled by, many carrying large glass "Jumbo" mugs full of beer.

Signage on the side of the tent boldly stated, *No Beer—Get Water Here* and *Women's Christian Temperance Union* and *Free Medical Clinic.*

Teddy and Dr. Cozine had agreed to provide free medical treatment to those in town for the Fall Fest, many of whom were far from home, and with such a crowd of revelers there were bound to be accidents.

Vernice took great pleasure in occasionally filling one of the brewers' Jumbo mugs with ice cold water. They had a large barrel sitting in a tub of ice. It galled her that she had to buy the ice from Englert, but nonetheless they were making their presence felt. They had people in shifts marching in front of the tent with signs of condemnation and righteousness.

The signs read: *Beer Is The Slippery Slope, NO BEER, Drink Beer—Break the Law, Brewers are Sinners, Backsliders, and Lawbreakers.*

Most people were laughing and enjoying themselves until they read one of the signs and a frown would come over them. Invariably they would lock eyes with Vernice and they would immediately look away, shamed by the beer they were carrying. Others scowled at her and continued on their way. Some stopped and handed over their beer mug only to watch it be poured on the ground and refilled with water.

Vernice would hand them their water with a thin smile and a nod of the head. "Turn from your wicked ways and have life."

Teddy was in a tent off to the side with three tables and his carry bag of equipment. Matilda had volunteered to be his assistant though she'd had no nursing training. She simply wanted to be with Teddy no matter what he was doing. She was afraid to tell him the sight of blood made her squeamish.

The second patient to come through the tent was a fourteen-year-old boy who had fallen from a horse and suffered a deep cut along his eyebrow. Blood flowed in copious amounts and when Teddy flushed it with water, she saw how deep the laceration was. It turned her stomach a bit, and she wavered enough that Teddy noticed.

"Are you alright?" he asked.

She nodded through clenched teeth and held the towel as instructed on the wound, determined to make him proud and be a good doctor's assistant.

The boy did the best he could to endure the pain while Teddy quickly stitched it up.

Once he was done the boy stood to go. "What do I owe you, Doc?"

"Nothing, son. This is a gift from the Ladies of Temperance," Teddy replied.

"Thank you, Doc."

After the boy left, Teddy and Matilda found themselves alone for a minute. Matilda glanced out the doorway and saw no one approaching. She crossed the room to where Teddy was washing his hands, leaned in, and stole a kiss, which Teddy gladly returned.

After a moment, Teddy pushed her away. "We're going to get caught!"

"Who cares? We'll be married in a month."

"I know, but what if your father or Vernice walks in?"

Matilda frowned. "I know. I can't wait till we're married." She kissed him again.

"Me either." Teddy pulled away at the sound of someone entering the tent.

Fall Fest was roaring long into the night with the sounds of singing and laughter echoing for miles around. The northside was alive with good times and commerce long after Teddy and Matilda had closed their tent and gone home for the evening.

Conrad stepped out of the Union tent and spotted Francisco standing on the front step to the brewery looking over the crowd. He waved at Conrad. Francisco stood patiently while Conrad pushed through the crowd on his way toward him.

"Hello, Mister Graf. We are ready for the show in the morning and I would like to take you up on your offer of a beer," Francisco said.

"Did you get the whiskey? I had it sent."

"Yes, our drunkard Jumbo thanks you. You have made my job all the more possible."

"We are drinking in these tents tonight, enjoying the fine weather. Come with me and we will share a brew." Conrad pointed to the tents that were jammed full of people enjoying themselves.

"Is there anywhere we could go that is private? I have a couple of my friends with me and we must be hidden from the masses until tomorrow."

Conrad furrowed his brow. His public house was full of people, as would be J.J.'s place. He thought of Dostal's Second Floor Club, but knew it would be full of swells and Dostal would be entertaining. "Are you sure you can't be seen? Everything is packed with the circus in town."

Francisco pulled a figure up from behind him. Conrad hadn't even noticed he was there. The person gently pulled back his hood. Conrad jumped back a step, "Egads! What the...?"

The man's face was entirely covered in hair, no skin showing, but his eyes were human without a doubt. The hairy man covered himself again.

"Now do you understand?"

Conrad was wide-eyed. "Yes, follow me."

He unlocked the front door to the brewery and motioned them to enter. Three cloaked figures followed Francisco. Conrad was afraid to see what else was hidden under the shrouds.

As he was locking the door, Conrad noticed Sammy the errand boy walking by. "Sammy! Come here." The boy rushed over. "Run and tell J.J. and any of the teamsters to join me in the caves for a special meeting right away." Conrad handed him a coin.

"Yes, Mister G," the boy said, and he was off running through the crowd about his task.

The mysterious guests followed Conrad into the elevator and down into the caves. The lamps were blazing when they arrived at the bottom, providing a golden light.

Jimmy was standing at the entrance. "Hey, Mister G. What's up? Need another keg?"

"No, we're fine for now. I'm here to have a beer with some new friends, will you join us?"

"Absolutely, sir. You know I never turn down a beer." Jimmy's eye still had a slight droop from the beating and probably always would.

A dusky man with long hair stepped forward holding out his hand. "I am Francisco of Corsica."

"And I am Jimmy of um…Ireland, or Iowa, I guess," Jimmy laughed.

"These are my friends." Francisco motioned to his followers. They each carefully pulled back the cloaks covering their appearance. The first was the man covered in hair.

At the sight of him Jimmy jumped back. "Jesus, Mary, and Joseph!"

They laughed at Jimmy's fear. "Don't be afraid, he almost never bites!" said Francisco. The hairy man growled and made a scratching motion with his hands. "He's known as the Dog Faced Boy, but he's not a dog or a boy."

He stuck out his furry hand to Jimmy, who tentatively shook it with an uncomfortable glance at Conrad.

"His name is JoJo."

"Jimmy, get JoJo a beer," Conrad said.

"Next, I introduce, Skeleton Man." said Francisco. The man was of average height but could not have weighed more than fifty pounds. His drawn face was hollow like a skull, yet his eyes were alive and bright blue. Bony fingers hung from thin wrists, while wisps of light hair fell from his head, adding to the appearance that he was a walking skeleton.

"Hello," the skeleton said with a shockingly low voice. Jimmy handed him a beer.

"His name is Isaac Sprague," Francisco continued. "And lastly, Manaaki." He was a massive man made of muscle. His shirt fell open at his chest and he had no hair on his body other than a fierce black beard. Every inch of his skin, including his bald head, was covered in intricate black tattooed designs. The man had a long, flat bone penetrating each side of his nostrils, adding to his terrifying appearance, and what looked like shark teeth hung from each ear lobe.

"Don't worry, if you give him a beer he's harmless. Otherwise, I make no promises," Francisco laughed.

Manaaki growled when Jimmy handed him a beer.

"Now you can see why we must drink in private," Francisco explained.

Conrad nodded. "Yes, I do."

"We don't let P.T. find out either. Depending on the day, or present company, he's against drinking, and we only have a few more shows to finish the tour." JoJo took a solid drink, leaving foam on his furry lip. "No reason to upset him, which is why we can't invite Little Tom."

The circus crew chuckled at that.

"Who's Little Tom?" Conrad asked.

"He's been with P.T. for years. They are inseparable. He's known as General Tom Thumb, and at his peak he was a solid three feet tall, but he has always been an asshole. He tells P.T. everything." Francisco grinned. "We are of the opinion that P.T. doesn't need to know everything about every minute of our lives. Am I right?"

"Yes. That's right!" the menagerie chorused.

"Annie would have joined us, but she's found a new man and stays in at night."

"Annie?" Jimmy echoed.

"The bearded lady. You'll see her at the show. Top notch lady."

The odd group settled into the chairs around the table.

"What is this place?" Manaaki asked.

Skeleton Man pulled out a deck of cards and several cigars. He sat at the table and began shuffling.

Jimmy stared. It was eerie in the lantern light. He really looked like a living skeleton.

"We call them the beer caves. It's a constant temperature in here and it is good for the beer," Conrad explained.

Manaaki took a drink. "Beer is good."

"Thank you, it's a family recipe."

The sound of voices coming from the tunnel leading to Englert's brewery bounced off the walls.

Jimmy snickered. "Wait till J.J. sees this!"

"Hello, the cave!" J.J. hollered, stepping into view with Tom and Gunnar just behind. At the sight of them, JoJo put his chin in the air and let loose a howl as if he was a wolf calling the moon. It echoed in the chamber and sent shivers up the spine of everyone present.

J.J. stumbled into the room and couldn't hide the terrified look on his face. He could see there was no danger because both Conrad and Jimmy were laughing hysterically. Conrad gathered himself and tried to talk, but he couldn't stop laughing as he made introductions, beginning with Francisco.

"Thanks for inviting us, Conrad. I thought something was wrong with you calling a meeting on such short notice at this hour," J.J. said.

"No problems tonight. Just thought you might want to share a beer with our friends." Conrad raised his glass, and everyone followed suit. "To new friends."

JoJo and Isaac lit their cigars and smoked as they dealt a hand of poker to those seated at the table.

Manaaki regaled the crowd with stories of his childhood in New Zealand and all the men he had killed in battle as the son of a great Maori chieftain. His father had been murdered by a rival king and he'd fled, as they wanted to kill him as well.

"Someday I will return to my home and kill my enemies," he said. "For now, the circus is my home."

"In America, we can't simply kill our enemies," J.J. laughed.

"No, though I wish we could!" Conrad roared.

Jimmy couldn't take his eyes off the skeleton man. "Does it hurt?" he finally asked.

"No, not unless I fall or something, just like you," Isaac answered.

"Do you starve yourself? How do you look like that?"

"Although I eat as much as possible, it doesn't matter, I still look like this. It's a syndrome. Stay back or you could catch it," he said with a serious face.

"Really?" Jimmy stepped back right away.

Isaac stepped forward and grabbed Jimmy's hand firmly. His bony grip was like iron and he refused to let go, no matter how hard Jimmy pulled. Isaac burst into laughter, as did all of his circus partners. "No, I'm just messing with you. You can't catch it, you have to be born with it."

Jimmy looked visibly relieved and struggled to regain his composure, gently rubbing his hand where Isaac had grabbed him.

"I'm sorry, I love that joke," Isaac said. "I have three sons, and they are all normal weights. It's just me that I know of. One of a kind."

"Have another beer, Jimmy," Conrad said. Jimmy finished the one in his hand and obliged himself to another, hoping he hadn't just caught the skeleton disease. He thought he should go to confession as soon as possible to be sure he wasn't being punished for something.

After a few more beers the caves echoed with laughter and the crew of misfits and brewers enjoyed the company, conversation, cigars, and cards until finally Francisco glanced at his pocket watch. "It's late. Thank you for such a time. We will not forget our visit to the beer caves of Iowa."

"Thank you for bringing the show to your town," JoJo said.

"The show will be the highlight of our year," J.J. said. "I've dreamt of building a permanent venue for special performances like you see in Chicago and New York, but I haven't done it yet. We need more entertainment here."

"If you ever build it, we'd be happy to come back as long as we get to drink beer in the caves," JoJo said.

"Anytime, anytime," Conrad offered as they returned to the surface in the elevator.

Other than Francisco, each man carefully placed his hood back over his unusual appearance to keep the crowd from noticing their differences. The hour was late and the street was mostly empty. The singing had died down to a lonely few and a harvest moon hung low in the night sky. The strange fellows exited the brewery and followed Francisco, vanishing into the night.

Only Jimmy remained. "There's a night we'll never forget," Conrad said.

"That's for sure, Mister G. That's for sure. Goodnight, I've got to get some sleep." Jimmy disappeared into the northside on his way home.

# 15

THE first show was at eight AM. It was the only show that didn't have a line. Shows began on the hour at eight, ten, twelve, two, four, and six. The massive tent held hundreds of people comfortably and no one was disappointed.

With billing like, *The Greatest Show On Earth*, the opportunity to let some patrons down was high, but Mr. P.T. Barnum did not leave anyone wanting.

Conrad carried Otto on his shoulders, while Anna held Simeon's hand, slowly pushing forward in the close quarters crowd. The line extending from the main entrance to the circus tent was long, but Conrad had made other arrangements. They slipped around the tent and entered through a side entrance, circumventing the long wait for the ten o'clock show.

Conrad had to admit he was nearly as excited as the boys to see what the infamous Mr. P.T. Barnum had to show, and he was looking forward to seeing his new friends.

After a late night, he'd captured a couple of hours' sleep and was ready for the day. Max, the bartender at the Public House, was accompanying the Graf family. Conrad had purchased a couple of extra tickets for him and his young wife as a bonus for all the long hours and faithful service he regularly gave the Union.

The best seats in the house were waiting for them. Front and center had been reserved as the crowd was pouring in fighting for the best seats. Conrad had purchased the seats in advance and at a premium. They say money can't buy happiness, but it could buy the best seats in the house and no line. Conrad had no desire to wait in line or sit in a bad seat.

"Thank you, Mister G," Max said as they found their seats and he realized how prime they were.

"No problem, Max. You've earned it a million times over. Enjoy the show."

Barkers in bright red uniforms were shouting to the crowd. "Find your seats, buy some peanuts, and get ready for the greatest show on Earth!"

"Peanuts, get your peanuts!" Vendors walked amongst the crowd selling bags of peanuts with a picture of an elephant printed on the side and the letters JUMBO.

"Can we get peanuts?" Simeon asked.

"Of course." Conrad bought three bags for everyone. He handed a bag to Max and his wife and Conrad and his family shared the other two. The boys were sucking the salt from them and tossing the shells to the ground.

The loud bang of a metal cage door slamming open followed by a warning siren came from the far end of the ring. One of the barkers called out, "Don't feed the monkeys! They've escaped! Folks, please don't feed the monkeys as we round them up!"

Monkeys poured out of the cage, sprinting every which way. Seven or eight monkeys were running rampant in the ring with seemingly inept handlers trying to capture them. Conrad could see immediately it was part of the act. "Barnum has started the show!" he said to his boys, whose eyes were wide with excitement.

He pointed for Simeon to look across the ring at a monkey that was climbing the ladder to the trapeze while a handler feigned trying to grab the monkey. Simeon's eyes were as big as saucers. Out of nowhere a monkey jumped into Conrad's lap, and Anna screamed. The boys jumped back in fear, as did Max's wife.

The monkey grabbed a handful of peanuts, shoving them into his mouth as he leapt back into the ring.

The barker yelled with a smile on his face, "Please, no feeding the monkeys!" It took a moment for the entire Graf family to recover from the surprise, but the show had already lived up to its billing.

A man in a yellow shirt entered the center of the arena. He blew a shrill whistle and dumped a large pile of bananas on the center of the middle ring. Every monkey in the tent ran full speed toward him and formed a circle around the bananas.

"Everyone knows monkeys love bananas. Watch what our monkeys will do for a banana!" the barker in yellow yelled.

One-by-one, each monkey did a back flip. The man in yellow tossed each one a banana after they did their flip. The monkeys sat patiently, holding their banana. Once each monkey had a banana, the man in yellow took a bow. The applause shook the tent.

The man in yellow looked at his monkeys waiting as trained. "Okay, monkeys!" he shouted. "Peel your banana and you can eat it."

Each monkey began carefully peeling his banana and once the peel was off, they ate the fruit. Then the man in yellow pointed to the end of the tent and as he trotted off, his monkeys followed along in a perfect single file line.

"Daddy, I love monkeys!" Simeon said.

Conrad smiled at his son, as did Anna.

A drumroll began and the lights were dimmed. Gas lanterns were being manipulated with mirrors like Conrad had never seen. Circular spotlights flashed around the room until one man stood alone in the center ring and all the light focused upon him. Cannons exploded and smoke filled the tent.

He dramatically removed his hat and bowed low before the audience that was holding its breath to what they knew and hoped to be true. This was *Barnum!*

He stood straight and all could see he was not a tall man. He was not slim. He had wild hair that was mix of darkness and gray streaks. He raised one arm high over his head and turned to face the crowd.

He picked up the cone that stood next to him to amplify his voice as he spoke, so all could hear.

"Welcome to P.T. Barnum's Greatest Show on Earth!" He waited while the crowd erupted in clapping. "Welcome the Great London Circus, as well as Sanger's Royal British Menagerie! You are in for a treat worth every penny you paid today. You will see death defying feats high above the ground, you will see magical productions with no Earthly explanation, and you will see a collection of oddities so unique you would be tempted to call me a liar if you hadn't witnessed it with your own eyes. Some of you may have come today for one reason alone, and that reason would be to see something you've never seen before, to see something you'll never see again, am I right?"

The crowd clapped and screamed their agreement.

"Did you come to see the one, the only, JUMBO?" he waited on the crowd's applause as an experienced showman should. "Jumbo is the only real African elephant in America and today he is here!"

The crowd erupted again.

"Are you ready?"

"*Yes!*"

Barnum had them in the palm of his hand. He obviously knew what he was doing, and Conrad had to admire it as a thing of beauty and showmanship.

"Are you ready?" The crowd again shouted *yes!* "Then let's get this show started!"

Lights erupted all around and people began running in many directions to each of the three rings. No matter where you looked your eyes were not disappointed.

Two women in tight clothing stood upon the backs of two white stallions prancing around the outside of the ring, raising each knee high and holding their tails just so. The horses were gorgeous in their own right, but stunning in their movement. They wore no saddles or bridles, yet seemed to follow the commands of their standing riders who balanced on their backs with bare feet waving at the crowd as they passed.

Most any man who had ever trained a horse watched in awe. As if the white beauties were not enough, they were followed by a creature foreign to the American continent. Three chariots being pulled by small black and white striped ponies sped around the ring as if they were racing gladiators of Rome.

The speeding zebras were amazing to behold. Each driver was a man no larger than a boy of five or six, yet they were men with full beards and all things manly. Each small man was dressed in an outfit of a royal sort and they snapped whips at their odd-looking steeds sliding around the curves, tipping the chariots up onto one wheel and slamming into one another while the audience gasped.

All the while, the center ring filled with impressive athletes in their own right. A massive man covered in tattoos lifted a wagon over his head and then tossed it aside as if it where nothing. He then clasped a long spear and tossed it the length of the ring, sending it straight into the main pole.

"That's Manaaki! He's one of the ones who came to the Union," Conrad said to Anna, leaning toward her so she could hear him over the crowd.

Barnum announced a husband wife pair in tight purple clothing who trotted to the center ring and began climbing the tall poles leading to the high wire that stood taut above. People in the crowd bit their lips in nervous anticipation.

"The amazing Corianos!"

At each end of the tent, the side rings displayed a show unique to the world. At one end a man with flowing white hair walked to the center of one ring with two great cats at his side heeling like hunting dogs.

One was orange and black striped, while the other animal was tan with a dark mane. The man with the white hair wore all white clothing trimmed in yellow, shimmering like the sun. He carried a long black whip which he cracked, and the big cats roared in response. A beautiful young woman dressed in red entered the ring and placed a large circle on a pole.

The man in black tipped back his head to take a liquid into his mouth, leaned forward, and blew straight toward the ring. The liquid ignited, blasting a flame forth from his mouth.

The fire lit the ring and the crowd applauded at the impressive display. If Conrad had been skeptical about the show, that feeling was gone now. It was already the greatest show he'd ever seen.

The man in black cracked his whip and the two cats took turns jumping through the hoop of fire. All the while, the zebras raced around the arena with their drivers slamming into one another violently.

Everywhere he looked, strange sights abounded. Clowns on stilts, little people juggling, monkeys dressed in human clothes walking dogs, a woman with pale hair and albino white skin riding a massive pig twice the size of a normal swine tacked with a complete saddle and bridle as if it were a horse.

At the other end of the arena a man stood in the center and arched his head back straight while he wiggled and cajoled a three-foot broadsword, allowing it to slide down his throat while several sheep ran circles around him, each with a small dog standing upon its back.

Conrad glanced over at his family. They looked exactly like he felt. Amazed. They stared at the great spectacle with their mouths gaped open in wonder.

As if no one was even watching, the man in purple who had climbed high aloft stepped out on a long wire strung between the two tall apparatus and began to carefully walk the wire with no net. He was definitely high enough for it to be a fatal mistake were he to fall.

The woman in purple screamed and clutched her chest, drawing attention to what she was staring at. The man on the rope had reached the center and stood frozen. All could see he had no rope to catch him if he fell. He bobbled the pole he carried and tried to gather it in then lost it, slipping to the ground below. The crowd cried out for his loss.

This stunt was very real and could cost him his life right in front of the entire crowd. The anxiety was palpable as the crowd wondered had he dropped the pole as part of the act or was he in real trouble?

His right foot slipped, and he wobbled. Every woman in the tent cried out and most men as well when it appeared he really would fall. Everyone hoped this was part of the act. He carefully pulled his foot back up and balanced once again. He attempted to take another step, but wobbled horribly and fell. With one hand he grabbed the wire as his life hung by a finger's grip.

The crowd collectively held their breath waiting on life or death. The man grabbed the wire with his other hand and began swinging back and forth until he got momentum. With a great swing he swung back up to the top of the wire and he stood wobbly at first, then raised both hands in victory.

The crowd cheered at his success. The woman scaled the ladder and reached the top just as the man made it across. The crowd cheered when they hugged in safety on the platform.

That joy turned to anxiety when the woman climbed upon the man's shoulders. He turned back to the wire, ignoring the crowd's chants of "*No! Don't do it!*" The man stepped out on the high wire with the woman on his shoulders.

Conrad grimaced, thinking *I hope they don't die in front of the kids!*

The tightrope walked reached the middle with no problems, then he stopped and wobbled. He slowly went to a knee on the wire with the woman upon his shoulders. He collapsed onto his rear at the same moment the woman somersaulted forward as if she was falling and flipped onto the wire, standing by herself unaided.

The crowd erupted in cheers once again.

She took the man's hand and helped him to his feet. They stood and bowed to one another. Then the woman bent back over herself and did an entire roundoff, ending on the platform safe as could be. The man acted as if he was suddenly unsteady while the woman tossed him a rope.

He began to inch toward the safety of the platform and stumbled and fell. The crowd gasped; his death seemed eminent. The rope caught at the last second, saving the man from falling to his death. He swung around the pole and let go of the rope, and with a flip to the ground, he landed on his feet.

He stood victorious with his hands held high as the crowd cheered all the more.

Barnum had taken over calling at one end while another barker had assumed control of the other. The various acts would perform in one ring and then move to the other end and perform yet again.

Barnum began to bring his menagerie to the ring. First, Skeleton Man ambled to the center ring, followed by JoJo the Dog Boy darting around the ring. General Tom Thumb and Manaaki led the way for the magnificent Bearded Lady. She marched to the center ring proudly with her chin held high, all the oddities around her. Then an absolutely unexpected thing happened. She sang a song of love in Italian as if she was an opera star from overseas. Her skill and talent were obvious to even those who knew nothing of operatic talent. She nailed her final note and the tent settled to silence.

The entire crowd was dumbfounded and could only stare at her dark black beard, knowing they had witnessed something they would never see again. After the short silence ended, the crowd leapt to their feet and gave a wholehearted and deserved standing ovation. Annie, the Bearded Lady, bowed.

The lights changed focus to the tightrope area. No one had noticed but the tightrope had been replaced by two trapezes and a man and a woman in sparkly cream-colored uniforms stood ready on the platforms, ready to perform their death-defying leaps, flips, and swings that no normal person would dare attempt.

Double flips and triple spins left the already impressed audience stunned into submission. The crowd gasped each time the young woman flew through the air and clasped the hands of her strong partner, saving her from falling to a painful death.

After they were done, Barnum marched to the center of the arena, waiting for his crowd to quiet.

Once they did, he spoke loudly, but slowly. "I have one last thing to show you before I let you go back to your lives. I have one last thing to show you that you will remember till the day you die. I purchased this animal from the zoo in England and it didn't make the Queen very happy. She felt it was an English specialty from the days of monarchy in Africa.

"I wanted to tell her that Americans don't serve the Queen anymore and neither would this animal!" he shouted, eliciting a loud patriotic cheer.

"This great beast didn't come from England. Oh no. It came from the dark continent where prehistoric creatures still roam the Earth. He has come all the way from Africa and his name is JUMBOoooo!"

The crowd stood up, and all the lights focused on the end of the tent where the massive elephant entered. He was huge, all of fourteen feet tall and weighing several tons. His gray hide covered an animal that strode with confidence, raising his trunk and bugling a sound previously unheard on the plains of Iowa.

Conrad leaned over to Anna, who was smiling ear-to-ear at the amazing show and snickered. "The elephant is drunk," he whispered.

Anna laughed. "What are you talking about?"

"I supplied the handler with gallons of whiskey for Jumbo. He eats whiskey biscuits, hundreds of them! They keep him drunk all the time."

Anna laughed heartily. It was a long time since they'd had so much fun or laughed so hard.

The massive elephant bent a knee and three small acrobats and a monkey wearing a hat ran up his leg and right onto his back. He rose to his feet and marched around the tent while they waved at the crowd, performing tricks as Jumbo strolled.

Jumbo returned to the center ring and sat back on his rear, raising his front feet up and waving. The acrobats and the monkey slipped right off the back.

"Jumbo says thank you for being a fantastic audience, and if you're lucky we shall see you again," Barnum said, taking a bow. Jumbo stood to all fours and then knelt as if taking a bow as well.

"I love the elephant!" little Otto exclaimed to his parents.

"We do too, Otto. He's amazing!" Conrad said to his little boy.

The show ended with each act running into the center ring and taking a bow to the standing ovation from an overjoyed crowd. Barnum found his spot in the center ring to take one final bow. The barkers returned and directed everyone to leave out the south end of the tent since the new audience was coming in from the north side.

Once they had exited the tent, Conrad tossed Otto up onto his shoulders and the family walked back toward the northside.

"That was amazing!" Max gushed. "I can't thank you enough, Mister G. We'll never see anything like that the rest of our lives." Max's wife nodded her agreement.

"That was so fantastic!" Anna said. "Did you like it, boys?"

"Yes, Mama! I loved the monkeys!" Simeon said.

"I liked Jumbo," said Otto.

"What was your favorite part?" Anna asked Conrad.

"Seeing my friends from last night. Barnum didn't lie. That *was* the greatest show on Earth," Conrad said. "I am seriously shocked. I've never seen anything like that!"

They noticed Father Edmonds talking to people in the line for the next show, which wrapped around in front of St. Mary's and most of the way to the Methodist church.

"How was the show?" he asked the Grafs when they approached.

"Fantastic," Anna said. "I hope you're going?"

"I have a ticket to the four o'clock show," Father Edmonds said.

Conrad grinned. "You won't be disappointed."

Anger surged through Conrad when he heard familiar chanting getting louder from the west.

"NO BEER! NO BEER! NO BEER!"

Vernice was working her way through the crowd toward the front entrance of the tent.

"Doesn't she take a day off?" Conrad griped to Father Edmonds.

"Do you?" he replied with a wry smile.

Conrad almost had sympathy for her and her followers since the crowd was not sympathetic to her cause. Many held Jumbo beer mugs in their hands while she marched with her signs condemning their behavior.

He noticed the young lady Teddy was going to marry carrying a sign as well. She looked a little shaky in the face of the crowd. Conrad frowned when he noticed a few men shouting at them as they pushed their way through. He almost intervened, but they made it through without incident and staked out a corner on the edge of the tent.

"Sinners, repent!" they shouted. "Turn from your wicked ways! Drinkers are lawbreakers!"

Conrad turned his back on them. He had no desire to be angry today. He'd just had possibly the best time of his life and he didn't want to ruin it. They strolled back into the northside, leaving Vernice and her protest behind. Conrad bought food from a vendor and they found a table that was empty. They sat enjoying a fine lunch while enjoying the music from the festival stage. The German polka was a perfect soundtrack for the day. The Grafs couldn't stop talking about the amazing things they'd seen.

A loud bang was followed by the wail of a siren coming from the Barnum tent.

"That's the start of the show," Conrad said. "They're probably chasing those monkeys around."

The barkers were calling out in voices garbled because of the distance from the tent.

Anna giggled. "I can't believe that monkey jumped on you."

"And now the zebras are racing," Simeon said.

"That's right, Simeon," said his mother. "Can you believe all the things you've seen today?"

"A singing lady with a beard!" he said.

"She sure could sing like an angel," Conrad said.

"I want an elephant," Otto announced.

"Well, if we had a zoo here that would be the only way, Otto. You can't keep elephants as pets."

"Why not?"

"They drink too much!" Conrad quipped. Anna joined in and they shared a knowing glance at what they knew about Jumbo the drunk elephant.

Conrad smiled at Anna in a surreal moment, as if for a brief second he glimpsed his family and the fact that everything was changing. Deep in his heart he wished things could remain as they were at that very moment and as they had for hundreds of years, but somehow, he knew that was impossible.

By noon the next day, the entire circus was loaded on rail cars and were leaving the station on their way to the next show. The Fall Fest tents came down and the brewers each sent several men out to pick up trash and sweep up broken glass.

There was lots of broken glass from many dropped Jumbo beer mugs. By Monday the northside looked like it always did, and life went back to normal, but everyone continued to talk for weeks about all the amazing things they'd seen at *The Greatest Show On Earth.*

# 16

"IT'S happened," J.J. said, sitting down for the weekly meeting.

"What's happened?" Dostal asked.

"The court challenge to the amendment. It's happened. It's going to the Iowa Supreme Court."

"Who told you that?" Conrad asked.

"I walked Lucas to the train today. He's on his way back to Des Moines. It will be in the papers tomorrow. He is cautiously excited. He said it's all going according to plan so far, but with these things its always dodgy."

"What plan?" Conrad asked.

"They have judges in Scott County favorable to our plight," said J.J.

Conrad nodded. "That would be nice."

"You know the Koehler and Lange Brewery?"

"Yeah, I met them at the state meeting a few years ago," Conrad answered. "Seemed like good fellas."

"They're good men. They supply beer to the Turner Hall Saloon in Davenport owned by John Hill. John is a friend of the cause. He usually helps with their big festival, Koenigfest. Anyway, he refused to pay Koehler and Lange for beer delivered and drank."

"What the hell? He's no friend," Dostal growled.

"It's all part of the plan. A ruse. Koehler and Lange filed suit against Hill to force him to pay up. Hill contended that he has no obligation to pay for a product that is not legal under the constitution thanks to the amendment and they went before District Court Judge Walter Hayes. A good friend of Lange.

"Koehler and Lange demanded payment claiming the amendment was not valid since it was in two different forms when it passed the two separate sessions of the legislature, making the entire amendment invalid," J.J. smirked.

"Invalid entirely?" Conrad shook his head. "No way."

"Yes. Then Judge Hayes ruled in favor of the brewers that the amendment was invalid, and Hill was ordered to pay the brewery. The ruling was instantly appealed and it's going to the Supreme Court in December." J.J. paused and took a sip of his beer.

"Then what?" Conrad pressed.

"The Supreme Court either strikes down the amendment like the lower court just did or they overturn the lower court's ruling and the amendment stands."

Conrad snorted. "Either way, we're still selling beer."

"Yeah, but only because I'm on the city council and we control the northside and half the town. What if that changes? What if Vernice turns the tide against us? No. We need that amendment overturned. No question about it," J.J. said.

"What did Lucas think? Are they going to void it?" asked Dostal.

"He thinks we have a great shot. Since the lower court ruled in our favor, we have a better than good shot of the higher court upholding the ruling, and it's going to be in Davenport, which is helpful for us. He did say they were sending in the best lawyers in the state for both sides to argue before the Supreme Court, so it will be a fight."

Conrad took a drink and sat back in his chair. "So we wait and see. Maybe this can all be over soon."

"I hope so," Dostal said. "Depending on what happens, I'm going to add onto the Great Western and increase our capacity."

J.J. glanced at him. "Aren't you content to be the biggest already?"

"Even if you're not the best," Conrad said with a smile.

"Quantity isn't everything," said J.J. "It's not only about the money."

"You guys keep telling yourselves that," Dostal scoffed. "I have no shame in profiting as much as I can. The more I produce, the more I can sell."

"Oh, we know that you have no shame," Conrad said. "We know what drives you."

"You're no different!" Dostal all but shouted.

"Easy fella, we're only kidding," Conrad said. "You guys have all sorts of other businesses. The Union is all I have, and I'll fight for it till my last breath."

"Conrad, you have other ventures. The Union bakery and Bushnagle's Ice Cream Shoppe." J.J. pointed out. "Don't you have some farm ground?"

"Yes, I own the building and I have financed Bushnagle, but he's slowly buying me out. It's all nothing without the Union."

"If you want to expand your interests, I'd be happy to talk about diversifying with you," J.J. said. "When Louie came here, he started a saloon right in our house on Dubuque Street. He ran a stagecoach stop and an inn, and we farmed. You know I want to build a theater."

"Thanks, J.J. If this amendment falls, I'll be just fine running the Union. If not, we better talk. I'm not much for theaters. Brewing beer is all I know," Conrad said.

"I love to brew beer, but it's not like you can't do other things too," J.J. countered, determined to kindle Conrad's entrepreneurial spirit.

"Let's just get rid of this amendment," Conrad said.

"Agreed," Dostal stated as a matter of fact.

Fall gave way to winter and the river once again was a sheet of ice and snow clinging to the hardwoods. While winter was not without its beauty, the cold and snow simply made everything more difficult. Along with his growing ice business, J.J. added wood supply to his list of growing ventures to augment the seasonal aspect of the ice business.

"They need ice all summer, wood all winter, and the Englerts are here to provide it all," J.J. explained.

"Well, they need beer all year long," Conrad said with a smile.

The *Koehler Lange vs. Hill* case was argued in December and the Supreme Court had gone into its chambers with no hint of how it would rule. The new year, 1883, came in cold and quiet across Iowa. No promise of exciting circus visits or anything out of the ordinary at all on the horizon, only the ice-cold prairie.

No matter the weather, building continued as best it could to provide shelter for the seemingly unending supply of new faces coming to town. Immigrants from Europe found peace and prosperity on the fertile hills between the Mississippi and the Iowa Rivers. The state university erected several new buildings, as did the Sisters of Mercy Hospital. Residences filled the streets and town lots sold at prices unheard of only a few years ago. Speculators and landowners became wealthy men.

Iowa City got better every year. It became known as a town of beauty, both cosmopolitan and enlightened to the pride of every resident. For eastern Iowa, it was the pearl of the prairie. Every trade and shop a person could dream was found right here. Iowa City had become a true rival to Galena and Chicago without having to travel as far.

Conrad Graf, J.P. Dostal, and J.J. Englert sat together eating a fine beef stew at Dostal's Second Street Club as per their weekly meeting.

"I'm tired of this cold," Dostal complained.

"It won't be but a couple months and we'll be back in spring," J.J. said, the eternal optimist. "March is spring."

"No, it isn't," Conrad argued.

"Well, it's not winter," J.J. said.

"Yes, it is," Conrad stated. "March is winter."

"No, it is not. Green plants sprout. You spend at least half the month of March with no coat. That's spring."

"It's winter," Conrad insisted. "There's still frost in the ground."

"No."

Dostal raised a hand. "Stop it, you sound like my kids."

"Fine. It's winter," Conrad conceded. "I have some exciting news."

This caught both of his friends by surprise, because he never had *exciting* news. J.J. even gave up his argument. Conrad returned to his stew without continuing.

"Well, what is it? Do we have to beg it out of you?" J.J. asked.

Conrad looked up, smiling ear-to-ear. "Anna told me this morning that she's pregnant."

"Congratulations!" Dostal said with genuine happiness.

J.J. raised his glass. "To the birth of another fine Graf! The future of the Union Brewery is intact!"

Conrad smiled, unable to contain his joy. "We thought we were done. It's been a few years since we had Otto and no more babies followed."

"Might I suggest the name John? It's a fine name. You can't go wrong with it," J.J. stated.

"I agree," Dostal said. "John is a fine name."

"Dostal, you don't even go by the name John," Conrad laughed. "Heck, neither of you do."

"John Conrad Graf has a ring to it," said J.J.

"Anna likes William if it's a boy. It could be a girl, you know."

"For Anna's sake, I will pray it is a little lass. Can you imagine a house full of four Graf men?"

"Lord have mercy," said J.J.

Conrad raised his glass. "Mercy indeed."

"Did you know that Teddy's wife, the teetotaler, is pregnant as well?"

"I had heard that," Conrad said. "She's got him on a tight leash. He doesn't come to the Public House anymore."

"He knew what he was signing up for with that Methodist gal," Dostal snickered.

"She apparently found something for him to do at home!" J.J. exclaimed.

Sammy the errand boy appeared at the top of the step and surveyed the room. At the sight of the brewers at their table he trotted over to them.

"Hello, Sammy, what is it?" Conrad asked.

"I have a telegram. I was supposed to take it to each of you, so I'm glad to have found you together."

"What is it?" Dostal asked.

"It's from Congressman Lucas. It says 'January 18, 1883. Victory. The Supreme Court issued their ruling upholding the lower court. It was five to one, thereby voiding the prohibitory amendment! Hoist a brew to victory. E. Lucas." Sammy looked up at the brewers with a smile growing across his young face.

The men sat in silence for a moment and then erupted in shouting, laughing, and general merriment. They stood from their seats, making a scene for the rest of the patrons to wonder at.

"The prohibitory amendment has been repealed!" Conrad yelled to the entire room, which sent the remaining patrons into their own joyful moment.

"Ed!" Dostal yelled to the bartender. "A round on the house for everyone!"

News of the amendment being declared unconstitutional spread like wildfire. The northside took to the streets with shouts of happiness that could be heard for several hours and the pubs were full that night as everyone wanted to enjoy a beer free of constitutional worry.

The City Council removed the monthly levies upon the bars and brewers at the next meeting. Vernice was in attendance, though she did not say a word. She contented herself to stare with a dark hatred at J.J. and all of the council as they reveled in their victory.

On April 21st, the legislature confirmed the Supreme Court's ruling and wiped the amendment from the books. The Great Western Brewery, City Brewery, and Union Brewery all launched expansion projects on the heels of their constitutional vindication. Their businesses enjoyed substantial increase the entire year, aided by the constant population explosion Iowa City continued to enjoy.

Dostal and J.J. both branched into other endeavors, as was their nature. The Great Western added production of mineral water as well as increased beer production, while J.J. finished his larger icehouse north of town and purchased a large stand of timber to provide for his logging business.

Conrad stuck to what he knew, the brewing of beers. However, he did expand with an idea that proved most lucrative, and in time, all three breweries offered the service. The Union began a local delivery service to residences...*at night.*

This allowed beer to be delivered discreetly under the cover of darkness to people who wished to partake but were too ashamed to enter a pub or be seen picking up beer at the brewery docks.

Conrad had no idea the pent-up demand for such secretive home consumption and the desire for a discreet delivery service. He was utterly unprepared for the huge influx of orders. He was forced to increase production to its maximum. He added four more drivers and purchased two large new wagons to accomplish the routes. He was pleasantly surprised that more than a few he'd labeled as teetotalers had added their names to the discreet list under the promise of anonymity.

The entire year was marked by growth and the brewers gained in wealth and influence as their product was in strong demand. Conrad's wife had a baby boy who, contrary to J.J. and Dostal's opinion, they named William. Teddy's wife also gave birth to a healthy boy they named Louis to honor the Englert patriarch. With construction continuing at a brisk pace, the northside was a dream come true for citizens of every station.

Even Conrad, who was cynical by nature, began to let down his guard and enjoy life with everything going well, at least for a time.

With the spring of 1884 everything was about to change.

# 17

THE 20th General Assembly of the Iowa Legislature was called to session. Johnson County was proud to send a solid slate of intemperate democrats to Des Moines. The seat held by Lewis Wolfe opened up when he did not run again. He was replaced easily by democrat, Cyrus Ranck. Ranck was a quiet man and was as well-liked by the community as any lawyer could be. He'd come from Pennsylvania, graduated from the law school in Iowa City in '71, and never left.

Before he became a congressman, he amassed quite a fortune in his legal practice. He made his home on the growing west side of the river on a beautiful property, owning several acres on Benton Street where he built a home and a large barn. He was known for keeping to himself while not at work. Although a member of no church, he was agreeable to good works in the community and gave a large sum to the Foundation.

His vote was considered safe down Democrat party lines. While he never visited the northside nor took a strong side in the warring factions of temperance, his vote was always against temperance.

The only Republican from Johnson County, John Shrader, lost his seat to Iowa City businessman Moses Bloom, entirely due to his vote for prohibition. That vote made him virtually unelectable in Johnson County.

Moses was loved by the northside and made his home on Dodge Street, but he was no Catholic. Moses was born in Alsace, France, and was Jewish. He became the first Jew to hold a seat in the Iowa Legislature, which he was very proud of until the day he died.

He owned and operated a clothing store on Clinton Street just south of the St. James Hotel to which he owed his fortune. Known as a great orator, he was a friend to the northside breweries and staunchly against prohibition. He somehow managed to avoid the scorn of the Ladies of Temperance while he fattened hundreds of cattle on the mash remains from the Iowa Distillery, which he quietly operated on South Gilbert Street.

Moses was a welcome change from Senator Shrader, the only elected official to have been for the prohibitory amendment. It was widely accepted that Shrader's vote for the amendment did more than permanently damage his electability. It put a black mark on virtually every Republican and began a more than thirty-year stretch that saw only one Republican ever elected from Johnson County.

Edward Lucas had agreed to one more term and easily won his seat again as the senior representative from Johnson County.

With such a fine slate of anti-prohibition politicians in Des Moines, it felt like a kick in the gut when the news came that the legislature had passed a prohibitory law. With the prohibitory amendment destroyed and business booming it seemed the struggle against the temperance movement had passed on. The teetotaling legislators in Des Moines had other ideas. They used their majority and simply passed a law that effectively outlawed the sale and production of liquor statewide with the stroke of a pen.

The members of the Beer Mafia didn't see it coming and it was a difficult blow to bear. Their businesses were experiencing exponential growth and they generally saw the temperance battle as behind them.

They were wrong.

Dostal and J.J. entered Conrad's office without knocking. Dostal slammed the door shut which didn't matter. They were talking so loudly it was heard in every office in the brewery.

"Did you hear what they did?" Dostal yelled.

"Yes, I heard," Conrad said quietly.

"It's unbelievable," J.J. bellowed. "How could this happen?"

"What are we going to do?" Dostal shouted.

Conrad was surprisingly calm and simply sat listening while they ranted.

"I can't believe this. I've just put in an order to add a third brew house," J.J. said.

"I agree. I'm increasing every month. I can't brew it fast enough," Conrad said.

"Well, aren't you mad?" J.J. asked.

"Yes, I'm furious."

"You don't look it!"

"Because I don't care."

"What the hell do you mean, you don't care?"

"I mean, they can pass whatever law they want. Vernice can spit in my face and march down Market Street with her signs, and I won't stop. They can't stop me."

"They can make it illegal," Dostal said. "They just did."

"They made it illegal in '82 as well if I remember and we are still brewing. I will still be brewing this time next year. Mark my words."

"They are going to be coming after us again," J.J. said.

"Let them come," Conrad said. "The people are on our side, and more every day. Who's buying all this beer?"

J.J. glanced at Dostal, frustrated.

"This is going to be different. I can feel it," J.J. said.

"Maybe so. If they want war with the northside they can have it. While they've been calling us the mafia for years, they haven't seen nothing," Conrad said. "If they want us to act like a mafia, they better look out."

"Sounds good to me," Dostal growled. "I've had it."

"Better get the crew together again and see if they are up to it," said J.J.

"Sounds good, but I won't be ordering them to do anything I won't do myself this time. If these temperance hacks want a fight, they're going to get it from me personally. I'll be the one to toss the match. They know where to find us." Conrad had an edge of cold anger riding his voice. No one who heard him doubted his resolve.

"I heard they decided to put the new law into effect on July 4th," J.J. told them.

Conrad snorted. "I had not heard that. Independence Day? Seriously?"

"Yes, I heard that too," Dostal piped up.

"They do want a fight after all. Starting it on that day of all days. That's a slap in the face of freedom." Conrad grinned. "I say bring it on. I'm not afraid to get bloody."

Articles ran all the month of June throughout the state discussing the prohibition and preparing the citizenry for the new law to take effect.

Every brewer was producing at full tilt as customers were buying in bulk and building up private stores in their barns and basements to weather whatever may come.

Vernice printed flyers and distributed them by hand to any who would take one stating:

VICTORY! IOWA DRY!

A JULY 4th TO BE PROUD OF

ALCOHOL FREE!

Conrad sent Sammy and a few of his friends around to tear down any they could find. He also had them distribute a flyer of his own.

FREE BEER!

CELEBRATE JULY 4th

AT THE UNION PUBLIC HOUSE

FREE BEER ALL NIGHT!

The argument that was once settled was once again the only topic of conversation to be had.

Vernice walked into Sheriff Coldren's office. He glanced up at her and laid his pencil down. She took a seat, and it was obvious she meant to talk.

"Sheriff, what are you going to do about these brewers?"

"Nothing yet. They aren't doing anything illegal," Coldren replied.

"On July 4th they will be."

"Maybe. We'll see."

"You're a fool if you think they are going to just stop their brewing. You don't think that, do you?"

"I don't get paid to think. I enforce laws that are broken. You are talking about a law that is not yet in effect and about crimes that have not been committed."

"Well come this Friday, you better be ready."

Coldren simply rolled his eyes at her scolding.

"Have you seen this?" she slammed one of Conrad's flyers down on his desk. "You better be ready to arrest him."

"Arrest him for what?"

"Selling beer of course."

"It says here, *free beer*. It's not a crime to give it away free," Coldren said. "Maybe he's just emptying his reserves so he can comply with the new law."

Vernice stared at him with contempt. "You are a pitiful man. I've been recruiting someone new for sheriff. You can be replaced, you know."

"Don't I know it. And please do, this job is thankless and does not pay nearly enough for the abuse."

"I thought you were a teetotaler?"

"I was. This job has driven me to drink."

Vernice frowned. "That's not funny." She stood to her feet. "You better get ready, 'cause this law is here to stay and those brewers are going down."

Vernice didn't wait for Sheriff Coldren to respond. She turned on her heel and marched right out his door, slamming it hard as she left. It slammed so hard it bounced open and he watched her go, shaking his head.

"Damn her," he muttered under his breath. "She's the kind of woman who makes you love your wife."

He got up and closed the door, ran his fingers through his hair, and took a seat at his desk. He felt guilty for a moment when he pulled open the bottom right desk drawer. He grasped a small flask and unscrewed the lid. "Here's to you, Vernice," he whispered, tipping the flask up and taking a solid drink.

He slid it back into the drawer and went back to his paperwork, a gnawing pain growing in his stomach. He had no idea what he was going to do on Friday. The vast majority of the town loved the brewers and J.J. had almost singlehandedly financed his last re-election campaign, leaving him feeling more than a little conflicted. He wished they'd never passed that damn law.

As darkness fell on July 4th, fireworks were launched from the state university steps out over the river. A large crowd had formed, since the fireworks were a family favorite. Within minutes of them being completed the crowd dispersed. They wanted no part of what was likely to happen. Everyone knew a storm was coming on the beautiful cloudless night.

Lights were glowing on the northside and the line out the front door of the Union Public House was growing by the minute.

Max and the other bartenders couldn't pour the beer fast enough. Jimmy, Tom, and several others kept bringing up new kegs from the caves to try to keep up with demand. He'd never seen it like this. No food and no payment meant it was a constant stream of Graf's Golden Brew as fast as it could be poured.

Only one beer at a time left many feeling shorted when they had to get back in line for another free beer or head to Louie's or Dostal's, who were not offering their beer free. Max ran out of glassware first. That meant he couldn't serve anyone who didn't have a glass. People were getting testy.

Two men got into a scuffle in the front of the Public House and as they fought, they crashed through the front window. The sound of glass shattering incensed the already angry mob.

They started chanting, "Free beer, free beer, free beer!"

"Jimmy, bring up all you can," Max commanded.

"Mister G didn't say to do that," Jimmy protested.

"We have no choice! They'll tear us down!"

Jimmy disappeared with several other workers and they brought up keg after keg and rolled them out to the street so the angry mob could serve themselves.

After several hours the crowd was satisfactorily drunken and slowly dispersed. Max finally locked the front door.

"Is there any beer left?" Max asked Jimmy. "I could use one."

"The north cave is entirely empty. But we have some more, follow me." They disappeared into the caves, leaving the glass and debris scattered around for Conrad to see in the morning.

The next day Conrad stood looking at the destruction.

He smiled and shook his head. "Let the fight begin."

He ordered the mess cleaned and the window boarded up. He also ordered his brew master to step it up to full capacity to replace the beer consumed by the mob.

Hans was already at full capacity.

The next day a flyer was spread around town that was simply a list of names. Sheriff Coldren read it and his stomach flipped.

> Herein is a list of evildoers and lawbreakers. those listed
> below took part in the drinking of beer and destruction of
> property in defiance of our prohibitory laws. They should all
> be arrested by Sheriff Coldren immediately.

The list was more than a hundred names long and began with the three brewery owners. From there the list was almost man for man the members of the

July 4th mob. Almost instantly, rumbling began of informers amongst the group or someone who had watched and made a list to report.

Conrad placed the flyer down on the table in front of Dostal and J.J. "Somebody told on us."

"You told on yourself announcing the free beer," J.J. snapped.

"Someone told them who was in the mob, I mean. I'll bet it was Swafford or one of Vernice's lackeys."

"I heard that Joe Lund was back in town. Remember him?" Dostal said.

"I remember," Conrad said. "It could be him."

"What next?" J.J. asked.

"Nothing. I'm going to keep on like nothing's different. Make them come after me. What do you think of that?"

"Sounds good to me," Dostal said. "Damn them for doing this."

"I agree. I'm not going to comply," J.J. said. "This is unacceptable."

Conrad shook his head. "So much for our new politicians going to Des Moines to fight for us."

"It's not their fault. They don't have a majority, you know that. Do you think Moses would vote for temperance?" J.J. said in their defense.

"No. I know he wouldn't do that. I'm just angry," Conrad argued.

"They smashed out your glass I saw," Dostal said.

"Yeah, they got a little out of hand." Conrad smiled. "Didn't think that all the way through, I guess. Free beer on the fourth of July was not really the best idea."

"We need a list of our own," J.J. said.

Conrad looked confused. "What do you mean?"

"We can put together a list of everyone who ever marches with Vernice and those we know are against us."

"Yeah, I could do that," Conrad said.

"Then what?" Dostal pressed.

Conrad glanced at J.J. and said, "We'll send the boys to make them a little nervous. Let them worry to walk alone. Stuff like that, but no damn cabin fires or dead Indians."

The others nodded their agreement.

"Do it," Dostal said.

J.J. threw up his hands. "Yep, it's time."

That night as Vernice slept her house was pelted with rocks, breaking out all the windows that faced the street. She saw no one and heard nothing but the sound of glass breaking as she screamed into the night.

The next night, both Swafford brothers found a rope hanging from their front porches with a note reading, "To the informer, death. – Citizen." Within a week all of the main players in the local temperance movement had been visited.

Teddy opened his door to find a dead rabbit laying on his mat with the word *traitor* smeared in blood on the wood porch.

A week later, Sheriff Coldren walked into the Public House at eleven in the morning. He found a small crowd of patrons and Conrad talking to Max at the bar.

Conrad met the sheriff in the middle of the room. "Would you like a beer, Sheriff?"

Coldren chuckled. "Boy, would I. No, I'm here to give you this."

He handed an official looking paper to Conrad who quickly read it. "What's this mean?"

"You're still brewing beer and selling it. This is your written warning to stop doing it. You're in violation of the new law."

Conrad held up the warning in front of the sheriff. Everyone held their breath wondering what would happen next. He tore the warning to shreds and tossed the pieces against the sheriff's chest.

"That's what I think of your warning, Sheriff," Conrad said.

Coldren definitely wanted that beer now. "I was afraid you might do that. Consider yourself warned. If you continue, you'll get a citation and more. It's time to stop, Conrad. It's over."

Conrad laughed out loud. "Maybe you're over, but *we* are not done with anything. We're just getting started. Good day, sir." He turned his back on the sheriff, who let himself out and turned left on his way to City Brewery, hoping to serve J.J. Englert his warning.

He found J.J. drinking a beer in Louie's.

"Hello, Sheriff, what can I do for you?"

Coldren walked up to the bar and handed the warning to J.J. "Councilman Englert, here's a warning to cease the sale and production of alcohol on these premises."

"Oh really?"

"Really."

"Was this your first stop?"

"No, I stopped in at the Union first and gave one to Conrad. I have one for Dostal too."

"How did Conrad take your warning?"

"Pretty well. He ripped it up and tossed it in my face."

J.J. smiled. "You got off easy." J.J. ripped up the warning and slid the pile of paper back to Coldren on the bar.

"The next one will be a fine or worse, you know?"

"I understand. Have a good day, Sheriff."

"And you," Coldren said.

As Coldren was leaving, J.J. called after him, "Dostal is out of town today. You won't find him over there."

Coldren set his last paper on the table by the door. "You can give him his warning then. I've an idea what he would do with it." Coldren continued on out and turned down Gilbert Street, wiping the sweat from his brow. He couldn't tell if he was sweating from the humidity or his nerves. He was just glad it was done.

A week later, Justice John Schell issued cease and desist injunctions and turned the warnings into citations, with a one hundred dollar fine for each brewery and one for each pub.

Coldren had had enough delivering unwelcome documents to the northside so he summoned his most trusted deputy to his office.

Tom Fairall entered and took a seat. Coldren glanced out his window, fighting off the feeling of cowardice.

"I hate to ask you to do this, Tom, but we have to serve these papers to the brewers and they're not going to like it."

"What are they?"

"Cease and desist papers and a fine. They've got to stop brewing right now or this is going to get a whole lot worse."

"So you want me to deliver these?" Tom asked.

"Yes, sir," Coldren looked out the window again. "We got it to do."

"I want to take Parrot with me. I'm not going alone on this."

"Fine. Sam is a good deputy."

Tom stood and picked up the documents walking out of the office in silence. Sam Parrot was just coming in the front door.

"You're coming with me," Deputy Fairall said.

"Where we going?" Parrot asked.

"The northside." Fairall strapped his sidearm around his hips.

Parrot went to his desk and picked up his badge. He placed it on his chest and he buckled his gun belt around his waist. "Okay, Tom, let's go."

They went to the stable and saddled up. Tom had a knee that prevented him from walking that far. The two men rode in silence, dismounting in front of the Public House. The place was busy since the day was coming to a close. Men were getting off work and having a beer and a meal as they had a thousand times before.

Silence fell on the crowd when the two men with badges on their chests and guns on their hips boldly strode in.

Conrad stepped out from behind the bar. "Have you come to arrest me?"

"No sir, but I have orders for you." Deputy Fairall handed the papers to Conrad.

"My wife says I'm not too good at taking orders."

A subdued laugh made its way around the room as Conrad smiled at the deputy.

"It means you are in violation of the prohibition law. Conrad, you have to cease production and sale of alcohol immediately. The judge has already fined you. If you persist, you'll have to come before Judge Schell on the 14th of August."

"You can tell the sheriff and the judge or whoever you want I will not cease making beer. I've been making it all my life and I don't give a rat's ass what your paper says. I'm gonna keep making it *and* selling it."

The crowd erupted in jubilant laughter.

The deputies waited patiently until the cheering subsided.

"Then I'll see you in court on the 14th. Have a good night." Deputy Fairall turned and left with Deputy Parrot, backing slowly out of the room, keeping an eye on the crowd and a hand on their pistols. Once they were in the street they exhaled loudly.

"That was fun. Only two more to go," Parrot said.

"No wonder Coldren asked us to do this," Fairall groused.

The deputies found Dostal in the Second Floor Club. He took his papers and simply stared, seething with rage but holding his tongue.

The last stop was City Brewery. They found J.J. in front of Louie's with a small crowd of friends behind him.

"I heard you were making the rounds," J.J. said. "Thought I'd be easy to find."

"Good news travels fast," Fairall said.

"Bad news even faster," J.J. said.

Deputy Fairall glanced at his paperwork. Strangely absent was the order to appear in court. It was only the citation and the fine. He wondered if it was a mistake, then realized that J.J. was a councilman. Apparently, it paid to be in a position of power.

"Here's your citation and your fine," Fairall said.

"Have a nice day, Deputy," J.J. said.

"Your friends are to appear before the judge. I guess *your* position couldn't save them," Fairall said with a slight bit of anger showing through. He hated corruption more than anything.

J.J. frowned. "What's that supposed to mean?"

"Pays to be a powerful man with a known name I guess," Fairall said.

"Get going, Fairall! You've done your good deed for the day!" J.J. shouted and walked into Louie's.

Anger flashed all across the northside as news spread of the fines and injunctions. Almost all of the people for temperance had rocks or beer bottles tossed at their homes that night. The breweries continued to sell a lot of beer to their patrons, whose thirst only grew with their indignation. It was as if the force of the new law was tightening around them like a noose, causing a desperate feeling of hopeless anger.

The next two weeks were rife with shouting and unruly behavior. Teddy had endured enough and he finally showed up at Louie's ready for a fight.

He stepped into the middle of the room and kicked over a table. "You all know me. You all know who put the dead rabbit on my porch, broke out my windows with rocks, and called me a traitor! Who was it?" he shouted. His sleeves were rolled up, his fists up, and he stood balanced on the balls of his feet. He looked more like a prize fighter than a Methodist doctor.

No one doubted his sincerity, and no one answered his demand. "I'm not kidding! Who did it? Step up and say it to my face, you sonsabitches!"

No one moved. "No one? Nobody knows who did it?" He spun around, glaring at the crowd. Several fellas looked at him with disgust but didn't move.

Teddy noticed one of them glaring. "Was it you, tough guy? Scaring a woman with a baby and running off like a coward? Was it you?"

Everyone knew that Teddy was favored by Louis Englert, the founder, and no one wanted to go against that. The man was shaking with anger, but he was half the size of Teddy and also was smart enough that he didn't want to take Teddy on in his rage.

"You tell whoever did it I'm looking for them. And you better make sure nothing like that ever comes to my house again, got it?"

Another man stood up and walked over next to Teddy. Teddy spun to confront the man and noticed he was taking up a shoulder-to-shoulder position of support. He recognized him as Ludy Novak.

"Anybody else messes with the doc, he'll have me to deal with too!" Ludy shouted, balling up his fists.

Just then J.J. walked in the front door with Frank.

In a moment he sized up the situation and marched straight toward Teddy. He grabbed him firmly by the shoulder and led him to the back room.

"A round of drinks for everyone, on the house!" Frank called, immediately relieving the tension. Everyone cheered and released a deep breath.

Frank walked up to Ludy. "That was good of you, Ludy. You're a good man." Frank tossed his arm around Ludy's shoulder. "How's the boy?"

Ludy grinned. "He's walking and his mama's pregnant again."

"Another Novak," Frank said.

"Can you have too many?" Ludy cracked.

The adrenaline was wearing off and Teddy was shaking by the time he sat down in the back with J.J. "Do you know who did it?"

"No," J.J. said. "It could have been any one of them."

"They better leave me alone," Teddy snapped.

"They will after news of this spreads. You've got more balls than any Methodist I ever knew." J.J. went behind the bar and poured two beers.

"They scared Mattie to pieces. She won't leave the house."

J.J. set the beer in front of Teddy. "I wouldn't if I was her till this blows over. She's known to march with Vernice."

"That's not against the law."

"I know, but if you know what's good, tell her to stay in for a bit. I'll spread the word as well to leave you alone. It shouldn't happen again, but we've lost control of the mob. This is a dark time and I can't promise how it ends."

Teddy picked up his beer. "It's been awhile since I've had one of these." He took a solid drink and exhaled loudly. "Ah, dang that's good!"

"Of course it is. City Brewery is the best. No matter what old Dostal or Graf say."

Teddy was calming down. He finished his beer and accepted a second. He was enjoying himself even.

"I've missed you, J.J." he said. "Doctor Clapp too."

"After this is over, we'll get together. I'll have you and Matilda over to the house for a proper dinner. I promise."

"That would be great. She is curious about you."

J.J. smiled. "A married woman too. Since my wife died, it's usually the widows, the spinsters, and the ladies of the night interested in me. I am the most eligible bachelor in town." He laughed at himself.

"I'm sure there is a good Catholic woman somewhere who could be Mrs. Englert the second."

J.J. looked down into his beer. "Mrs. Englert the first is going to be hard to top." He paused. "I don't think I ever will try for a number two."

"You never know," Teddy said. "You could fall in love with a teetotaler."

"Bite your tongue. You know that's impossible and absolutely not funny in light of our current situation."

After the beers were done J.J. collected his jacket and walked Teddy to Dubuque Street safely out of the northside.

"I don't need an escort," Teddy said.

"I noticed that earlier. I'd hate for you to hurt your hands. Lots of good work to be done with them around here yet," J.J. said.

"I had a great time talking with you. See you soon," Teddy said.

"Maybe not soon, but after this is settled, especially if I'm not in jail." With a wave, J.J. headed back toward his brewery. Teddy disappeared into the night, making his way home.

**18**

MONDAY the 11th of August was hot. August in Iowa could be so hot and humid the air literally felt wet. Sweat was a constant companion and a cold beer was one of God's gifts to the world. Some believed that the dog days of August might be the very best days to drink a cold beer.

The windows were open on the second floor of Dostal's pub and a light breeze was passing through west to east, making for an almost enjoyable atmosphere. The brewers had their elbows on the table, leaning in close and talking as if they wanted to be sure no one else heard.

Although the room had only a few patrons that were more than a table away, they whispered, nonetheless.

"Wednesday is the day. We go to trial on Thursday. It's now or never boys," Conrad said.

Dostal slapped his hand on the table. "We have to send a message."

"The message is, we aren't going to be bullied, and we aren't going to stop brewing beer. If they want to spill blood over it, here we are. Let's do it. That will teach them a lesson, and with J.J.'s political skills we'll get this put to bed," Conrad said.

"You might overestimate my political skills." J.J. smirked. "We might need a new sheriff. This one appears pretty set on enforcing the law."

Conrad laughed. "Should we run an advertisement? Wanted, one good sheriff not interested in upholding the law. Must be willing to follow orders. Sincerely, the Beer Mafia!"

The three men laughed out loud at the idea and it cut the tension a little bit.

"That is actually a good idea," Dostal laughed.

"In all seriousness, what's the plan?" asked J.J.

"We go to the judge's house. We drag him out and we tar the son-of-a-bitch," Conrad stated. "That should take the spark out of any other judge wanting to sign off on charges against us, don't you think?"

"Yes." Dostal nodded. "That should put the fear of God into them."

"Let them know that no matter what they do in Des Moines, we're not doing that around here," Conrad railed. "Beer built this town and beer will keep it alive, no matter what the temperance hags think."

"Be sure to tell the boys only tar that judge," J.J. cautioned. "We're not killers."

Conrad shook his head. "No, we're not killers, but we are past needing to use force. If I get the chance, I may string up those Swafford brothers. I know they're the ones behind this. They whisper in old Prosecutor Maine's ear and they get Judge Schell to do their bidding, which is really Vernice behind them. I can't promise I won't hang those sonsabitches if I get the chance."

"Let's just beat the heck out of them. No need to hang them," J.J. suggested.

"Did you hear what the so-called peaceful temperance folks did to that guy down by Burlington?"

"Of course, we all read about it in the *Post*," J.J. scoffed.

"That was Vernice, you know. She's no angel. That was ordered from here. They went down there and burned that guy out. When he tried to move his pub across the state line into Illinois they sent their fanatics down there and they beat him and burned his place to the ground on the Illinois side. They don't care about the law either. The article didn't mention that guy never woke up from his beating. He's not dead, but a month later, and he just lays there," Conrad said, pointing his finger at them. "These aren't nice people. They only understand violence."

"We're not burning anybody after what happened at the cabin," J.J. argued.

"I know, but I heard the Illinois fire was that Joe Lund again. I think that guy likes fire. I think he likes to hurt people. He might have killed that Indian boy. Watch out for him," Conrad said. "That's all I'm saying."

"We hear you," Dostal said. "We should tell our crew to keep an eye out for him. He could do something and make it look like us."

"I'll tell Tom to tell the others," said Conrad.

"So," said J.J., "we're agreed about Wednesday?"

"Yes," Conrad replied. "Let's bring whoever will come from our pubs plus our crew and march to his place at dusk. The whole neighborhood should see us and know we mean business. The politicians in Des Moines will see we are serious."

"Agreed. We leave from Brewery Square at dusk," Dostal said. "We gather all we can from our pubs and hopefully we'll have a big group of angry people. A real mob!"

"I'll have Tom get a wagon ready to bring the tar," Conrad said. "This judge will think twice before messing with us again."

Wednesday, August 13th, Conrad walked into the Public House with Tom Bontrager on his right and Jimmy O'Connor on his left. They had their sleeves rolled up and they looked serious.

"Mister G!" Max yelled from the bar. "Good to see you, boss."

"A round for everyone," Conrad called.

The room was filling up and men were having a good time. A free round was always welcome and added to the joviality of the atmosphere.

Tom, Jimmy, and Conrad stepped up to the bar and Max gave them all fresh beer.

"Pour yourself one, Max." Conrad took a swill. "Ah, that's a fine batch!"

"They're all fine, Mister G. Graf's does it right." Jimmy grinned. He was entirely back to his old self. The droopy eye and a lazy leg were the only reminders of his beating. He was having headaches, but he hadn't told anyone about that.

"Are you ready, boss?" Tom asked.

"More than ready. How about you?"

"It's been a long time coming. These teetotalers deserve what they get. We just want to be left alone," Tom said.

"Watch out for that Lund," Conrad reminded them. "I told you he's back."

"I always do. I'd like to talk to him about that fire," Tom said.

"I'd like to beat him some more," Jimmy said with a laugh. He took a big drink. Jimmy was the least violent of the men on the crew, yet any mention of Joe Lund riled him up.

Conrad clapped his hands. "One more round and let's get these boys moving."

"One more round might do it, but two would do better," Jimmy cracked.

"Two it is then," Conrad agreed.

Once Max had refilled everyone's brew Jimmy raised his glass. The others followed suit. "Bloody beers this night."

Tom even laughed a little as they clinked glasses together. "Bloody beers!"

They took their drink and Conrad wiped his whiskers free of the foam. "You alright, Jimmy?"

"Right as rain."

Conrad clasped his shoulder. "Okay. If you say so." He glanced at Tom and they shared a knowing glance. Jimmy might never be fully alright. It didn't matter though—it was time to set things right.

"Well, let's get this party started." Conrad climbed up on the bar, looking down on a captive audience of friends, admirers, and employees. He knew them all well. They were friends who'd been sharing life together for years on the northside. He knew their wives, their children. They went to mass together, drank beer together, worked together—they were as close a neighborhood could get.

"Fellas, I've had enough!" Conrad hollered.

"Yes!" a few men shouted back.

"Tomorrow, I go to court. They mean to convict me, and for what?"

"Nothing!" several men shouted.

"They mean to close down the Union."

"No!"

"And not just the Union. The Great Western, and City Brewery, all of us! It's now or never, boys! Do we let them shut us down?"

"Hell no!" they shouted.

"Or do we fight back?"

"We fight!"

"That's right, we fight!"

This sent the crowd into a chanting frenzy.

"Fight, fight, fight, fight, fight, fight!"

Conrad raised his hand to stop them. "I know where the judge lives who is going to do it. I say we go there and send him a message, right now! *Who's with me?*"

Every man in the room was with Conrad.

*"Who's with me?"*

"I am!" everyone shouted.

Conrad jumped down off the bar and slammed back the remainder of his beer, which happened to be in one of the old Fall Fest Jumbo mugs. Every man in the room did the same with his mug and followed behind Conrad, marching out the front door.

He took a hard left down Market Street. As they passed Linn Street, crowds appeared both from the City Brewery with J.J. in the front and from the Great

Western with Dostal leading. The three groups came together as one, marching with the three brewers in the front, a mass of angry acolytes behind.

Tom Bontrager appeared with his wagon containing one large barrel of tar and a bunch of rope. He also had twenty or so axe handles with cloth tied tight and wrapped around the end. He dipped them in the liquid tar and lit each one, tossing the burning torch out into the crowd.

The torchlight lit the way as the mob marched on with the sun setting in the west painting the sky blood red. They traveled more than a mile east and well outside what would be called the northside before they came to the home of Judge Schell.

The crowd numbered between one hundred fifty and two hundred men, easily encircling the house, shouting obscenities and demanding Judge Schell come out.

Neighbors came out of their homes to watch the disturbance and the crowd only grew. Rocks began to pelt the house, shattering windows, and the scene continued to deteriorate.

"We want the judge! We want the judge! We want the judge! We want the judge!" was the refrain of a hundred plus men demanding satisfaction while raising their torches.

There was movement inside the house, but no one came out. Rioters who were armed pulled their pistols and began shooting into the air as the thirst for justice heightened. No one could be sure, but a few bullets may have penetrated the house itself when the unanswered demands infuriated the mob.

"We want the judge! We want the judge!"

A slight pause swept over the crowd as the front door opened. A man sheepishly shuffled forward, obviously afraid of the violent crowd. He stepped to the edge of the porch and faced them.

It was not Judge Schell, but the city prosecutor, A.E. Maine.

Conrad shouted. "Maine, you traitor! Go get the judge! We're not messing around!"

Maine ignored Conrad and held up a sheet of white paper he appeared to be reading. "Go away. This is legal. Conrad Graf and John Dostal are to report to Justice Schell's court to answer for failing to submit to the lawful cease and desist orders duly served by a legal depu—"

"We're not under your law!" Conrad yelled.

Tom Bontrager stepped up onto the porch and ripped the paper from Maine's hands, dragging him down the steps. The mob fell upon him. He cried out in terror as every inch of his clothing was forcibly torn from his body. He was a naked overweight man of middle age and nothing could stop the mob from exacting justice.

Punches and kicks bruised his hide and he was dragged over behind the wagon. The barrel of tar was violently tipped over, running all over his body. Men rolled him around and smeared him until he was literally covered in the sticky black tar. Maine continued to cry out as he endured the mob's wrath.

The night erupted with the undeniable sound of a shotgun blast. Every man turned to the porch to see Deputy Fairall and Deputy Parrot standing ready for whatever may come.

"Give us the prosecutor!" Fairall yelled.

Parrot leveled his shotgun at the crowd as they slowly fanned out around them waiting for an opening to attack.

"I said bring me Maine!" Fairall shouted and fired his shotgun again into the air. He ejected the two spent shells and jammed two new cartridges into place. Every gun in the mob was pointed at the deputies as they stood fast.

"What the hell are you doing here?" Conrad yelled.

"We want the prosecutor!" Fairall shouted again.

No one noticed, but A.E. Maine had struggled to his feet and was staggering toward the porch.

"Who told you we were coming?" J.J. shouted.

"I said we want Maine. Give him up now and no one has to die tonight," Fairall demanded.

Parrot noticed the tar-covered Maine was stumbling toward the porch. Without thinking of his own safety, he leapt into the throng and ran toward Maine.

The crowd collapsed upon him. His shotgun went off and someone screamed in pain. Miraculously, Parrot managed to grab a hold of Maine's arm and began dragging him toward the porch. A fist hit Parrot in the chin, sending him flying. He dropped his shotgun and felt a sharp pain in his right thigh—a knife blade entering the flesh just below his pelvis and tearing a gash halfway to his knee.

Deputy Parrot cried out in agony as Fairall leapt from the porch, firing his shotgun. He grabbed hold of Deputy Parrot, who somehow had maintained a firm grip around A.E. Maine's tar covered body. Fairall drove hard with his legs, pushing back with all his strength toward the porch. Both the Swafford brothers appeared on the porch with weapons leveled at the crowd.

"Back off!" John Swafford yelled as his brother fired a pistol into the air.

The pause the gunshot elicited from the crowd was all Deputy Fairall needed. He took the opportunity and made it back up onto the porch with both the tarred prosecutor and his wounded deputy.

All of the men on the porch backed their way into the house, closing the door behind them. Inside the house, screaming could be heard and movement flashed by the broken windows.

Outside, the mob was incensed at losing their prize and more shooting and rock throwing commenced. After a long time the door cautiously opened once more.

Deputy Fairall returned to his perch on the top step.

The mob had no idea, but telegrams had gone out to sympathizers in Ames, Marengo, Muscatine, and Davenport asking for support in the uprising underway in defiance of the new law. Friends of the brewers jumped into wagons and mounted horses, striking out in the middle of the night to lend their support.

Deputy Fairall looked a terror. His face and clothing were marred with a mixture of blood and tar, but he had lost none of his courage. He held a shotgun in each hand pointed at the crowd. "All of you go home. Get out of here. This is over!"

"You're over! *You* go home!" J.J. yelled.

"Give us the judge!" Dostal shouted.

"We want the judge!" Conrad chimed in.

J.J. raised both fists. "Give him to us or we'll break down the door and take that bastard!"

"I'll shoot every sombitch that comes up on this porch!" Fairall yelled. "We can all die tonight! C'mon!" His eyes appeared crazed—he had crossed over the line.

"Shoot us then." Conrad stepped forward. "Shoot me! 'Cause we're taking that judge one way or another!"

"You can die first, Conrad." Fairall aimed one of his shotguns right at him and leveled his second one on J.J. "And you can be next, Englert!"

C.G. Swafford appeared next to Deputy Fairall and raised his hands to the crowd. "Have mercy! Justice Schell's mother is upstairs on her deathbed. Disperse! You're going to kill an innocent woman. Go away!"

No one knew whether he was telling the truth about the dying mother or not, but it caused a portion of the mob to turn away into the night. No one wanted to kill an old lady already dying.

Swafford disappeared into the house while the mob argued.

Some men wanted to leave, others wanted to storm Fairall and hang him from the closest tree. Fairall slowly backed inside and eventually the mob lessened. The Swafford brothers saw their opportunity and snuck out the back of the home, making their way along a creek bed leading toward town. They knew nothing would stop Conrad from hanging them if they were caught.

Max noticed them slipping into the woods.

"Conrad," he said, "I saw the Swaffords heading toward town."

"Just them? Not the judge?"

"It looked like just the two of them."

The mob began to falter, men disappearing back toward the northside.

Conrad grabbed J.J. by the shirt. "Can you keep a few men here in case they try to sneak out? I think the judge is still in there."

"Yes, I'll watch the house. He won't get out. If I get the judge, I'll find you. I'll still want to take this house."

"Where's Dostal?"

"I don't know. Maybe he headed back to town," J.J. stated.

Conrad was enraged. "I'm going to get them damn Swaffords."

Graf left the Schell house with most of his Union men following behind him carrying torches and causing general terror everywhere they roamed. Even northside citizens clung to their loved ones, locked their doors, and loaded their firearms just in case the mob turned on them.

Conrad and his band of rioters stopped at the Public House and drank a few beers as fast as they could pour. The march had caused a powerful thirst and beer was all that could assuage it.

Young Sammy the errand boy ran into the room. "I saw the Swaffords over by Church Park!"

Without any command every man in the room jumped into action and ran the block to the park looking for the Swaffords. No one took notice of the dark angels watching the fray from the tower of St. Mary's weeping as anger and bloodshed ruled the night.

"There they are!" Jimmy shouted.

The entire mob of men saw the Swaffords running west toward the capitol. Drunk or not, the mob caught them in short order.

Conrad burst through the crowd and leapt onto John Swafford, pinning him to the ground with his knees, swinging, fist after fist crashing down upon his face. Conrad kept punching as if all his anger from the last few years was bottled up in his fists and pouring out in blasts of rage.

Jimmy noticed that Swafford's face was a malaise of red blood and mashed flesh. He thought Swafford was likely dead from the abuse as grabbed Conrad's shoulder and shouted, "Stop! Conrad stop, it's enough!" Conrad let fly one last punch and then slid off to the ground, exhausted from his onslaught. He was drenched in sweat and spattered with blood.

John Swafford lay on his back coughing up blood. Ropes were flung through the air, dropping down over branches, and the hangman's noose was ready. The crowd dragged C.G. Swafford to the front and slipped the noose over his head, cinching it up. Several men pulled hard on the far end of the rope, knocking C.G. off his feet.

Swafford's hands were free and he clawed at the rope while it viciously pinched off his wind as he left the ground. His feet kicked wildly as he rose higher and began to black out. The end was near.

Out of nowhere a crowd of people entered the park from south. They ran toward the hanging party shouting, "Stop! Stop that! Let him go!"

The sound of a shotgun blast added an exclamation as the crowd charged the brewers group. The brewery men bolted in fear, substantially outnumbered. Jimmy lifted Conrad to his feet and they took off to the north as fast as their feet could carry them.

They didn't stop running until they had reached the front of the brewery where they only briefly paused. Shouting from Church Park could be heard. Everyone assumed they had released C.G. from his hanging and had discovered the battered John Swafford on the ground.

"Go! Head out, boys! Good work!" Conrad shouted.

Each man took off in his own direction toward his home, the night of terror coming to a close. Conrad slipped down Linn Street, turning onto Bloomington Street a short while later. He stopped in the shadows, placing his hands on his knees in an attempt to catch his breath. His grand home stood before him in the moonlight.

He clenched and unclenched his fists, which were covered in blood and ached horribly. He couldn't tell what was his blood or what was Swaffords.' The night was hot, and the sky was a sea of stars. Conrad noted the three stars of Orion's belt as he slowly crept up his back step and quietly slipped in his rear door to find Anna sitting in the kitchen with a candle and a Bible.

At the sight of him she broke into tears. "Thank you God. Thank you."

He stumbled and fell in a state of exhaustion. She ran to him and took care of his need, regardless of what he'd done. She was there for him, he was the father of her children, which to her meant they were blindly loyal to one another no matter what his deeds.

Tom appeared from the woods behind the Schell home to find a small crowd remained behind with J.J. patiently waiting in case the judge showed himself.

"Where's Conrad?"

"He went looking for the Swaffords. He's probably at Church Park by now," J.J. replied.

Tom didn't acknowledge the news. He hopped up into the wagon containing the tar and slapped leather to the gelding, who trotted off into the darkness. The moon provided enough light to clearly see the steeple of St. Mary's marking the way home.

Tom slipped down Dodge Street and cut past the houses and the new building that made up the Sisters of Mercy Hospital. He saw a flash of light out of the corner of his eye and stopped for a moment. What was it?

He was planning to continue on, but it flashed again. Tom hopped down from the wagon and moved toward the light. He noticed a man close to the hospital building bent over and working with a fire.

"Hey, what are you doing?"

The man jumped at the sound of Tom's voice and spun around.

"What are you doing?" Tom repeated.

"None of your business," the man snarled.

With dawning realization, Tom recognized the face of the shady figure.

It was Joe Lund.

Joe lunged toward him. A flash of metal in the moonlight was the only warning before a sharp pain exploded into Tom's side. He fell backwards, the attacker toppling with him. Tom clawed at the pain and they fought over the knife. Joe attempted to stab him again. With a hard kick to the groin Joe went over his head. Tom rolled with him and found himself on top of Joe. He grabbed at the knife as Joe slashed again. Tom caught it in his hand, the blade slicing into his flesh.

Fear and survival instinct took over, and somehow he wrenched the knife free. Tom held the knife and, in an instant, slammed it hard against Joe's chest, penetrating his sternum. It stopped when the knife guard rested on his shirt, darkening with blood.

Joe cried out, exhaling his last breath. He stiffened for a few seconds before his body fell limp beneath Tom.

Tom stood and stared at the body for a moment, his mind a swirl of emotions. He hadn't meant to kill him. He had to. Joe would have killed *him* if he hadn't done it. What now? He should go find a deputy. But they wouldn't believe him, not on this night.

His reality foggy, Tom glanced up and down the street. He saw no one, and in one quick motion he tossed the body into the back of the wagon and covered it with the tarp. He climbed aboard and turned the horse south. He pulled his hat down and hunched forward. Blood was running down into his pants from his wound. He passed the Close Mansion and the Linseed factory.

He smelled the unique odor of the factory as much as saw it and noticed a figure in a window of the mansion holding a candle. He wondered if it was Emma. She had always been nice to him.

Tom looked away and kept going. In a matter of minutes, he was in a grove of maples on the edge of the river. He pulled Joe's body from the wagon and pushed him out as far as he could into the current. The strong water caught hold and with one last shove Joe was gone. Tom washed the blood from his hands and wrapped his terrible hand wound with a rag from the wagon. In a moment the wagon was heading back north.

He was having trouble staying awake and somewhere along the trip he'd lost consciousness. The horse had simply found his own way back to the stable behind the brewery. Tom came to and managed to release the horse into the corral still partially harnessed. He leaned against the wagon, a terrible throbbing pain in his side. He scooped some tar from the back of the wagon and rubbed it into his wound. The pain was intense. He muffled his cry as best he could.

He was so wobbly. Tom just wanted to sit down for a minute to catch his breath. He climbed into the back of the wagon and lay back, just for a minute. Darkness enveloped him and would not let go.

# 19

MORNING light found the doctors busier than the lawyers. Swafford had been taken to Dr. Cozine's office, who called for Teddy to come assist. They tried to save Swafford's face, not to mention his life. His nose was obviously broken, but the real problem was that most of his cheekbones and perhaps his jaw were fractured as well. If he lived, Dr. Cozine had no idea if he would ever see, eat, or talk normally again.

Deputy Parrot was taken to Dr. Clapp, while Conrad dressed his own wounds on his knuckles with his wife's help.

Just before dawn, the first man to the brewery found Tom Bontrager passed out in the back of the wagon covered in blood. He was faintly breathing so they hitched the horse to the wagon and towed it to the Sisters of Mercy. The tar had effectively plugged his wound, saving his life. The knife had entered his abdomen on the side, narrowly missing his most vital organs, but causing severe bleeding to almost fatal levels.

A.E. Maine was taken to the State University Medical Hospital and was in terrible shape. The tar had cooled and almost permanently adhered to his skin. Several students watched as the senior department head, Doctor Anton Smith, attempted to remove it a little piece at a time.

They discovered that gently heating the tar aided in its removal, yet it caused immense pain to the patient. Water had no effect at all, either cold or hot. They were working down a list of chemicals hoping one would aid in its removal. The only thing that was sure was that A.E. Maine's life would be forever altered. He whimpered and trembled as they worked upon him.

Deputy Fairall sat in Sheriff Coldren's office.

"You did good, Tom. You saved a lot of lives last night," Coldren said. "Judge Schell for sure."

"Yeah, maybe. If Parrot makes it."

"He's going to be fine, it missed the artery. God knows how, but it did."

"That's good. He's a brave kid. I wouldn't have made it without him, and Maine would most likely be dead. Probably Schell too." Fairall looked out the window and exhaled loudly.

"What is it?"

"I need a leave of absence. I have to take my wife to her sister's in Ohio. She can't take this," Fairall said.

"I need you here," Coldren stated.

"I know you do, but we had a noose hanging on our porch and our windows have all been pelted with rocks. Not one of them remains intact. You know I can handle it, but it's too much for her. She's afraid to leave the house, afraid when I leave the house, and afraid to stay in the house."

Coldren shook his head. "I'm sorry, Tom. You're my best."

"Thanks for saying that. We leave tomorrow on the train. I don't know for how long. I'm sorry."

Coldren shook his head. "I'm sorry too."

"What did they think was going to happen?"

"Who?"

"The politicians. You can't just outlaw something like this. Johnson County voted two to one to keep the beer flowing. Hell, the whole town is built around it. How are we supposed to enforce this?"

"I don't know. The best we can, I guess, but it's not worth getting killed over, that's for sure," Coldren said.

"Last night was pretty close. Maine is covered in tar from head to toe," Fairall said. "It looked bad."

Coldren grimaced. "That would be horrible."

Deputy Fairall stood up and laid his badge on the desk.

Coldren slid it back toward Fairall. "You keep it. I believe you're coming back, and your job will be here for you."

Fairall smiled. "I hope so."

"Have a good trip to Ohio," Coldren said.

"I'll have a beer. No prohibition out there!"
"Have one for me."

An emergency session of the City Council was called to address the riots. They met behind closed doors with the county supervisors.

In the end, the breweries and pubs were charged stiff fees but were issued permits to operate once again in spite of the state law. A total of six permits were issued. The only brewer not issued a permit was Conrad Graf. He continued on in spite of this oversight and no one ever attempted to halt Graf's Golden Brew from production or consumption, despite his lack of a permit.

Although the breweries continued to operate as they had before, the violence of the beer riots hung like a shadow over the northside for many years. Even so, no one dared to try to stop the Beer Mafia ever again.

# Picture
# Gallery

Union Brewery, Hotz & Geiger
(Courtesy of the State Historical Society of Iowa)

Cave remnant, thirty-five
feet under the old Union
Brewery, present day
(Courtesy of Marlin Ingles)

Simeon Hotz
Co-founder of Union Brewery
(Courtesy of the State Historical Society of Iowa)

Anton Geiger
Co-founder of Union Brewery
(Courtesy of the State Historical Society of Iowa)

Union Brewery Advert Logo

Union Brewery Building, present day

Former Dostal Mansion at the corner of Van Buren and Bloomington Streets, now the Sisters of Mercy Hospital.

The John J. Englert home at 318 East Jefferson Street, currently a private residence.

John Dostal of Bucyrus, Ohio, one of the former owners of the ill-fated Iowa brewery, is here for a visit with his sister, Mrs. C. Hohenschuh. The shattered, fire blackened walls of the great plant once owned by him and his brother brings a pang of sorrow to him as he looks upon them.

John Dostal has left for Denver where he will transact business. The new proprietors of the big brewery took possession yesterday, and are busily-engaged today, getting into shape for a prosperous season. The new-comers are welcome to Iowa City, as they bring with them a reputation for enterprise, progressiveness and wide-awake business methods.

Dostal clippings, date unknown.

The Conrad and Anna Graf home at 319 East Bloomington Street, currently a doctor's office and residence. (Used with permission of owner)

Left picture: Oakland Cemetery,
Iowa City
Above picture: J.J. Englert headstone

The Great Western Brewery, J.P. Dostal, circa 1900
(Courtesy of the State Historical Society of Iowa)

Old State Capitol Building, Iowa City
(Painting by Bertha Shambaugh, 1903)

Iowa City postcard, late 1800s

Chalmer Close Mansion on Gilbert Street

Left picture: Louis Englert (1810-1892), founder of City Brewery
Above picture: Dr. Clapp (Courtesy of UI Library)
Bottom picture: Clinton Street and the St. James Hotel, late 1880s (Courtesy of the State Historical Society of Iowa)

Above picture: Baker Property on the corner of Market and Gilbert Streets circa 1899 (Courtesy of Doug Alberhasky)
Left picture: John's Grocery (Present Day), formerly Baker Property, corner of Market and Gilbert Streets (Courtesy of Doug Alberhasky)

Left picture: St. Mary's Catholic Church, Iowa City
Above picture: United Methodist Church, 1884
Bottom picture: Rittenmeyer Home

Above left: P.T. Barnum: Barnum and Bailey's Jumbo Tour did visit Iowa City as portrayed in the story. The visit is documented in the travel routes of the circus to be September 27, 1881. This was a month prior to the Lizzie Stein murders. For the purpose of dramatic flow, the circus visit was moved to 1882 in the story.

Above right: Isaac Sprague, known as the Living Human Skeleton when he traveled with Barnum Circus. At age forty-four, he was 5'6" and weighed forty-four pounds. He had three boys, all of normal weight. He died in Chicago in poverty in 1887.

Above picture: Fedor Jeftichew traveled with Barnum Circus as Jo-Jo the Dog-Faced Boy.
He was 5'8" and had only four teeth. He spoke English, German, and Russian, and died in 1904.
Bottom right picture: Annie Jones, known as the Bearded Woman, was a main attraction for the Barnum Circus. She was a beautiful singer and went on to fight for the rights of "special" people. She died in 1902.

Jumbo the Elephant was an African Bush Elephant born in the Sudan. He was purchased from the London Zoo to the fury of Queen Elizabeth in 1882. He became Barnum's main attraction until his death in a train accident in 1885, after which Barnum toured with his bones! He really did eat hundreds of whiskey biscuits every day.

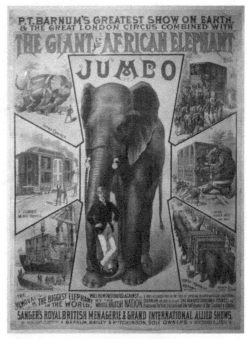

Barnum flyer from the Jumbo America Tour

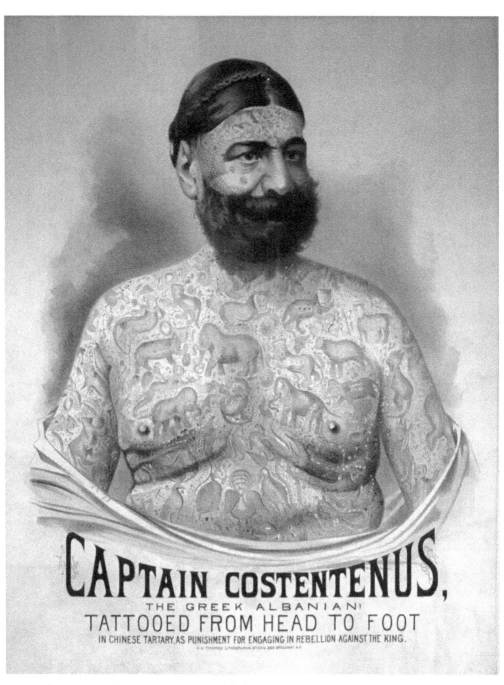

**CAPTAIN COSTENTENUS,**
THE GREEK ALBANIAN,
TATTOOED FROM HEAD TO FOOT
IN CHINESE TARTARY, AS PUNISHMENT FOR ENGAGING IN REBELLION AGAINST THE KING.

Captain Costentenus was known as the Tattooed Man. He was a Greek Albanian prince tattooed as punishment while imprisoned by the Chinese Tartars. The character Manaaki was modeled after him.

THE LATE HON. MOSES BLOOM

Moses Bloom

The Englert Theatre, 1912

Present day Goosetown Café, formerly Union Bakery and Pub Building, 203 North Linn Street, Iowa City

Englert Family, John J. Englert (top left)

Above picture: Union Bar in the 1920s, the Public House in the story and currently Goosetown Café. (Courtesy of Doug Alberhasky)

Right picture: Pro-beer activists

Brewers in Iowa City, 1880s
(Courtesy of the Johnson County Historical Society)

**The Iowa Prohibition** experiment largely ended in 1894 with the passage of the Mulct Act, which legalized what most localities were already doing in granting local permits to operate bars, taverns, saloons, and breweries despite the state law prohibiting it. Prohibitionists in Iowa remained active up until national prohibition, even passing another strong prohibitionist law in 1916.

**The National Prohibition** of 1920 brought all sale of alcohol nationwide to a halt and ended most breweries throughout every state in the nation. States were forced to firmly enforce the national prohibition. The nation could have learned from Iowa just how unpopular and what an absolute failure a forced prohibition would be. Prohibition ignited massive sales of illegal alcohol and fueled large criminal networks ushering in a time of gangsters, speakeasys, and lawlessness. Prohibition ended nationally in 1933.

**John Swafford** survived the terrible beating he received at Conrad's hand. He and his brother filed suit and demanded the arrest of all three of the brewery owners. The case was brought before a grand jury in Iowa City with no result. The Iowa City Grand Jury refused to make indictments of any of the brewers and was accused of being a "stacked jury" by several newspaper accounts.

The Swaffords attempted to have their case moved in hopes of finding a legitimate and fair jury. First the Marengo courts declined. Finally, a trial was granted in Marion. Swafford sued Graf for twenty thousand dollars and settled for seven thousand, which in today's money is approximately $165,000.

The three brewers shared the cost, equally paying the fine and smiling as they walked from court.

**The Great Western Brewery – 330 Market Street.** After a time, J.P. Dostal sold the brewery to his sons and they operated it as Dostal Brothers Brewery. Eventually, it was sold again to Fred Kemmerle and Andrew Feely, who renamed it the Iowa Brewing Company. They were regionally famous for their Erlanger beer. The building was a total loss and burned down under mysterious circumstances sometime prior to December 27, 1904. A clipping from the *Iowa City Press Citizen* mentions the charred remains of the once mighty brewery on page 7.

Dostal was rumored to have moved his interests to mining in the Leadville, Colorado region.

The Bluebird Diner and George's Pub currently sit where the Great Western Brewery once was.

**The City Brewery - 315 Market Street** owned and operated by J.J. Englert and Frank Rittenmeyer was closed due to national prohibition. Englert was an avid entrepreneur and successfully diversified his business to provide ice and wood for years to come to happy customers. John Englert's son Willie realized his dream of a modern entertainment venue for the Midwest and built the Englert Theater, which opened in 1912. It remains open to this day located at 221 E. Washington Street, providing excellent entertainment to Iowa City.

**The Union Brewery – 227 E. Market Street.** Owned by Conrad Graf, the Union Brewery, located on the corner of Linn and Market Street, remained open until national prohibition. In an attempt to survive, the brewery unsuccessfully switched to making sodas. The brewing of soft drinks failed due to the high amount of residual yeast spores in the brewery, rendering the site unfit for producing "soft" drinks because they kept fermenting. The iconic building is the only brewery building that still remains and is the centerpiece of Brewery Square. Currently the brewery is the location of La James International College of Hairstyling and offices. Below the old brewery, several of the original beer caves still remain, and some have been mapped by local archeologists.

**St. Mary's Catholic Church and the First United Methodist Church** both share the entire south half of the block of the old Union Brewery site, and their buildings are both stunning in their architecture. Both churches still host weekly services as they have for more than one hundred years. It is rumored that they get along quite well in the modern age despite their antagonistic history.

**Baker's (Hall) Corner Pub and Alert Hose House #1** at 401 E. Market Street is currently home of Iowa City favorite, John's Grocery, owned by the Alberhasky family. They boast one of Iowa's largest specialty beer selections to the blessing of their northside heritage. The building was erected in 1848 by Samuel Baker. He sold dry goods and beer until his death in 1884.

**The Lizzie Stein murders** happened at the corner of Market and Dubuque, which is now Casey's Gas Station. Mrs. Hess survived the terrible wounds inflicted by her son-in-law. With her husband Peter, she lived out her life in Iowa City, enduring the terrible loss of their family. Details are in the *Iowa State Press* found in *The History of Johnson County* page 447.

**Father William Edmonds** came to Iowa City in 1858 and served for thirty-two years as head of the Iowa City Parish. He is credited with establishing forty-four new parishes in the surrounding communities. He also oversaw the building of St. Mary's Iowa City in 1867, as well as many other churches, including St. Patrick's in 1879 and St. Wenceslaus in 1891. He was instrumental in the founding of Catholic parishes in Solon, Oxford, and many more.

**Dr. Elmer F. Clapp** was born in New York in 1843. He served in the Civil War in the 11th Regiment of Illinois and became a professor of anatomy at the state university in Iowa City in 1871. He practiced medicine and surgery in Johnson County during his long career in medicine. Dr. Clapp was president of the board of directors for Mercy Hospital and he is credited with aiding immensely in its founding.

**Sisters of Mercy Hospital** began in 1873 when four Sisters from Davenport came to Iowa City to provide services in Johnson County. They began in the Mechanics Academy Building on Linn Street. They moved to the former Dostal Mansion in 1885 and Mercy Hospital still operates at this location today.

**The State University of Iowa officially became the University of Iowa** in 1964, but has been officially registered as the State University of Iowa since it began in 1847. The Old Capitol Building remains the center of pride in what is regarded by all as a beautiful campus that is known for its fantastic educational opportunities and enjoyable Hawkeye sports.

**The Union Bakery and the Union Public House** formerly located at 203 N. Linn Street currently house Goosetown Café and residential apartments.

**Church Park** is currently owned by the University of Iowa and is home to several buildings, most notably Van Allen and Seashore Halls. It is no longer a park.

The **Women's Christian Temperance Union** movement continued on for many years and was the driving force behind national prohibition in 1920, which obviously ended in total failure. The group, however, also became the central component of the fight for women's suffrage. Thanks to their dogged devotion and stalwart efforts, women won the right to vote in 1920 and the whole world would say that has been a success.

**Vernice Armstrong** was a fictional creation based upon Carrie A. Nation, the most ardent of the Women's Christian Temperance Union, who was known for entering bars in Kanas with her axe and destroying everything. Vernice is actually much more reasonable than her real-life counterpart.

**Joe Lund** was also a fictional creation based upon the dark side of human nature. There really were groups of men called the Sons of Temperance. Iowa City had one founded in 1847. Also, in 1882, the Cadets for Temperance was a group made up of as many as eighty to one hundred boys and men. They were sometimes known as the Total Abstinence Society. See page 408 in *The History of Johnson County* 1836–1882.

**Jimmy O'Connor, Tom Bontrager,** and all the Teamsters at the disposal of the three bosses are fictional characters based on real men whose names are lost to history. Every time there was violence at the behest of the brewers, it was said to have been done by one of the brewers' "Teamsters" or one of their "men." The teamsters would have been fiercely loyal to the brewers, rough men from faraway lands who were unafraid of action and violence. They were working men who would never be named in a history book and their deeds would go undocumented.

**City Prosecutor A.E. Maine** was a real man who was tarred by the mob. He lived out his days following the beer riots in obscurity and avoiding politics or public life altogether.

**Sherriff Coldren** was also a real man who did his best in a difficult time. He left the sheriff's office shortly after the riots. Nothing else is known other than he died in 1894.

**Deputy Fairall and Deputy Parrot** were real men of history. They were accurately portrayed in the novel. Nothing else is known other than Deputy Parrot was stabbed in the leg during the standoff at the Schell home. Deputy Fairall was instrumental in stopping more violence.

**The Chalmer Close Mansion** still stands at 538 S. Gilbert Street, a symbol of a bygone age. It was built in 1874 and is a steam heated 30,000 square foot Italian style home with fourteen rooms and eight fireplaces. Mr. Close made his fortune in the linseed oil business.

## WE WANT BEER!

Thanks to the fact that prohibition has been long repealed and the explosion in popularity of craft beer, many new breweries have opened for business in Johnson County, Iowa, and nationwide. I am quite sure the original brewers of Iowa City— Dostal, Graf, and Englert—would approve of America's newfound infatuation with locally brewed specialty beers of which they would be known as forerunners.

# ABOUT THE AUTHOR

S.C. "Steve" Sherman grew up an Iowa farm kid. He still lives and works in Hawkeye country with his wife Amy, and their four children, Mollie, Cole, Brock, and Sariah. Steve is a sought-after speaker and guest on radio and TV and loves outdoor activities and larger-than-life stories. He has written across several genres, enjoying his foray into each one. His novels include: *Leaving Southfields*, a historical fiction; *Hell and Back*, a spiritual thriller; *Moxie*, a young adult fantasy; *Mercy Shot*, a political thriller; and *Lone Wolf Canyon*, a modern-day western.